The Great Leader

Also by Jim Harrison

JIM HARRISON

The Great Leader

A Faux Mystery

Grove Press
New York

Printed in the United States of America

FIRST EDITION

ISBN-13: 978-0-8021-1970-4

Grove Press
an imprint of Grove/Atlantic, Inc.
841 Broadway
New York, NY 10003

Distributed by Publishers Group West

www.groveatlantic.com

11 12 13 14   10 9 8 7 6 5 4 3 2 1

To J. B.

"My sealed orders were to determine the shape of the world. The final report is that all presumptions are in error."
—John A. McGlynn Jr.
from *An Old Man's Rules for Hitchhiking*

The Great Leader

PART I

PART I

Chapter 1

Detective Sunderson walked backward on the beach glancing around now and then to make sure he wasn't going to trip over a piece of driftwood. The wind out of the northwest had to be over fifty knots and the blowing sand stung his face and grated his eyes. It was below freezing and the surf at the river mouth was high and tormented where Lake Superior collided with the strong outgoing river current. The wind and surf were deafening and Sunderson reminded himself how much he disliked Lake Superior other than as something admirable to look at like an attractive calendar. He had been born and raised in the harbor town of Munising and two of his relatives who were commercial fishermen had died at sea back in the fifties bringing grief and disarray to the larger family. The most alarming fact of prolonged local history was the death of 280 people at sea between Marquette and Sault Ste. Marie. How could you like a killer? In his long soon-to-end career

with the Michigan State Police he had never met a killer he
liked. His ex-wife who had loved even the crudest manifes-
tations of nature thought his feelings about Lake Superior
reprehensible but then she had never been held tightly by a
sobbing aunt at a funeral. With two sons and two daughters
his mother had only room to hold his crippled brother Bobby
who had lost a foot in the rail yard of the local pulp mill.

When he turned to take the narrow path back upriver
he found a piece of freshly charred wood and the damp
blackness came off on his fingers. In his rush to get through
the woods to the river mouth and possibly find the remains
of the floating pyre he hadn't closely studied the river banks,
which he did now with a little pleasure, glad to be out of
the wind, the roar of it now just above the thick alders and
stunted trees. He was on the track of a cult leader with
various aliases, a purported child sex offender, impossible
to prosecute as neither the mother nor the twelve-year-old
girl would talk to him. He didn't need a lot of aimless paper-
work miring up his retirement. Usually such offenders were
a furtive uncle, cousin, or neighbor. A cult leader seemed
beyond Sunderson's experience.

A half mile farther on he spotted a Phoenix Suns ball
cap stuck in a logjam and retrieved it. He managed to get
wet to his crotch retrieving the cap, which brought on a
fit of shuddering shivers that pinched his temples. There
was a smear of blood on the inside brim about which he
felt noncommittal. Indeed, on the morning of the day of his
retirement party five days later the state lab would determine that the blood was from a raccoon. His quarry, whom
he called Dwight, one of seven discovered aliases, was so

devious that Sunderson wouldn't have been surprised if it had been elephant blood. The Phoenix Suns ball cap made sense as Dwight possessed two diplomas from the tawdry degree mills of Phoenix, probably phony. The complainant in the sexual abuse charge, the father, had abandoned the cult and moved south to the spawned-out factory city of Flint and could not be found. It seemed obvious that the cult leader was faking his death to deter pursuit.

To still his shivering Sunderson had eaten the last of his baked bean and onion sandwich and taken a strong pull from a flask of schnapps. Of course drinking on duty was highly out of order but he doubted that there was another peace officer within fifty miles of this remote location.

He was tired and cold when he reached the longhouse, which was skillfully constructed of logs. These cult layabouts could have made solid money building summer cabins, he thought. If it weren't a hundred feet long it would have been a nice place to live nestled in a hardwood valley near a creek that emptied into the river. Before he made notes from seventeen witnesses that he considered uniformly unreliable he had made a mental note about the creek for future brook trout fishing should the cult abandon their dwelling with the disappearance of their leader, the Great Leader. Their name not his. The witnesses all looked hung over having had a wake for their leader where they doubtless drank vast amounts of their brackish berry wines, which he had tried on a previous visit. The worst was the blackberry and the best elderberry. He questioned idly what they would do with thirty cords of split hardwood stacked for winter when they abandoned their home.

These couples were packing their decrepit 4WDs: two Broncos and a Suburban missing most of its rusted-out front fender. The females were red-eyed from weeping but fairly attractive—at least by Upper Peninsula standards, which were none too strict—a consistent trait in Dwight's cult members. Sunderson liked to tease the Great Leader about this matter though it startled the adjutants or bodyguards always surrounding G.L. as his subalterns called him. G.L. aka Dwight enjoyed the teasing, pointing out that at the university in Marquette you could tell the U.P. female students from those who came up from downstate because the locals were far chunkier. G.L. was also amused when Sunderson had spit his blackberry wine on the ground thinking it tasted strongly of Robitussin cough syrup.

"What kind of fucking geek would drink this?" Sunderson had asked.

"My people," G.L. had answered, adding that all herbalists knew that blackberries increased sexual energy.

Sunderson nodded to several stragglers on the way to his vehicle parked near the bathhouse, dreading the bone-jarring, half dozen two-track miles out to the gravel county road. A certain air of lawlessness was always possible in the U.P. for the simple reason that unless it was a fairly serious matter no cop wanted to pursue it especially if the weather was bad. It was fun to send rookie cops off fifty miles in the winter to break up a fight in a country bar when by the time the bar was reached the fight would be largely forgotten unless weapons were in evidence, rare in the old days but more common in recent years.

A few miles down the bumpy road and two pulls from the schnapps flask plus turning the heater on high and he was at last truly warm. This made him sleepy and he had to pull off on a side road and take a short nap, which turned out to be long enough so that when he awoke the car was cold and the world was dark and a fine sleet beat against the windshield. He felt a slight edge of panic but then it was only six o'clock, which may as well be midnight this far north. A brother-in-law ran a chain of recreational trailer parks in Arizona and Sunderson had been invited to run one of them after his upcoming retirement but the idea nauseated him. He had, however, promised to look over a trailer park when he visited his eighty-seven-year-old mother in a place called Green Valley, Arizona, during the Thanksgiving holiday. Sunderson was nearly computer illiterate but at the office Roxie, the secretary he shared, had looked up Green Valley and it decidedly wasn't very green, especially the beige mountains of mine tailings to the west of the retirement colony.

He pulled off the highway near Marquette and bought a pasty, a Cornish meat pie, for dinner then ended up eating the pasty in his driveway in front of his darkened house thinking the microwave would ruin the crunch of its crust. Previously well trained he had become a slob in the three years since his divorce. He had become so deep in thought that he actually nipped a finger on the last bite of the pasty. He was unsure indeed if the G.L. was a criminal in the sense that there was prosecutable evidence against him. This was his first genuinely interesting case in many years. It had begun when a man had flown up from Bloomfield

Hills to Marquette in his private jet and shown Sunderson a piece of paper demonstrating that thirty thousand dollars had been drawn from his daughter's account. His daughter was the "queen" of the G.L.'s enclave. She was free, white, and twenty-five.

Sunderson had no interest in mysteries or detective fiction, those childish recipe books of mayhem, but it was not easy to see that a crime had been committed. Few citizens at large understood the triviality of a detective's job in this remote nonurban area—the city police handled their own pathetic crimes though Sunderson was occasionally called in for a stumper. As a student of history Sunderson favored Hannah Arendt's delicious phrase, "The banality of evil."

Sunderson sat down briefly at his desk to make a few notes but felt dullish after a big whiskey. He usually did his notes before a drink, when he liked to think that his brain was percolating, a sense that his mind was actually carbonated with the details of a case. A daily report to his chief was pro forma but was usually a list of the unproven suppositions before you eventually hit bingo.

1. Noted again that all cult couples have daughters around eleven, twelve, thirteen, or plus. Is Dwight, re: the rumor of sexual abuse, organizing his own breeding stock?
2. All members are closemouthed but will jabber profusely about the levels of spiritual development they wish to attain.
3. I have to find a lady to clean this fucking house top to bottom.

4. Little chance of resolving this case, a thousand to
   one against before I retire but curiosity has me by
   the balls. Historically America has always been full
   of cults, why?

It was to be one of the most horrid nights of his life in
mental terms. After another sturdy whiskey he put a large
afghan made by his ex-wife over his head and picked out a
Netflix ordered by Roxie who monitored his queue. There
was a fine-looking young Italian woman riding a bicycle
in a skirt, with the skirt blowing up her back revealing a
lovely butt in white undies that were drawn up fetchingly
in her butt crack. This drew the attention of men she passed
including a priest. The priest diverted Sunderson because
the previous August there was a tentative charge against a
priest for putting his mouth on a boy's penis during a church
swimming party but when Sunderson interrogated the boy
in the presence of his parents the boy was not absolutely
sure it was the priest because there were dozens of other
swimmers and the boy admitted the sexual event had happened underwater. The boy's father had stalked out of the
room in anger on seeing a generous lawsuit disappear. The
father was an insurance man and a well-known local chis-
eler. Sunderson certainly didn't tell the parents that there
had been another complaint against the priest, but then the
judgments of millions of dollars offended him, thinking that
perhaps ten grand should be tops for an improper blow job
or maybe twenty. The boy was 170 pounds and able-bodied
and Sunderson couldn't help suspecting the complainant as
much as the possible perpetrator.

The sight of the leering priest in the film and the obvious fact that they had needed a wind machine to blow the girl's skirt up her back dissipated Sunderson's nascent hard-on and he slept, waking with a yelp at 3:00 a.m. to a north wind rattling his house windows, also a tree branch cracking. He had lost all of the mental clarity of the day before, the lucid analysis of the hike down the river after the witness's testimony, and now he had become victim of a shit monsoon of dream images of the G.L.'s camp.

The seventeen witnesses had generally agreed that the floating pyre was anywhere from fifty to a hundred yards downstream when the flames appeared and a pistol shot was heard. Sunderson had stood before enough bonfires to know you couldn't see far beyond their brilliant light but in the dream the entire encampment was lit in the manner of those throbbing discos he hated to enter when he searched for a miscreant. It was up to each generation to be duped into lassitude by their own music. The faking of death had become obvious.

His panic on awakening from the night's lurid dreams was mostly caused by being wedged down in a corner of the big leather sofa with the afghan knotted around his face, a gesture toward suffocation. As a man with an extraordinarily ordinary mind the confusion he felt was blasphemous as if he had suddenly lost his arms while driving. The female cult members were dancing naked to tom-toms but were frightening rather than sexy and what was Roxie doing among them? Sunderson and Roxie met three times a month at his place for sex but she would park two blocks away and walk with her chow dog down the alley at night to keep their secret intact because she was married. A cult member was also roasting Sunderson's dog Walter on an open fire though the dog had been dead several years. Oh how he missed Walter. He fully expected his mind to clear with retirement but as it neared it was apparent that it would take a while.

He walked out on the front porch in his undershirt to feel the bracing sanity of being cold. It took less than a minute and he was pleased to see that a heavy oak limb had fallen on the newish Chevrolet Tahoe of the jerk across the street who was a swindling broker currently keeping a low profile. Back in the house he made a plate of Italian sausage and fried eggs. Resuming his Netflix he used a lot of his home-pickled horseradish root under the assumption that indigestion was a preferable reality to his dream life. Now the Italian girl was naked on her bed and said "ouch" when she plucked one of her pubic hairs after which she began to masturbate. It was electrifying despite his almost immediate acid reflux. Evidently Italian sausage and horseradish held unsympathetic qualities. It was time for a Gas-X pill and a tender nightcap of Canadian whiskey. He would save the rest of the movie for the hour before Roxie made her next stealthy night visit. Both of them were of Scandinavian parentage and favored an orderly adultery regularly scheduled every ten days. He would stand on his back porch and she would come down the alley on foot in inclement weather or on her pink snowmobile in winter. She was a member of a women's snowmobile club called the Snow Queens and was pissed off when he said the group's name illustrated the general lack of imagination in the Marquette area. He loathed snowmobiles referring to them as "crotch rockets." He also didn't care for one of her favorite sexual positions which was to sit nude on his clothes dryer turned to "cotton sturdy high" to feel the warm vibrations. He was 5' 9" and had to stand on a low stool for proper contact and feared pitching over backward at climax. Afterward she would cozy up on the sofa in his terry-cloth robe, smoke a number of Kools, and drink a Bud Light, and they would watch the eleven o'clock news. In contrast, on a trip to Italy with his wife he had been absurdly and elegantly stimulated by the draped forms of Renaissance women in paintings. Sexuality had so many layers and those at the bottom were pathetic indeed.

He tried to sleep but it was hopeless. The grimaces on the faces of the naked dancing women were utterly unlike any he had seen in his waking life except on a fourteen-year-old girl over in the Keweenaw who had shot an uncle who had been abusing her. She had a crazed glare and could not stop laughing. She used a 12-gauge shotgun with No. 8s in his lower abdomen, turning into red putty his offending organ and the surrounding area. There was no real effort at prosecution except for formalities because her rectum had to be surgically repaired. At the time he wondered what chance she had for a normal life if such a thing existed though now, six years later, she was playing basketball at a small college downstate and was a premed major. This said nothing about the state of her mind but Sunderson remembered so clearly looking up "maenad," the mythological women given to tearing men into pieces. Oddly, the most awkward thing about the abused murderer was her utter beauty.

He made coffee at 4:00 a.m. and went to the study, a literal cave of books that used to be in the basement but had been moved up to the former dining room after the divorce. His ex-wife, Diane, had joked that his book buying each month exceeded their mortgage payment which was only two hundred and fifty dollars. She had worked as an administrator at the large regional hospital and they had lived well on their combined salaries, no longer true for him alone but he didn't care because he had his books, nearly all historical in nature. He had been a brilliant student of history at Michigan State in East Lansing. He had been strongly encouraged by his professors to go to graduate school but he was mortally homesick for the Upper Peninsula, especially in May when the homesickness would become a palpable ache in the throat. He applied as a courtesy and received a graduate assistantship but one day on his way to visit a professor in faculty housing he had passed the Michigan State Police headquarters and stopped on impulse. In his Munising youth everyone thought the state police were zippy and along with being a UPS driver it was one of the best jobs in the U.P. He adamantly rejected the idea of teaching because he didn't want to be trapped indoors during his favorite brook trout month which was May. Other than history, brook trout proved to be his only other lifelong obsession. It was mostly their lovely remote habitats, some of the smallest and unobtrusive creeks and springs, and beaver ponds.

Within three weeks he had taken the recruit exam passing with the highest score possible, and at their urging went on to get a master's in criminology. He didn't mind being an ordinary trooper but his talents and knowledge of the U.P. were exhaustive and within a few years he was a detective in Marquette with a decided aversion for any administrative job.

His heart warmed when he sat at his desk, as if a heart could smile. The only slightly jarring note was the original Marilyn Monroe calendar, discreet by current standards, and also a photo of the actress Blythe Danner who used to figure large in his limited fantasy life. His friend Marion, a mixed-blood middle-school principal, had loaned him a book on Native American longhouses, which he had misplaced but now turned up under a pile of early logging monographs. At the onset Marion had told him that Chippewa (Anishinabe) didn't build longhouses but they were the chosen dwelling in the Six Nations of the Iroquois Confederacy — Cayuga, Onondaga, Oneida, Seneca, Mohawk, Tuscarora — and in certain Pacific Northwest coast tribes like the Salish and the Suquamish who built one five hundred feet long. This latter fact jogged his mind and he shuffled through the papers of the Great Leader's slender file finding the record of a Dwight Yoakam (an alias using a country singer's name) being charged for disturbing the peace in Port Townsend, Washington, the year before. When Roxie called for the details Dwight had alarmed a group of Japanese tourists by speaking in tongues. When Sunderson had impounded Dwight's old mint Nash Rambler for the day on the flimsy charge of larceny by conversion he had found nine current license plates in the trunk, one of them from the state of Washington. It was hard to explain to the Bloomfield Hills father that if his twenty-five-year-old daughter Portia, whom the cultists called Queenie, wished to give away thirty thousand dollars, mostly for propane heat for the longhouse and bathhouse, she was free to do so. The father, Sunderson thought of him as Mister Bigshot, got drunk at the Verling

House the night he was in Marquette and propositioned a waitress for a grand, or so said an informant. They bathed in the Jacuzzi of the Teddy Roosevelt suite in the hotel on the hill. He fell asleep so she pulled the plug in the drain so he wouldn't drown, removed the thousand from his wallet, and took her friends out drinking with a little cocaine on the side.

He didn't have all that much information on the Great Leader but he still refused to ask the FBI for help. They were both nosy and condescending and as the disaster of 9/11 indicated they didn't like to share the information they themselves ignored. Roxie had done the best she could in helping him build a file but in four days he would no longer be able to use her services. Despite his apparent intelligence he had never learned the computer mostly because of a lifelong aversion to electricity. When he was seven a cousin had been electrocuted having climbed the fence of the power station behind the pulp mill.

The ideal substitute for Roxie was the sixteen-year-old girl next door named Mona. She was an ace hacker and a detective friend of his who specialized in computer crimes told him that he kept her under surveillance. She mostly dressed in black explaining to him that she was a goth, which Roxie had explained to him but he kept forgetting the details. They talked a great deal partly because they were neighbors living solo. Her single mother was a traveling cosmetic salesperson so Mona was mostly alone though she said that she was never lonely. When they were both raking maple leaves a few weeks before Mona had teased him about blocking off his remaining dining room window with yet another bookcase. His Lutheran childhood still carried a miniscule weight but enough to make him ashamed of his motive. He could stand in front of the case and at eye level pull out Slotkin's treatise on violence in America and look across thirty feet of yard directly into her bedroom. Strictly speaking it wasn't illegal but what was it? A bare butt crack was mere negative space but then it could make the temples of a man very nearly sixty-five years old pound unpleasantly. The biological imperative was a distracting nuisance. Checking his watch he knew she would be getting up for school in fifty minutes and the question was did he have enough self-control not to take a peek, which often devolved into a fifteen-minute trance? Part of his mind ached with guilt over this dubious matter even though since he was in his own home peeking wasn't criminal. Sexuality could be like carrying around a backpack full of cow manure, especially for a senior frantically holding on to waning impulses.

He read the Great Leader's file backward in lame hope for new perspective. His quarry Dwight had started religions in four locations in the United States, and had attempted three more in other countries including Canada, France, and Mexico. He had only lasted three days each in Hattiesburg and Oxford, Mississippi, when the police advised him to leave in a hurry. In both Montreal and Arles, France, he had lasted a scant three weeks before he drew too much attention and with an alien passport it was easy to get rid of him. It had occurred to Sunderson that for the populace in general religious belief can have nearly the attraction of money. Dwight lacked the apparent greed of the raft of southern evangelists who had built empires but he had certainly managed to live well enough. As far as he could determine Dwight was still short of forty years old. The second time he visited the longhouse people were otherwise diverted and he had a quick peek through the curtains of Dwight's bailiwick, which could be called primitive regal, say the tent of Kublai Khan with a wealth of deerskins on the wall, bear skins on the floor, and a beaver skin duvet on the bed trimmed with mink pelts.

Sunderson wasn't well traveled enough to know if foreigners were in general as gullible as Americans. In America you didn't need credentials or if they were called for they could swiftly be created. A number of the Great Leader's current devotees were college graduates though Sunderson had come to the conclusion that most colleges were a mere continuum of the utter slovenliness of high school. In the seventh grade our students are competitive with Western Europe but by the twelfth grade we're in twenty-seventh place. When Sunderson had read this it made him happy as it helped explain why the United States Congress was so obviously ignorant of American history, not to speak of those sullen louts that had been in the executive branch. Bush would say, "History tells us," and then come up with something history doesn't tell us as pointed out by one of Sunderson's heroes, the journalist David Halberstam. When Halberstam died in an auto accident Sunderson had a private evening of mourning with the writer's books spread across his desk.

To peek or not to peek, that was the question. It was eleven minutes to zero hour when Mona's lights would come on. Was he so fatigued by a bad night that he lacked moral resolve? Probably. This was a wan attempt to recapture

the melancholic, philosophical mood he used to feel reading Kierkegaard in college. Of course even then he would
have dropped *Either/Or* like a hot skillet if a nude girl had
appeared before a window. Biology defeats philosophy in
the first round. What was this stomach-souring anguish of
sex? Even wise Socrates tripped over his pecker.

He tried to divert himself with history. The Congress
of Vienna in 1814 was the occasion of a speech by someone
—he needed to look it up—that warned against the dire
consequences of raising a mediocre man to power. Quite
suddenly he had to go to the toilet, threatening that there
would be no dawn Mona, but he accomplished the hum-
bling task in a trice. He was back within twenty seconds of
zero hour having synchronized his clock with her alarm as
closely as possible indicated by her turning on her bed lamp.
His neurons raced. A prof had said that the Enlightenment
wasn't very enlightened. He pulled the Slotkin volume and
her light came on. She flopped out of bed and stood. She
leaned over to scratch her tummy. Her butt was aimed at
me, thought Sunderson, either the gates of heaven or hell.
She stood and turned to the window, instantly quizzical. Oh
my god I forgot to turn out the light and she doubtless sees
the crack of light in my window. He ducked, then crouched
with his chest against the desk figuring that if he turned out
the light now she'd know he had been watching. What a
fool to forget the light! He felt the sweat on his forehead,
the navy blue shame of the geezer or near geezer possibly
caught at his ignominious vice. He had more than a touch of
acid reflux, which didn't help. When clothed Mona, usually
in goth black, looked too slender but in the nude her breasts

and bottom were ample. His old dick, sometimes a friend but now a foe, was pointlessly hard and deserved, he thought, to be slammed in the desk drawer for its implicit stupidity. How do we account for the theory and practice of our guilt?

His eye caught a few words from a piece of paper that belonged in the Dwight folder but had been carelessly stored. It was the testimony of a Carla G., the only person he could find who had become somewhat disaffected with the Great Leader's cult and returned to Marquette. She insisted that Dwight had moved headquarters from Marquette to Ontonagon for greater control but Sunderson knew it was the cheaper land over to the west. Carla G. was a shopper and claimed that was the reason for her departure but on further probing she began to cry and it nearly ruined his whitefish sandwich. They were lunching in the bar of the elegant old hotel, the Landmark Inn, and several women of the feminist persuasion glared at Sunderson as if Carla's weeping was his fault. She finally admitted she had quit the cult because Dwight had maintained that she was his true love but she soon discovered he was screwing the other members, sometimes even a few of the men, and possibly underaged girls. Sunderson practically gasped at this new detail and then her mind wandered off into details about the Great Leader's various masks and costumes. He had a half dozen or so tree costumes made of the bark of different trees in order to be invisible. He had a round mask with his face on all sides, with eye holes, and his features bleeding into each other so it looked like he could see like an owl. The last bite of the whitefish sandwich was hard to swallow. Out in the parking lot at her car Carla had embraced him in her thin summer dress putting her hips

and pelvis into it. She started crying again and said that her
father had abandoned the family when she was only seven
and all she could remember was all the spankings he gave to
her on her bare bottom. With a glint of something in her eye
she suggested that he come to her apartment. He said that it
would be improper for him to do so until late October when
he retired, and she said, "What do you mean?" as if he were
the naughty instigator. At that moment her cell phone rang.
She answered with an air of importance and a loud voice
squawked, "Carla, I want your ass on my face right now!" She
reddened and struggled with her car door. "That young man
likes you," Sunderson chuckled and walked away, absolutely
convinced that Carla was a fabulous liar about everything
and was in all likelihood a frontwoman and spy for Dwight
in addition to being nuts.

      In truth Sunderson was fair looking. Many thought that
though he was verging on sixty-five he could pass for fifty-
five. He was without vanity so this meant nothing to him.
"Sixty-five is sixty-five," he would reply. Roxie had said many
times that he looked "ratty" but that was because he had
bought no new clothes in the three years since his divorce.
When he had lunch with his ex-wife Diane a few weeks before
to settle a business matter she was appalled because both the
cuffs of his sleeves and his sports coat were frayed. She had
insisted on signing the house over to him because when her
parents from Battle Creek had died she had become "over-
loaded," plus she was now married to a retired surgeon who
shared her passions for art and nature. He had only met Bill
a few times, mostly because doctors don't normally hang out
with detectives and because often during their marriage when

invited out he had the slightly paranoid feeling that people would have preferred if only his wife had shown up. Near the end of it all he had asked just how she demonstrated her love for the arts and nature. They were having dinner and she broke into tears at the question and left the table for her small private room where she listened to classical music and looked at her art books. He didn't explain that his cold crankiness was caused by a child-beating incident that afternoon. A boy of ten had been unmercifully beaten by his drunken father. The boy lost several teeth and his nose was crushed flat. His mouth was too swollen to talk so he wrote, "I don't want dad to get in no trouble." It was out near Champion and when Sunderson and a trooper led the handcuffed man out the door Sunderson tripped him so that he pitched off the steps onto the sidewalk on his face. He never shared this sort of information with his wife who found so much unbearable. A hatchling robin fallen to the ground out in the yard brought her to tears.

On the way to work he was drowsy so he drove down to the harbor and stood out in the cold north wind that was pushing waves over to the top of the break wall. He felt forlornly on the wrong track with the Great Leader. His colleagues and captain in the state police teased him with, "Where's the evidence of a crime?" Everyone knew there wasn't a provable one and it was certainly an ironic way to end a fine career. His uncle John Shannon who was a commercial fisherman liked to say, "Every boat is looking for a place to sink." There were far more rumors of sexual abuse these days than day-old bread and in this case the mother and daughter were unwilling to testify.

He turned and looked at the huge Catholic church on the hill and received a modest jolt in his frontal lobe, not really a clue. The year before the divorce they had taken a vacation in northern Italy and his wife had been in a serene trance over religious art and architecture while he as an historian mostly saw the parasitical nature of the Catholic Church. This was what truly goaded him about Dwight who had managed to get seventy people to give up their lives and money. By living in primitive conditions in the "past before the past" as Dwight called it they would have a wonderful future. Was this any more cockamamie than the Mormons, or the Catholics for that matter? The idea that something so obviously stupid worked with people irked him. They beat on their drums, chanted in tongues, danced, and hunted and fished. As the members spiritually matured their pasts would reshape themselves. Dwight seemed to utterly believe in what he was doing and then one day he didn't and would move on. The little information Roxie had gathered on the Great Leader's activities seemed to center on the Mayan calendar, the nature of which Sunderson didn't yet understand. He suspected that it was true Dwight had had sexual relations with the twelve-year-old daughter of a cult member but there was nowhere to go with this. Sunderson was concerned that when you looked into the history of religion those in power generally devised a way to get at the young stuff, which seemed also to be a biological premise in other mammals. This was scarcely a new idea as Marion had noted. Just as Sunderson's hobby was history Marion, as a mixed blood, was obsessive about anthropology.

Chapter 2

It was Saturday morning and the miracle was upon him through the open window of his upstairs bedroom. There was a balmy though brisk wind from the south and it was sixty degrees, much warmer than it had been in two weeks. Marion had told him about the incoming weather when they drove to the party at a big log cabin on a lake near Au Train but Sunderson barely took notice so great was his anxiety and irritation over attending his own retirement party. He had a fantasy temptation about jumping on the afternoon plane to Chicago, staying at the Drake, and spending a leisurely Saturday at the Newberry Library. He certainly wasn't a party animal and shouldn't his feelings have been regarded? Of course not. Diane was paying for the cook who normally only handled occasions for Marquette's upper crust and certainly no one at the party had ever tasted her cooking. His ex-wife had also sent two cases of fine wine and a half case of top-shelf liquor to Marion who as a recovering alcoholic could be trusted with the bounty, he was so steadfast. This was a lot for fifteen men to drink but then the Upper Peninsula was a region of heavy drinkers and most of the men who were involved in law enforcement had arranged to be picked up by designated drivers. The *entertainment* was arranged by a younger officer whom Sunderson had originally disliked but then sympathized with over his rejection by the FBI because of a college prank. The FBI had altogether too many stiffs who couldn't think, in that pathetic euphemism, *out of the box*. A little old lady FBI agent had seen 9/11 coming and had she worn a necktie thousands of lives might have been saved not to speak of the grotesque governmental aftermath wherein the constitution was sadly bruised and the fraternity boys realized their ambitions about torturing brown people. There were thousands of bright career tracks for sadists who knew no more about the Middle East than a Lubbock insurance adjustor.

Sunderson hastily had a cup of coffee and packed two sandwiches made of the party's prime beef—it had been only the third time in his life he had eaten prime. He rechecked the gear in his day pack and decided to leave his service revolver behind. No more of that he thought though he would continue to possess a concealed-weapons permit in case any of the felons he had gotten convicted bore a grudge. On the way out the back door he had second thoughts and turned back, entered his studio, and pulled the Slotkin volume. It wasn't a school morning and the odds on seeing a nude Mona were slim but why commit the sin of omission? There she was topless wearing a skimpy pair of panties. He took the monocular out of his jacket pocket and focused on her butt cleft in which the panties were drawn up tightly. Of all things she was reading *Audubon Magazine*. He focused on her breasts, then her face, utterly startled because she seemed to be looking at him. Of course his studio door was open and the kitchen light shone brightly. He had always been a bit clumsy at surveillance. There was a niggling suspicion that Mona was putting on a show for him. He ducked and smiled, questioning whether this was a proper way for a retiree to begin his first full day of freedom, a towering item in itself, but then he had long since admitted that he wasn't particularly high-minded as he had proved the night before. A long day's walk in wild country was clearly in order no matter that the day had begun humbly with an intense but guilty view of Mona's butt crack. Like so many of us Sunderson wished to be brighter than he was, bright enough but not to the point that he could overcome his very human fickleness. Back in his sophomore year in college an acquaintance had loaned him Henry Miller's *Tropic of Cancer* but Sunderson had finished less than half the book so fearsome was the disorder of the lives of the characters. Sunderson was the first in his greater family to go to college and to finish college and to succeed in life you had to keep the lid screwed on pretty tight, not a frequent modus operandi for a young man hailing from the Upper Peninsula.

Two hours into his journey he stopped in Bruce Crossing for a hasty Bloody Mary having admitted that though his hangover wasn't in the top one hundred of his life it nevertheless existed and part of unscrewing the tight lid of his life involved the free following of impulses.

In truth his retirement party had fulfilled none of his anxieties. It began at seven with heavy drinks and hundreds of oysters, went on to rib roasts so fine that they were gorged upon, caramel sundaes, then two dancing girls in the over-heated cabin, and the party was over at ten.

A modest revelation occurred on the drive to Au Train when Marion told him that as the school principal he knew that the eighth-grade daughter of a cult member was preg-nant, at fourteen a different victim than the twelve-year-old. Sunderson pretended to be unconcerned and said that when he had seen the girl she had looked a tad blimpy and then he asked, "Who was the guilty party?" He was disappointed when Marion said that the girl had told the school counselor that it could have been any of four or five men but that her most persistent lover had been an Indian. Naturally Sunder-son wanted to hear that her only lover had been the Great Leader himself. A firm charge of statutory rape would have nailed the sucker assuming that he was not dead and could be found. Sunderson was confident that Dwight wasn't dead and had wondered if the man could fly a plane because an ultralight had been found by a grouse hunter two days before in a field near Bessemer a hundred miles from cult property. However, Roxie said that no pilot's license had ever been issued in the name of any of Dwight's aliases. He felt he was losing his incisiveness because he couldn't remember if the other victim was twelve or thirteen. Did it matter? What was truly boggling was that the mother wouldn't sign a complaint. What kind of religion condoned child rape?

When Marion pulled the car up to the cabin for the party he handed Sunderson an envelope from his ex-wife and turned on the interior lights. There was an intensely risqué photo of Diane he had taken the first year of their marriage with a Polaroid camera her parents had given them for Christmas. One evening, after they had drunk a good deal and smoked a whopper joint he had taken the photo as she lay naked and laughing on the sofa of their married student apartment. The photo excited him so much that they had made love twice and cooked midnight hamburgers for their poststoned hunger. In the morning he had furtively looked for the photo, which was gone, and she pretended she had no idea where it was. He had been furious and now more than forty years later he was looking at the photo. He handed it to Marion who said, "Jesus Christ but you were a lucky dog." Sunderson read the note that began with "Dear Big Boy," his nickname, but it only said, "Thought you might like this memento of our marriage." She had always had a remarkably tricky sense of humor and now he felt a hopeless sense of desire for her. He knew he lacked the courage to throw the photo away. It was a totem for his life, simply enough.

In just short of three hours he reached the turnoff from the county road on to the lumpy five-mile two-track leading to the longhouse, disappointed that there was a single set of tracks in the moist soil leading in but not returning. He did not want to see anyone and had hoped for a day of solitude, quite understandable in the aftermath of his retirement party. He had a cup of coffee and half a sandwich leaning against the hood of the ancient Subaru that he used for his excursions into the immense outback of the Upper Peninsula. A nearby elderberry held a noisy group of cedar waxwings eating their berry fuel for the trip south. The sandwich meat was so delicious he wondered what kind of cattle gave up such flavor. He felt a bit stupid that he hadn't brought along his fishing gear. The season was closed but he could have caught a few brookies for pleasure and released them and the thought of a brook trout's cool slippery skin reminded him of the young woman the night before. The dancing girls who provided the entertainment turned out to be Carla, the young woman he had interviewed at lunch, whose dad spanked her bare butt, and Queenie, Dwight's primary girlfriend from Bloomfield Hills who had provided the thirty grand toward the purchase of the cult property and other expenses. In Sunderson's experience such young women generally turned out to be less than they appeared, pretty but no content. This also confirmed his suspicion that Carla was likely still in the cult. He had been startled by their immense physical presence in the not very large room. They began by sitting facing the banquet table on a sofa before the roaring fireplace. They were wearing the demure attire of the sorority girls of his distant past: pleated plaid skirts and white blouses. Carla turned on their boom box to the Grateful Dead and they danced with frantic but somehow graceful energy. The music segued into "Born to be Wild" and they began laughing and wrestling on the sofa, tearing at their clothes until they wore only tiny half-slips with no panties and began to neck passionately. Then on cue the cook turned out the lights though the girls were still visible on the sofa in the firelight dry humping with vigor. Suddenly they jumped up and ran out the door. Someone bellowed, "Jesus Christ, I can't take it." Sunderson whispered to Marion, "I'm going out for a pee," and Marion said, "I'll bet."

Outside in the dim porch light Carla was standing near the woodpile staring at him and Queenie was dressing in the interior light of her Yukon. He felt a little faint as he walked slowly toward Carla who was hugging her chest in her slip and waiting patiently. They embraced and her back was slippery with cooling sweat. He wanted to go down on her but she turned her back and leaned against the woodpile. In a moment he was in like Flynn as they used to say and she whispered, "Slap my ass," which he did with gusto. It was a brief mating and then she ran off to her car. He stumbled and then sat down heavily on a pile of wood to light a cigarette. A number of men waved from the cabin windows but he didn't wave back now feeling a rush of embarrassment. Oh well, he thought, and when he managed to make his way back into the cabin the men absurdly sang, "For He's a Jolly Good Fellow." Sunderson poured a tumbler full of whiskey and drank it with another bowl of caramel ice cream after which he chewed on a bloody beef bone. In technical terms he was not fully conscious. Marion said, "You're entitled," thinking him morose rather than dumbstruck. Normally he was no more spontaneous than barbed wire.

His temples tingled in embarrassment as he finished the first half of his sandwich. Once a Lutheran, forever a Lutheran, his family's nominal faith, which mostly meant the women and children went to church and the men stayed home Sunday morning, went fishing or did yard work or shoveled the snow. Religion was merely there like cod liver oil, taxes, the beginning of school.

Now he heard a vehicle coming up the miserable road
from the compound, a two-track that only sportsmen with
4WDs would gamble on what with getting stuck being a
central facet of the U.P. experience. Sunderson was irritated
because he had called and requested that an Ontonagon
County deputy secure the crime scene with a piece of yellow
tape across the road. He had made the call the day before
but his real motive had been that he wanted to wander the
full section of cult land, 640 acres, in solitude unbotched
by grouse hunters or the bow hunters who had an early
deer season or those who drove their junkers around on
Saturdays working on a case of beer and pretending they
were looking for a big buck for the oncoming gun season
in November.

It turned out to be a realtor and client in a spiffy but
now mud-spattered newish Tahoe. He flipped his expired
badge in his billfold and they got out of the car, the realtor
reddening, and the client, a man in his fifties, yawning in
his expensive Orvis-type sporting wear.

Sunderson was fatigued with protocol and simply said,
"What's up? You violated a crime scene."

The upshot was that the deputy had neglected to tape
the entrance to the cult compound. The confrontation became civil out of necessity. The realtor said he had received
a phone call asking him to show the property.

"Who was the owner?"

"A guy named Dwight Janus."

"From where?"

"I don't know," the realtor said then began fiddling with
his cell phone. "The area code is five-two-zero."

"That's the Tucson, Arizona, area code," the client said gazing north down the two-track. "What a frightful road."

"What would you do with the longhouse?" Sunderson asked.

"Sit in it with my English setter and forget the world. You have any idea of grouse and woodcock populations in the locale?"

"Should be good. The cult shot and ate everything except birds. The Great Leader proclaimed that killing birds was taboo. He called them avian messengers."

"How delightful. It will be odd to buy a section of land for less than a pathetic house in Minneapolis."

The realtor was beaming. The recent financial collapse had brought his best efforts to a standstill and he had a son and daughter in college.

They all shook hands. Sunderson gave the realtor his own numbers to pass along under the pathetic idea that Dwight might call him. He was pleased to see them drive away and imagined the effort the client would make putting up NO TRESPASSING signs, which would be ignored by locals. He stood there at high noon with the eerie feeling that only his curiosity was still ambitious. It would be a pleasure to never arrest anyone again or write a report beginning with, "The stolen '73 Dodge was found abandoned two miles SW of Gwinn. The perp or perps left behind eleven empty beer cans and someone had shit on the backseat." Crime did pay but usually very little. He began smiling with the thought of his lovely library and then the fact that Dwight's most recent alias was *Janus*, a double-faced, fascinating prophetic figure from mythology. It was nearly as good as his claim that his

mother was named Nokomis from Longfellow's doggerel
Song of Hiawatha. Behind his pomp the Great Leader had a
sense of humor. Historically the mysteries of religion, sex,
and money tended to accumulate pontifical phlegm rather
than humor. And as a student of history Sunderson had been
mystified since college with the particularities of the relationship between money, religion, and sex—in fact, obsessed.

When he reached the gate of the cult's property he felt a
curious lightness descend upon him. He was properly suspicious of moods but figured this one had a pretty solid base.
Since childhood he couldn't remember ever having been
free of multiple obligations and here on an early Saturday
afternoon in late October he had no more duties than a cedar
waxwing, in their case, to fill their tummies and head south.

The trees were leafless and he intended to head up the
creek to check for beaver ponds for possible future brook
trout fishing but first he had to check out the longhouse.
Three of the four doors were lockless and open but the fourth
door in the back had its lock broken. What was the point?
The fresh tracks in the moist earth told him that the realtor
and his client had entered by the southward-facing front
door. The broken lock was senseless and therefore worthy
of investigation. The interior of the longhouse was cooler
than the balmy outside air and the floor was covered with
the discouraging remnants of domestic life: sneakers, baby
shoes, unmatched socks, plastic dishes, cut-rate skillets,
cotton gloves. In a food cache there was a case of canned
peaches apparently deemed not worthy of hauling out and
a few broken sacks of white flour, rice flour, and rice. Three
mice looked up at him from deep in the bag of rice. The only

thing he could determine that had real value in the long rect-
angular room were the six big potbellied stoves each with
a large wood box beside it. Some local human scavengers
were sure to carry off the stoves, which were easily worth a
grand apiece. The last stove at the back was the nearest to
Dwight's quarters where the door with the broken lock was
opened to the river thirty yards away down a slope. Dwight's
wood box turned out to have a false bottom and he cursed
himself for not having searched the abandoned longhouse
the week before. Someone had beat him to it, pushed the
logs aside, opened the hinged boards, and rifled the contents.
All that was left were environmental books and a stack of
journal notebooks unused except for one that had a name
and address inside the front cover: Philippe Desarmais, 13
rue Arenes. Sunderson recalled that Roxie had found a map
of Arles on the computer and that particular street led to
a coliseum still in use after two thousand years. With the
help of a French teacher at the local Northern Michigan
University Sunderson had written a letter of inquiry to the
Arles municipal authorities and had received an answer
in faultless English saying yes, the American Desarmais
had created a modest stir in the area before being "urged"
to move on. He had rented halls and gave well-attended
speeches (free wine, cheese, and charcuterie) proposing the
overthrow of the government of the United States, which,
during the first term of Bush Jr., did not seem irrational.
Dwight wanted the 512 tribes of Native Americans to be
able to reclaim their ancestral land and the capital of the U.S.
government to be reestablished in the more central location
of Chicago. According to the Arles authorities Dwight had

been there in April, out in the Camargue watching migra-
tory birds returning from Africa. During an interview with
an operative from French intelligence and representatives
of local police Dwight, who seemed to be a bit drunk at
the time, would not disavow the possible use of violence.
With European financial help he planned on arming Indian
tribes. The police, who had noted that Dwight spoke good
schoolboy French, had him pack his bags and then put him
on the train to Marseilles, which was being indulgent of
international riffraff.

Back home in Ontonagon someone had also taken the
bearskin and other fur decorations from the longhouse and
Sunderson wondered idly about the still enduring human
preoccupation with fur. Once he and Diane had made love
on a bearskin in a friend's cabin and the fur seemed to in-
vigorate him.

Sunderson stood at the open back door leaning against
the wall next to the doorjamb and noted a small latch on
the wall. He popped the latch and there was a tiny closet
containing a stack of bird books and, of all things, a dozen
expensive, lacy nightgowns.

The whole thing was giving Sunderson a headache so
he took an hour's walk up the creek and back. The wind
began clocking from the south to the west, which meant it
would likely be out of the north by nightfall bringing the
normal ghastly weather of the season. Sure enough there
were two fine beaver ponds with fine brookies rising to the
year's last insects. He meant to use his spotty introduction
to the realtor's client to gain access during the coming year's
trout season.

On the way out he noted that he still felt a delicious lightness reminiscent of his childhood when the last day of school brought on a near frenzy of happiness. He couldn't have been more than eight years old when he and two friends had begun camping out but then that was well before parents monitored their children so carefully. They would pack a few cans of beans, a skillet, salt and pepper, a loaf of bread, and a baby food jar of bacon grease to fry their fish catch. To Sunderson that beat the hell out of softball and besides he was too busy mowing lawns and washing cars for quarters to give him time to be on a team like the kids from better-heeled families.

He was nearly to his vehicle when he turned to have a last look at the bathhouse. He believed in thoroughness rather than hunches or intuition and it occurred to him that if Dwight's members survived on wild meat and foraging plus the usual staples of rice and flour there should be some indication of hunting like ammo or shell casings. Dwight was wise enough to limit the hunting to a half dozen Indian employees who had tribal rights in the area. They were doubtless aware of Dwight's phoniness. Sunderson had talked briefly to a game warden who had done some snooping and had said the cult was circumspect in this matter.

In the bathhouse were thatches of dried wildflowers hanging from the walls that pretty much absolved the place of the odor of human sweat. He turned on a shower that kicked in a demand generator for the pump. There was no hot-water tank so he presumed that they had settled for cold showers. There was a potbellied stove to keep the pipes from freezing. Even with the reputed free-for-all sex it must have

been a dismal place in the winter. He had heard that Dwight
made three-hour speeches in the manner of Fidel Castro.
Dwight had told him that monotheism was destroying the
world and that *his* people worshipped dozens of gods like
many ancient societies. On the verge of leaving the bathhouse he lifted the lid on one of the box benches noting that
the piles of expensive towels were the name brand favored
by his wife. He dug deep under each of the three benches
and on the third came up with an M-16 rifle wrapped in
oilcloth. On close inspection he noted this one was full automatic, making it a highly illegal weapon. It was easy to
shoot a deer with this because you could fire off a banana
clip of thirty cartridges in seconds. What to do? Nothing.
He was no longer a cop but a curious citizen and gun laws
are widely disregarded across America. His friend Marion
who had been a marine told him that a good shot could
stand at the end of a runway and conceivably bring down
an airliner by firing a full clip of an AK-47 into the under-
carriage beneath the pilots where the plane's brain center
was located. Sunderson had known many cops who owned
illegal, full automatic weapons and it was hard to take the
law seriously when owners were overwhelmingly nonfelons.

Sunderson finished his lunch and had his last cup of
lukewarm coffee. He glassed a distant hill with his binoculars. There was a mob of northern ravens circling and the
hill was reachable from an overgrown two-track near the
gate. This was doubtless the location of the cult's gut pile
and boneyard for the game they shot. He decided not to
visit primarily because of the queasiness engendered by
his hangover. Along with the modest ill feelings, he did not

want to see a pile of desiccated deer carcasses, probably a few beaver, raccoon, even porcupine thrown in. Marion had once made a porcupine stew that was quite good if a little fatty. He doubted that there would be any bear skeletons as the more traditional Chippewa (Anishinabe) were hesitant about killing bear for religious reasons. It had to be done just so.

The vagaries of a hangover included gratuitous guilt and he speculated at the speed the news of his misbehavior the night before would spread. As he hit the uncomfortable muddy potholes on the way out he could imagine that everyone at the party except Marion would be busy sending out the news of his coupling with Carla over the woodpile. Men in general were far worse gossips than women. There were a dozen or so Munising–Au Train area retirees out in Tucson and it was not unlikely that his iron mother would hear the story. She thought of herself as very religious but she loved bawdy gossip as long as it wasn't connected with a member of her own family. He didn't want to imagine his arrival in Tucson for Thanksgiving if she knew the story, which he suspected she would. The comic aspects of a sixty-five-year-old man being intimidated by his eighty-seven-year-old mother were not lost on him.

On the drive home he pondered his confusion about whether or not to learn how to operate a computer. Roxie had been badgering him on the issue because she would no longer be at his service. She figured she could teach him the essentials in a couple of weeks during the evenings but he was resisting on the basis of not wanting any more obligations. The phone was bad enough and he had noted the general slavery of e-mail in people he knew. His neighbor Mona, the goth hacker, had told him he could just do research and avoid e-mail. She needed pocket money and had offered to help him for ten bucks an hour. There had been a confidentiality issue but now that he was retired it was no longer relevant.

When he pulled into his drive just before dark Marion was finishing raking the yard and Mona was picking up windfall apples near his Jonathan tree, which yielded only every few years due to late frosts. Sunderson remembered that Marion's wife was in Milwaukee on tribal business and Marion was going to grill his signature Hawaiian pork chops. Mona put her hand on his shoulder and said she was going to make an apple tart. There was a new twinkle in her eye and he wondered again if she was wise to his window peeking. There was certainly no way to correct his stupidity in not turning out the lights. Of course this is what the Great Leader Dwight was talking about: to make the present and future a far better place to live you must change your past, which is to say, before window peeking make sure there's no backlight.

He poured himself a drink and watched Marion and Mona out the kitchen window. There was no dealing with Marion's peculiarities. Fifteen years before when Marion had quit drinking after a single AA meeting he felt he had to keep himself busy and so did such things as mow and rake Sunderson's yard, replace the garage roof, build new steps to the basement because the old ones had become rickety— though as a middle-school principal Marion had always made more money than Sunderson who still resented mowing or raking lawns for a quarter in his childhood.

Sunderson also resented biology when Mona came in and began peeling and coring the apples at the kitchen table. He sat down across from her and made his employment proposition. He would construct an exhaustive list of questions about Dwight and turn her loose on her computer. She was happy because her mother's on-the-road cosmetic business wasn't doing well during the financial collapse, and then she said blankly that her mother was conducting an affair with a rich old businessman in Charlevoix. She had read some of her mother's *filthy* e-mails and she then did a mocking imitation of her mother's chirpy voice, "Oh Bob, I love the way you lick my pussy for a whole hour." Mona added that she had found out via her computer that Bob had been making their mortgage payments for the last three months.

Sunderson felt his face redden as he stared down into his whiskey. The frankness of young women these days always caught him off guard and made him feel like a middle-aged antique, or like a diminutive football player without a face guard on his helmet.

Now Mona took off her sweater and she was wearing a beige T-shirt with no bra underneath. Not wanting to confuse himself further he inspected Marion's extra thick pork chops on the kitchen counter and out the window could see him cranking up the Weber grill with his usual mixture of charcoal with split oak for extra heat. It was then that Sunderson had the peculiarly unpleasant notion that he knew nothing about religion much less the spirituality that carried the outward form of religion. How then could he understand Dwight and his erstwhile followers when he

had no real conception of their spiritual impulses? He then
realized that if at gunpoint it was demanded of him he likely
couldn't define the word "spirituality." The idea was simply
enough not something that held his interest.

"Daddy, are you depressed about retirement?" Mona
embraced him from behind and he stared down at the tiny
gargoyle tattooed on her arm. At times she jokingly, or
so he thought, called him "daddy." She smelled sweetly
of the windfall apples and he felt her breasts against his
back. His embarrassment about lust was clearly a Lutheran
hangover from childhood when a Sunday school teacher,
an obviously gay young man, had told the roomful of little
boys that they must treat girls as if they were their sisters.
In other words Sunderson knew religion as a systematic
description of right and wrong behavior. Historical religion was mostly another power to be reckoned with. This
diverted him to a book he had read about the criminal
uselessness of the Catholic Church in saving Jews during
World War II. All of those bleeding Jesuses on the cross
he had seen with his wife in Italy had left him cold as an
ice cube while the emerging Venus at the Uffizi had given
him half a hard-on.

He turned but Mona didn't let go. She put her face in
his neck and said, "You didn't answer me."

"I've never been happier in my life," he lied.

"Oh bullshit," she answered as Marion walked in
through the porch door to the kitchen.

"Sixteen will get you twenty," Marion laughed, meaning that if Sunderson and Mona continued on to the biological conclusion he could go to prison.

"He's a stuffy old prick and would never fool with me,"
Mona joked. "I did get some gossip about him this morning, though."

"It's not true!" Sunderson barked, reddening. He had
been thinking about something the great luminaire Sir Fran-
cis Bacon said but it had slipped away. He couldn't help
but presume that Dwight understood the conflict between
religion and sex and had simply decided to meld the two.

"I'd trust him with a whole squad of naked cheerleaders," Marion said. He was expertly chopping a handful of
garlic. Marion tended to be obsessive about recipes and a
current favorite of a year's duration was a side dish of pasta,
minced garlic, olive oil, parsley, and a type of parmesan
that he ordered from Zingerman's way down in Ann Arbor.
Sunderson figured that since Marion had quit drinking he
had spent as much money on fine food as he himself spent
on books.

"I don't care what consenting adults do at retirement
parties." Mona patted him on the head, then slid her apple
tart into the oven. She walked into the living room and then
through the door into his studio. He imagined her pulling a
book from the case above his desk and gazing through the
slot into her own bedroom. He tried not to give a shit but
was unsuccessful. Roxie had showed him some extraordinary filth on the computer and he had wondered at the
time about the possible ill effects of the populace viewing
this sexual mayhem. Mona likely had a wider knowledge
of weird sex than he did. His wife Diane had said that the
computer would be the death of the erotic imagination of
our time. He was exempt from the funeral, watching Mona

stretch when she came out of his study. Her nubbin belly
button suggested to him the fact of human continuity. We
begin in one place with sore belly buttons and end in another,
in his case about fifty miles east of his birthplace.

Dinner was fine indeed though Sunderson drank too
much of his cheapish red wine and since Mona and Marion
were abstaining his wavelength differed from theirs. He
asked them to define "spiritual" but they both ignored him
as if he were proposing an inane parlor game. Mona and
Marion were talking about torture, which had been much in
the news of late but this was dropped when Marion began
exclaiming about the deliciousness of the apple tart.

"You'll find a husband, that's for sure," Marion said
with a mouthful of tart.

"It's more likely that I'll be looking for a wife," Mona
said blithely.

Marion was a little embarrassed but Sunderson didn't
catch on completely being sunk in the idea that he might
have been able to keep his wife if he had been spiritual.

"Why would you want a wife?" Sunderson asked
stupidly.

Mona's voice became cool and level. "When I was twelve
and living in Escanaba with my aunt while mother was in
beautician school in Lansing my two cousins would make me
blow them while they watched porn films. Girls seem nicer."

Sunderson squeezed his eyes tightly shut at the sheer
muddiness of human behavior while Marion became angry.

"You should have told someone!" he almost shouted.

"Who? Hey, you guys, I didn't mean to upset you.
These things happen."

The room fell silent as if each of them were sorting through possible things to say.

"I'm getting over it and everything else through witch-craft. I've cursed both of their lives and it's working. One spit on a cop and lost quite a few teeth." Now Mona was smiling and got up to clear the table. Marion ran dish water and Sunderson folded his arms on the table, cradled his head, and fell asleep.

Later, he wasn't sure how long, he heard their laughing voices and then felt Marion lift up the kitchen chair he was sleeping on and carry it into the living room where he was helped onto the sofa. Up until the age of thirty when he finished college at night school Marion had been a block mason and was still massively strong with the fifty-inch chest frequently found in Chippewa-Finn mixed bloods. Sunderson again heard Mona laugh.

"Look at the big baby sleeping," she laughed.

He awoke about six hours later at 3:00 a.m. knowing in his entire body that he must fly the coop, abandon his nest of nearly thirty-five years, at least for the time being. Staying here at this time would mean desuetude, a boneyard existence. He better leave early for Thanksgiving in Arizona. He decided to clarify his head by making notes, which always had a carbonating effect on his brain, or so he thought.

1. Just noticed Jack Beatty's overwhelming *Age of Betrayal: The Triumph of Money in America, 1865–1900,* on the coffee table. This book has been an off and on obsession. We have an oligarchy not a democracy. We are ruled by the moneyed class.

2. This said, my opinion is not worth a cup of coffee.
   We are helpless. When asked at lunch Carla said
   that Dwight was not particularly drawn to money.
   To him sexuality is the core of existence.
3. This makes me wonder how he can make a philosophical system out of sexuality.
4. I have to get out of town as I sense the possibility
   of a prolonged drinking binge, which could kill me.
   Almost did after divorce. The doc said I stopped
   barely short of doing myself in, which many do intentionally with booze.
5. Beatty's book can drive me batshit like the NPR
   morning news. All the issues become dumbfound-
   ing. I have to change to the Ishpeming country
   station and become the white-trash nitwit I occasionally am. Once a peasant, always a peasant.

The airline answered in a mere twenty-three rings. Yes,
there were plenty of seats available in these troubled times.
There were a few minutes of economic commiseration with
a sleepy man at the other end of the line while Sunderson
sipped his syrupy coffee feeling insincere because he had a
more than adequate pension and a fair amount of savings. He
could never sell the house because his faithful books needed
a dwelling. The books were an immediate problem because
he intended to travel light with one suitcase and had decided
to carry only two. Mona could send more when needed. At
the instant of thinking her name tears arose at her abuse by
her cousins mixed with an ample dose of guilt at his window
peeking. Jesus Christ what a nightmare. Luckily his sleep

had been dreamless except for a brief vision of trying to keep up with Diane on the sandy shores of a lake up near Big Bay. With a longer inseam and in better condition she could walk faster than he could. On this occasion she was chasing a male grebe that was buzzing along ahead of them on the water, keeping itself aloft in the manner of a dolphin skidding along the sea's surface by tail power.

The book choices were obvious: Charles Mackay's *Extraordinary Popular Delusions and the Madness of Crowds* and Richard White's *"It's Your Misfortune and None of My Own": A New History of the American West*. The American West was the major lacunae in Sunderson's knowledge for arcane reasons. As a boy their neighbors three doors down were the Mouton family who had four large sons. The Mouton boys were big, strong bullies and when all the kids in the neighborhood gathered for play at the main game of that period, cowboys and Indians, the Mouton boys were cowboys and everyone else had to be an Indian, hence a pummeled victim, and thus Sunderson carried into adulthood a marked dislike for cowboys and their culture. Of course he knew this distaste was childish and was aware of the West through reading Bernard De Voto but he could not overcome his early prejudices. When he explained himself on this issue Marion as a mixed-blood thought it quite funny as he felt the cowboys were the western *proletariat* and nearly as woebegone as the Indians.

He went into the study to fetch the two books and on impulse decided on a last good-bye look next door. It was 4:00 a.m. and to his surprise she was awake and nude on her tummy with her laptop open and beaming in front of her.

She turned, looked in his direction, and waved. Of course the lights in the studio were on. He dialed her number and watched as she rose to her hands and knees to pick up the desk phone.

"Hi. I knew you'd be up early because you fell asleep drunk at eight."

"I apologize." He was having difficulty breathing.

"It's just a game. No harm done."

"I shouldn't be peeking."

"Well, you have been and are right now. Men like to see nude girls. You're nice to me so what's the problem? I don't think you're a pervert."

"I was half awake part of the time. Why were you and Marion laughing?" He was desperate to change the subject.

"I told Marion that my story was bullshit. I don't have any cousins in Escanaba. It took a while but he thought my lie was funny."

"Why in God's name would you do that?"

"I like to explore men's emotions. I actually did have a bad time with my stepfather."

"I don't want to hear about it. I mean, Jesus Christ, you're like my daughter. Don't tease me please. Meanwhile, I'm taking an early plane. You have the key. Keep an eye on my house and I'm leaving the whole Dwight file on the desk. Hack away and keep track of your hours. I'll leave a couple hundred bucks."

"I'll come over and say good-bye."

"No. Please don't. I'm not too stable. I'll call every few days."

"Okay, but I'm not going to bite you. You're the best friend I have."

"Good-bye. I'll miss you." He hung up the phone but continued to look another minute wondering what it would be like to feel full of firm moral resolve. He was a little amused to remember the Bible story about King David seeing Bathsheba bathing and then sending her husband off to war so he could get his hands on her. Sunderson was sure he would cut off his own hands before he would touch Mona but then he wondered how one would go about cutting off his own hands? There was also the unpleasant thought of how Mona actually saw him. A college roommate liked to play a wretched blues song about a motherless child. What about a fatherless daughter? He had stopped short of explicitly fantasizing about making love to her knowing that it was morally wrong not to speak of being illegal. There was a specific cruelty to unattainable beauty that he felt now in his spine. Time to flee, he thought. A waffling geezer can talk himself into anything.

Chapter 3

Once aboard the plane for Chicago Sunderson had a striking sense of clarity and felt ashamed at how far he had slipped in the past few months. Starting in midsummer he had trapped himself in a male hoax of the far upper Midwest, the Great North, in which the attitude is, "I can handle anything." For instance, he was aware that the silly coda of his youth had helped doom his marriage: you had to be tough, taciturn, and when injured you said, "It don't hurt none," even if you were bleeding from your nose and mouth, and at funerals you didn't cry though you might when you were alone at night. Sunderson had noted that the educated women in Marquette tended to favor men who arrived at their remote city carrying a full load of extreme sensitivities. Certainly he had seen retirement and its problems coming but then he wasn't retired yet and had denied the possibility of any real difficulties. He had begun to lose the "grip" people talked about during a minor celebration he and other officers had held in honor of their breaking up what they thought was a major U.P. dope ring. They were in a working man's bar near the coal docks on the east side of Escanaba and Sunderson had untypically drunk too much while on duty and chain-smoked, and flirted with a dowdy, overplump, middle-aged barmaid. He was conscious enough to sense the concern of his colleagues but he still resisted taking a local motel rather than drive back to Marquette. The feeling had been uncomfortable indeed. He had always been able to have a few drinks and make the frequently long drive home. He had awakened in a shabby motel on a cold summer morning with the windows wide open and the door unlocked. For the first time he felt autumnal and after showering he avoided looking in the mirror. He ate his breakfast with slightly trembling hands and drove far over the speed limit back to Marquette in order not to be late for work only to discover it was Saturday. He was so unnerved that he spent the day on his hands and knees weeding his meager vegetable garden and Diane's perennial beds, which had been in decline since her departure. This make-work wasn't helped by Mona and three friends playing doubles badminton in skimpy attire in the adjoining yard. Men would say they were as horny as a toad but who among them knew if a toad was horny? An actual horned toad?

He drank no alcohol and smoked sparingly for six days until the following Friday when he was pitched off a tavern porch by a logger over in Amasa. He had to draw his pistol to arrest the man, something that he had rarely done. He should have called for backup knowing the logger's history of violence but despite his age he still thought of himself as physically tough. The man had beat up three college students the night before and Sunderson booked him in Iron Mountain. On the long drive home he had stopped in Manistique for dinner and his firm resolve had liquefied into a couple of calming whiskeys. At the restaurant he had seen a realtor out on bail on a drug charge for distribution. Rather than just society's edge scum, more and more middle-class men throughout the country were becoming involved in the drug business for the simple motive of money. Most of them were on the rather remote capital end of deals and hard to convict.

He indulged in a Bloody Mary at O'Hare and on the longish flight to Tucson slept for the first two hours waking up with the peculiar sense of having been smeared, a brand-new feeling, not quite like a roadkill but like a man whose peripheries had been squashed, blurred, by the loss of his defining profession. Midway through high school his dad who worked at the paper mill, a step up from his earlier career of cutting pulp logs, had told him, "Like the rest of us you'll never have much but make the most of it." Unfortunately, now he continued to lose order in his mind while he continued to try to control it to the point that any order was a false order.

Fortunately the feeling of being smeared gave way to the light-headedness of the morning before on the way to the cult property. He had become nothing but he was free. He would no longer break into a dilapidated house trailer and find three ounces of marijuana, three grams of meth, and the usual needleworks. He had once been cited for breaking

a perp's arm but the young man was so skinny from meth
that when Sunderson grabbed his arm when he was trying
to crawl out the back window of a third-story apartment
the snap was audible. What was he going to do, fly? Unlike most in his profession Sunderson did not see the dire
threat of narcotics as a societal rot that must be expunged
or society would be imperiled. When a guy with four DUIs
runs over a kid and receives less time than a college kid
with a half-pound of pot intent on selling the silly weed to
other dipshits you have a justice problem. It was easy in the
current economy to have fantasies about being a member
of a secret cabal of detectives who travel through the world
assassinating the world's most destructive criminals who,
obviously, were all members of the financial community next
to which a Mexican drug cartel seemed murderous but childishly simple. Drug cartels didn't destroy the world economy,
but then what were his conclusions worth? Hadn't he been
put out to pasture? His mind had become a Ping-Pong table.

In the Tucson landing pattern he came near to eupho-
ria over the idea that with his extensive historical prepa-
ration he was just the man to study the crime of religion.
Sometimes you had to get out of town to see things clearly.
Prosecution was as childish as the profession he had left.
At least Dwight hadn't swindled widows by giving them a
hope of heaven where they might rejoin their mates who
had worked themselves to death. As the plane jolted to the
ground he felt a momentary loss at not being able to find
any of the cult's tree costumes. How grand it would be to
stand beside a brook trout stream masquerading as a tree
though there was the alarming thought that a bear would

rub against your bark. Several years before their divorce
Diane had pushed him into attending a reading by a U.P.
author who had found a stump, mammoth in size, in a gulley in the back country south of Grand Marais. The man
claimed that he often sat within this huge, hollow stump.
Sunderson had been envious to the point that he totally
ignored the contents of the man's reading of his fiction and
poetry. Sunderson had no interest in fiction sensing that his
room full of historical texts were fiction enough. The writer
had said that the stump was his church.

Because of the time change it was only noon when he
found himself in his room at the Arizona Inn, which was
an extravagant mistake. Sunderson had remembered the
name because Diane used to stay there when visiting her
parents in their retirement home in north Tucson. She and
her petulant mother didn't get along well enough for Diane
to bunk with her parents. His room at the Arizona Inn reminded him uncomfortably of Diane's parents' home near
Battle Creek. Everything was immaculate, the furniture
old and expensive. The toilets were fluffy and you weren't
confident it was a proper place to take a crap.

There was an urge for another nap, which troubled
him. He wasn't ordinarily a napper but it was his consciousness that was tired rather than his body. He checked the
pricey room service menu then walked a few blocks to a
restaurant called Miss Saigon he had noted in the car. He
had a splendid bowl of Vietnamese *pho* with tripe, meatballs,
pork, hot chopped peppers, lime, and cilantro. The irony
about Vietnam is that the war closed down and Sunderson
was in a medical detail in Frankfurt helping to take care of

the thousands of burn victims. The Frankfurt hospital fed *pho* to the veterans. Sunderson worried for a year about being transferred to a field hospital in an area of action. He was also afraid of snakes and had heard many stories. The grotesque thing was how much burned flesh stunk and how many times he vomited. He returned to MSU with a glad heart and the U.P. with actual joy.

His morale was high on his walk back to the hotel. A good meal would do that. In the room there was a call from Mona on his voice mail and he was startled to hear that she had tracked Dwight from Choteau, Montana, to Albuquerque to a location about thirty miles south of Willcox, Arizona, near a village named Sun City where Dwight was currently looking for the bones of Cochise with a group of six followers all of whom had dark hair. Dwight would no longer accept disciples who looked decidedly Aryan.

"Jesus, how did you get all this info?"

"Three hours of hacking. I got it from credit card records. Your secretary Roxie didn't know shit. Want a Map-Quest of where Dwight is staying, also an aerial photo?" Mona had met Roxie only once but thought of her as a *lowlife*.

"Sure. Fax it here." Sunderson was still unnerved by the information she had garnered through her computer, obviously through illegal means but then what with computers was truly enforceable?

"I miss you, darling."

"I've asked you not to call me darling."

"Don't worry. I don't want to fuck you. I just want to be pals."

"Before I come back I want you to put up venetian blinds in your bedroom. I'll pay for it."

"Okay, but I'm real surprised that you can't control yourself."

"I never was very religious." Sunderson struggled to change the subject. "I'm actually controlling myself," he said defensively. "I'm just looking at you like you were a painting." This was lame.

"It's funny but the most sexed up kids at school are the Bible thumpers. The rest of us started early and now it's a yawn."

"Keep up the good work." Sunderson hung up abruptly. Sexual issues unnerved him to the point that he would nearly prefer to find a dead body. A few days ago when Roxie had left the office to pick up sandwiches he had fielded a call from the wife of a prominent citizen. She was sobbing having learned that her fourteen-year-old son was sexually active, and his *slut* of a girlfriend, also fourteen, had sent him a nude picture of herself on his cell phone. It took a half hour to calm the woman down by which time his Italian meatball sandwich had lost its heat. As his dad used to say everything was fucked up like a soup sandwich. Why did they all have to have cell phones? Down at the marina park last summer a whole group was busy text messaging rather than playing and there had been several accidents involving kids walking into traffic while listening to iPods or watching TV programs on their cell phones.

He tried to stop his brain from nattering against the way things were what with having no more control than he did over his own impulses. His friend Marion, who was as

addicted to reading in the field of anthropology as he was in
history, had quoted Loren Eiseley to the effect that older men
like themselves become antiques in the face of the fantastically
accelerated social evolution induced by industrial technology.
He had been becoming a fish out of water back home and
even more so in Tucson where he was a fish in the desert.

He sat at the desk in the hotel room pondering this matter, which made him sleepy. Above the desk was a Frederic
Remington print of a bunch of cowboys rounding up cattle
in a mountain valley. He had never been on a horse and had
no intentions in that direction. It looked desperately uncomfortable. He remembered his embarrassment as a boy during
the Saturday matinee at the movie theater when Gene Autry
pulled up his horse during a roundup and began singing,
more like braying, "When It's Springtime in the Rockies."
Even worse was Roy Rogers with guitar in hand and a foot
up on a straw bale singing to a group of appreciative wildly
painted Indians in ceremonial headdresses. Why was he
letting a hotel painting lead him off into the void?

Mona had managed to get Dwight's cell phone number but Sunderson wanted to collect his scattered thoughts
before he called and then he decided it would be better to
simply arrive out of context, which might unnerve the wily
Dwight. He could also accuse Dwight of impregnating the
twelve-year-old girl but then that might spook him into
running forever. Marion had been helpful when Sunderson
had questioned the Native American motif in the Great
Leader's projects, strongly evident from the slim files that
also touched on Choteau, Montana, and Arizona. Roxie
had said, "What's all this Injun shit?" Marion doubted if

more than 10 percent of the populace as a whole had deep
religious feelings but Indians were a fresher source for the
sucker shot. People were still genetically primitive and
responded to drum beats. Religion is fueled by the general sense of incomprehension about life, and ceremonies
that were equally incomprehensible had been discovered
by charlatans. Marion gave him the work of the scholar
Philip Deloria that dealt with the way whites would ape
Indians culturally. Sunderson and Marion had been friends
for over twenty years but Marion refused to talk about his
own nativist religion, which he claimed shouldn't be subject
to a white man's idle curiosity even if it was a close friend.

Near Marion's retreat shack back in the woods a half
mile from any other dwelling there was a fine, if small, brook
trout creek that began a mile upstream in a large spring
and beaver pond. He and Marion had shoved a twenty-foot
tamarack pole in the spring and hadn't reached bottom.
Marion said that this was what was sacred about the particu-
lars of the natural world. Sunderson said that some ancient
Greeks believed that the gods lived in springs and Marion
said, "Why not?" Marion's intelligence was peculiar. One
evening the month before they had been surfing through
the satellite channels after watching the Detroit Lions lose
their thirteenth in a row and happened onto a program called
Celebrity Medical Nightmares. Further on there was a soft-core
porn channel playing *Super Ninja Bikini Babes*, and Marion
remarked that in our culture both men and women were
working toward enormous breasts, men by bench-pressing
and women by surgery. He wondered what this meant and
Sunderson was at a loss.

He was beginning to feel irritable about having to go to his mother's for dinner down in Green Valley about forty miles to the south. The phone rang and it was the desk to say Mona's faxes had arrived. He left the room in a hurry then slowed down when he saw a woman examining the extensive flower beds. He put a hand to his chest because his heart abruptly fluttered. With her back turned he was sure the woman was Diane but then of course not. Her hair was a lighter brunette and she was slightly shorter than Diane's five foot nine. He passed close enough to catch her scent, an unknown quality. She turned and smiled and he said, "Gorgeous flowers." She nodded then knelt beside a bed to examine the flowers more closely. She was faultlessly neat like Diane who had even folded her undies like one would handkerchiefs. Diane had always arrived at breakfast impeccably dressed for her job, then toasted her English muffin applying a scant amount of cream cheese and Scottish marmalade she got by mail order. She was always fresh as a daisy while he struggled to make passable sausage gravy at the stove. She even peeled fruit precisely while he had difficulties with something as simple as starting a roll of toilet paper. He had to abandon their king-size bed because his snoring kept her awake and he had refused to wear the anti-snoring mask contraption his doctor had recommended. His doctor, who had moved up from Kalamazoo, was shocked at the number of men in the Upper Peninsula who thought of themselves in fine physical and mental shape when by any outside standards they were walking wrecks. Sunderson smoked and drank heavily and his cholesterol always hovered around three hundred. He was very strong for his

age but this had nothing to do with his diminishing life
expectancy.

Sunderson sat under a pergola on the hotel lawn, the
official smoking area, and read the faxes with growing anger.
He had no idea how many cult members had taken out home
equity loans before the current financial plummet and turned
the money over to Dwight. Mona had also discovered that
Dwight had taken a Rent-a-Jet from Choteau to Albuquerque and then to Tucson for the exorbitant total of twenty
thousand dollars. Mona had also written that Dwight had
purchased five hundred peyote buttons in New Mexico. She
found this out by prying into Queenie's checking account,
which used a simpleminded code for peyote. Sunderson
thought idly that he might turn over this information to
the DEA but then they were too busy tracking shipments
of heroin and cocaine from Mexico to be interested in this
peripheral drug mostly used by the Native American church,
a widespread religious organization among Indians, and
besides the DEA would be interested in where he got the
information. He suspected that law enforcement agencies
would be wise to hire world-class hackers like Mona and
probably some of them had already done so.

Mona had sent him MapQuest directions to his mother's
house but he was inattentive when he reached Green Valley
which, all in all, was rather brownish. On the drive down
on 19 through Papago property he had been mystified and
captivated by the weird flora, the saguaro, cholla, paloverde,
and the spiny ocotillo. Sunderson wasn't a traveler, another

sore point in his marriage. Other than a long flight to Frankfurt for army hospital work he had only been west of the
Mississippi once and then only briefly to Denver to retrieve
an extradited prisoner. He was somehow pleased to note
that the Rocky Mountains looked fake. Southern Arizona
was another matter mostly because Marion had loaned him
a book about the Apaches called *Once They Moved Like the
Wind*, which left him with the obvious conclusion that the
Apaches were the hardest hombres in the history of mankind. Dwight and his followers were unlikely to ape such a
recalcitrant tribe, preferring "nicer" Indians.

His mother's house was a small stucco bungalow right
next to a large home owned by his sister Berenice and her
husband Bob whom Sunderson considered a nitwit, albeit
a wealthy nitwit, having managed to acquire a dozen RV
parks. Bob's Cadillac Escalade was parked out front, sixty
grand worth of nothing and Sunderson had the irrational
urge to ram it with his Avis compact but then giggled at the
impulse like a child.

He was barely in the front door before his mother
hissed, "Shame on you, son." She was seated on the sofa
wrapped in her wildly colored macramé throw, the air con-
ditioner on so high on this warm day that she needed the
blanket's warmth. Berenice had given her a home permanent and her hair was such tightly wrapped white nubs
that her pinkish knobby skull was revealed. "You have
disgraced our family, son."

"Mom, you have no idea of the tensile strength of some
women there. They go to the gym every day. She had me
in a bear hug."

"From what I heard in e-mail and on the phone you were behind her in plain view." His mom was smug with self-righteousness.

"The night was black and cold and snowing. No one could see a thing. I was carried away with passion." Sunderson had decided that a strong offensive was best and could see that his mother had become doubtful in her attack posture.

"We're having your favorite chicken and biscuits," Berenice interrupted.

"Darrell Waltrip is kicking ass," Bob said, turning from his NASCAR event on the television, then noticing Sunderson. "There's room for you in the company," he added.

Sunderson sat down beside his mother and took her stiff hand. She turned away, still unwilling to let him off the hook.

"I e-mailed Diane and you can tell she's upset about your behavior."

Sunderson tried to imagine the language his mother had used to describe his behavior to Diane, and then Diane's trilling laughter when she read the e-mail. Berenice brought him a stiff whiskey on the rocks for which he was grateful. He spilled a little when Bob bellowed, "Waltrip won!"

Sunderson ate too much of the stewed chicken and biscuits but then so did everyone else. His mother dozed off at the table after her last bite of lemon meringue pie. Looking at her he dwelt on the mystery of her giving birth to him sixty-five years before.

"She's not doing too well. Her heart is weak," Berenice said, clearing the table. "And you look like you could use a vacation. Couldn't you go fishing someplace down in Mexico?"

"He could start work tomorrow," Bob piped up, finishing his second piece of pie and rubbing his tummy as if he had accomplished something noteworthy.

He had left his cell phone in the car and noted that Diane had called for "no reason," or so she said in her message. He called back before he got on the freeway back to Tucson. While they talked he watched an octogenarian shuffling down the street with his walker. Sunderson resolved to shoot himself in the head before he would live in a retirement colony. Diane joked about his "scandalous missteps" with Carla. She had always been amused rather than judgmental about human foibles, but then her voice weakened and she said that two days before her husband had been diagnosed with liver cancer. Since he was a doctor himself he had become immediately depressed about the inevitable prognosis. "I'm so sorry," Sunderson offered. "Things had been going so well," she said before hanging up. She had only been married half a year.

Heading north on the freeway he saw clearly again that like so many his marriage, the central fact of his life, had failed because the marriage and the job didn't go together, couldn't coalesce, couldn't coexist in a comfortable manner. The simple fact was that when you worked all day monitoring the least attractive behavior of the species you're going to carry the job home. Diane, a very bright woman indeed, couldn't believe in the fact of evil, which always reminded

him of Anne Frank's deranged statement that people were
essentially good. If you're a cop long enough even song-
birds are under suspicion. The daily involvement with minor
league mayhem did not predispose one to large thoughts.
His brain short-circuited again. His unused first name,
Simon, only served to remind him of the Mother Goose verse,
"Simple Simon met a pieman going to the fair." He signed
his name S. Sunderson and no one he knew had the guts
to call him Simon, except his mother. In his childhood any
grade school boy that used Simon got his ass kicked while
the girls tortured this sore point as did his sisters Berenice
and Roberta. The family called Roberta "Bertie" because
of the eccentricity of his parents calling the little brother
Robert who had been the family's long-term headache until
he died of heroin in Detroit where he was the soundman for
a Motown band. When Robert was a boy he'd had a terrible
accident at the big saw at the pulp mill and Sunderson and
the rest had all stood in a circle looking at Robert's lower
leg on the railroad siding. When the ambulance came the
driver put the appendage in a small burlap bag. This item
was large in Sunderson's accretion of emotional mold.

When he reached the Arizona Inn in the twilight he saw
that Diane's near doppelganger was sitting near the vacant
Ping-Pong table under the smoking cupola. He barely had
the courage but joined her and was rewarded with a broad
smile. This made him happily nervous so he lit a cigarette.
To his surprise she lit one of her own.

"I rarely smoke but at dinner I had an argument with
my mother. I'm fifty-five and she's eighty but she tried to
make me eat my spinach." She laughed at the absurdity.

"I had an argument with mine, too," he admitted.

"About what?"

"I misbehaved at my retirement party in the Upper Peninsula of Michigan and the news reached her by phone and e-mail all the way out here."

"What did you do?"

"It's too indelicate to admit." He felt himself blush.

"Please. I'm an Episcopalian but I'm an adult. I want to hear some naughty talk," she laughed.

"I sort of made love to a dancing girl out by a woodpile. There were witnesses looking out the window of the cabin." He was pained to admit this but he liked the fullness of the laughter that ensued.

"You *sort of* made love! What did your mother say?"

"She said shame on you son."

More laughter and Sunderson leafed through a large book she was looking at. It was a coffee table book about petroglyphs in the Southwest.

"That's wonderful. My name's Lucy. My mother served spinach, a vegetable I hate, at my birthday dinner. Maybe you're like Kokopele, a mythic Indian with a fondness for ladies?" She showed him a petroglyph of Kokopele, the humpbacked flute player. The light was growing dim and she invited him to join her for coffee and a brandy. He followed her on a longish walk through gardens past rooms and bungalows a little worried that he wouldn't find his way back to his room, which he saw as a deliciously childish worry.

"Keep your hands off, buster. I'm happily married," she said at the door.

"I'm not happily divorced," he replied.

He wondered where her bed was because he was standing in an elegant living room with a couple of Chinese screens while she called room service. He had never felt so far away from the Upper Peninsula except maybe at a Frankfurt whorehouse forty years before.

"My parents were friends of the owner and used to stay here so my dad reserves the same room for me."

They sat at a table slowly turning the pages of the petroglyph book. He had seen a similar book at Marion's house but had never bothered taking a look. When the room service waiter came he called her "Mrs. Caulkins." Sunderson noted her conversation style was very much like Diane's, light and deferential with an occasional edge of the abrasive. She spoke of the drawings on stone as the "roots of religion," also "totemistic," a word Marion used. She drank her large brandy more quickly than he did.

"My mother is making me gulp. Why are you on edge?"

"I didn't think it showed."

"It does. You're like my husband when he heard he was going to be audited by the IRS."

"I retired two days ago and I already feel a little useless." He was hesitant at first but then went ahead and explained his recent life including the Great Leader, Dwight. With a bit of probing on her part he added the reasons for the divorce.

"I've seen that a half dozen times. A couple begins quite romantically doing a lot of things together and then it begins to die if the man becomes overabsorbed in his work. It can go the other way. A friend of mine started working in an animal shelter and found it more interesting than taking care of her husband who was anyway less than fascinating. Another friend saw her kids off to college and then went back to finishing her nursing degree. Now she's a surgical nurse and lives in New York City and her husband is still down the road from us in Bedford wondering what hit him."

Sunderson was looking down at the beautiful table before them feeling the full impact of his own shabbiness. His desk at the office had always been the most grungy of any of his colleagues with its accumulated gummy spilled coffee, dust, and scraps of paper. Roxie had never been permitted to touch the desk or he might lose track of what he comically called "important papers." Now he thought of the old saying *pigs love their own shit* as he looked down at the finely made table and the frayed, soiled cuffs of his sport coat. There was a longish, more than awkward silence as if they were both asking themselves, "Why are we depressing each other?"

"Marriages get moldy real slowly," he said, then paused to take out the flask of whiskey from his coat pocket. She nodded and he poured into their empty brandy glasses thinking that she had likely never drunk cheap whiskey. Sure enough she winced at her first sip.

"My God what is this, paint thinner?" She laughed and took another sip. "Sorry, I interrupted you."

"I was saying that marriages slowly get moldy and then are no longer mutually vital. You just keep dancing the same polka steps."

"I never danced the polka. We fox-trotted out East or waltzed."

"I could show you but I'm sure that Tucson is not a polka town. Anyway, we had a lot of fun camping in the summers in our twenties and thirties. It's wonderful to make love in a tent. In the winter we'd do a lot of cross-country skiing. When we got into our forties we stopped doing both. In the summer we'd rent a cabin, which wasn't the same as a tent, and in the winter we'd vegetate."

He had made himself nervous and finished his ample whiskey in a single gulp. He could no longer bear her nominal resemblance to Diane and imagined her living in a colonial house with daffodils in the yard in the New York City suburb of Bedford. He got up to leave.

"Please don't go just yet." Her eyes seemed to be misting and her voice was less strong. "When you spoke about your new hobby of investigating the crime of religion, I found myself agreeing intellectually but emotionally I have to protect my own religion. We lost our baby girl, our first child, Lucy, when she was five months to a defective heart. My husband insisted she be called after me because he loved the name Lucy. Probably because of dreams I had the irrational belief that my little daughter became a bird and that her soul passes through generations of birds. I even became a bird-watcher though I had never much noticed them before Lucy's death. We raised a son and a daughter but with them my feelings were never as intense as they were with Lucy. We knew that we were going to lose her for three months but I never accepted it."

"We never got beyond a couple of miscarriages," Sunderson said lamely. He began to finally feel the extreme fatigue of having awakened at three a.m. and also a niggling twinge of desire for her. It seemed crazed that he could hear this terrifying loss and it made him want to make love to the mother. He remembered that Diane, who knew so many nurses in her work as a hospital administrator, had said that they tended to be very sexually active because they're around death so much. "At least fucking stands for life," she had said, shocking him because it was the only time in their marriage she had used the word.

"I can't believe it." She suddenly burst into laughter.

"Believe what?" he asked timidly, already sensing that she had read his thoughts about her similarity to Diane.

"It's outrageous. And funny. Maybe flattering." She paused, and then added with mock seriousness, "You better go now."

He took her seriously and headed for the door. She followed and put an arm around his neck.

"I'm so sorry," he said.

"Just teasing. I have a bottle of wine that's perfect for a Sunday night."

He slumped down in a chair by the door, looked at his scuffed shoes, and then watched her expertly opening the wine. Since Diane had left he had been strictly screw top. He made his way back to the table. The wine was a soft burgundy called Clos de la Roche and she said it was hard to get but her family knew the family that owned the vineyard. It was gradually occurring to him that she was rich, which had a dampening effect since he was an old-line left-winger and laborite, his sympathies deeply enmeshed in the fortunes of the union movement. He was honest enough, however, to admit that he had never really

known a rich woman and the few he had met in Marquette
were civil enough.

"How much would a bottle of this set you back?" It
was certainly the most delicious liquid he had ever drunk.

"Oh God I could only estimate. My dad has it sent to
me. Several hundred dollars a bottle I suspect. My dad's
from an old New England family though he's a democrat.
He says his family made a lot of money in the spice and
slave trade and whaling so it's his duty to try to correct
certain ancient injustices. He's always loathed my husband
Harold who started as a broker and is now an investment
banker. My dad refers to him as Swindler Harold. My dad
was pleased when Harold's firm went bankrupt. Harold
has been in a depression for a couple of months. I support
the family with my money but I could never leave Harold
because the kids love their hopeless dad. Harold wants
me to invest in a company he wants to start to recondi-
tion sailboats but dad has control of my money and won't
allow it." She paused, almost frantic. "This must all sound
strange to you."

"It does sound remote. When my dad was dying of
cancer at age sixty he was worried because he was three
thousand bucks in debt. I paid it off with a loan from my
wife. He didn't know the money came from Diane but was
proud that I had a good job." He was pleased that they were
talking nonchalantly about their families. "I never thought
much about money because I had enough to buy books and
live fine and now I'll get by on my state pension okay."

They were silent and drowsy drinking the wine and
he suspected that his sexual feelings for her came out of

the usual loneliness and that the wine had the curious effect of making her look even more like Diane. When you're sixty-five, he thought, a fifty-five-year-old woman looks young.

She asked him if he'd like to go look at petroglyphs with her father early the next morning and at first he said no, that he was moving out to more reasonable quarters, would see his mother a few more times, then head out to find the Great Leader Dwight. She looked quite disappointed like Diane looked when he refused to go along with what she wanted to do so he changed his mind by saying "one more day won't hurt" and then she smiled.

"Why do we seem to like each other?" she asked at the door.

"I have no idea," he lied. He certainly wasn't going to say, "You bear a resemblance to a woman I loved and lost."

"Once, on a plane, I developed a crush on an anthropologist I was seated next to. I was *turned on* as the young people say. I told my daughter who thought it was hysterical. She asked, 'Why didn't you go for it mom?'"

Sunderson thought of this on his way back to his room, quite lost until he was helped by a night watchman. It was a troublesome night indeed as if he had just been on a fifteen-hour drive and couldn't stop moving when he got into bed. Once he woke up weeping but twice it was laughter, and belly laughter. The tears were caused by a reality-based dream of when he had returned from a three-day meeting at state police headquarters and found her gone on a late Friday afternoon. He was in immediate tears as he had skillfully, he thought, remembered that it was their seventeenth anniversary and he had bought fifty bucks worth of cut flowers, a pointless gesture as it was late June and she had better flowers in her perennial garden. Some of their camping equipment was gone from the porch and it seemed odd that a woman fleeing from marriage would take this sort of gear. As a detective he might have figured out he was dulled from the four-hundred-plus-mile drive up from Lansing and a hangover from sitting in a disco rock bar watching college girls wiggle their toothsome asses. Fetching a beer from the refrigerator he saw the note. "Hoped you'd call last night but you must have been busy. Also hoping you remembered I'm camping this weekend at our spot near Big Bay. Your dinner in the blue Creuset is a *blanquette de veau*, a veal stew. I also made a salad dressing, etc. See you Sunday. Love, D."

He played a little game that was usually successful in countering insomnia. He constructed a series of mental notes that wouldn't be that hard to remember in the morning. At the university he had always memorized potent quotes from historical texts to use in blue book essay exams, so his memory had never been a problem. The only issue in using notes to battle insomnia was that the brain without benefit of light tended to be errant and freely waffled into the irrelevant.

1. As Mom used to say when I was slow to do chores, "Stop fiddle-faddling," an expression no longer in use. Dad was more direct, saying, "Get your head out of your ass and get to work," a difficult physical maneuver. Fifty years later I'm still my parents'

child. Fiddle-faddle. If I'm going to nail Dwight to the wall I better get started with full energy. Carla is possibly the key due to her volatility as in all witnesses who struggle to explain themselves to themselves. Despite everything Dwight teaches she wants him for herself.

2. A dim memory of Berenice giving her allowance to the Lutheran pastor for the African Mission effort. Mom was angry when Dad said that the clergy were "God's pickpockets." Back to money and religion. The central business of Lucy's life seems to be inheritance. A portion of her emotional content died with her infant daughter.

3. A clear memory of ten years ago when Diane gave me Judy Crichton's *America 1900* for my birthday and also made a fine stewed rabbit she said was a French recipe. At first the book seemed insufficiently scholarly but then this was a relief. I recall a passage from a 1900 *New York Times* unsigned editorial insisting that we hadn't moved an inch forward from the Dark Ages. Ten years before in reaction to the Ghost Dance movement the *Chicago Tribune* stated that it might be wise to kill all of the Lakota. I had this sobering feeling that I was spending my life running around the Upper Peninsula applying tiny bandages to mostly superficial wounds.

4. The idea that history gives perspective is partly a hoax because it only functionally gives you perspective on history! Imagine if Congress were actually knowledgeable of American history.

It didn't work. Here he was in a hotel room in Tucson
drying his tears after he mistakenly thought Diane had left
him, still feeling the fool. He turned on the light to change
the pattern of consciousness. With Diane he had always
felt a little vulgar and brutish and now Lucy was doing
the same thing to him. Curiously his colleagues and many
people thought him to be too refined and bookish to be
a detective but they were victims of television and crime
novels. He'd never wanted to be a tough-guy cop partly
because the first two years of his state police career he had
been stationed near Detroit where there were a phenom-
enal number of tough cops, real bruisers, first among them
the "Big Four" who were called in for particularly violent
situations. He was off duty after a Detroit Lions–Green
Bay Packer game, always a volatile item, and had seen the
Big Four cruise up in their black Chrysler sedan to settle a
brawl between fans, locals, and a group of big krauts that
had come over from Milwaukee. Sunderson stood well
back watching with amazement as the lead man of the Big
Four, an immense Polack named Thaddeus chewing a ten-
cent rum-soaked Crooks cigar, waded into the brawlers
and began throwing them left and right fairly high in the
air, grinning as he worked. Later on a gory case Sunderson
had had dinner with Thaddeus in Hamtramck, duck blood
soup and fried muskrat, and the table next to them had
been noisy and Thaddeus had said to them, "Shut up we're
talking about the fucking United Nations." And the men
fell silent. Thaddeus was melancholy that evening because
a pimp had cut a nipple off of an Amazonian black hooker
he loved. It was a famous pimp who was named Mink

because he wore a mink coat even in July. Thaddeus had said, "That fuck is gonna go off a bridge. He don't know it yet but he's a floater," meaning a dead body in the Detroit River. When Sunderson was transferred and he and Diane drove north there were tears of relief when they reached the Straits of Mackinac. The least fun possible was picking up a severed head in a drug slaying down near the Flat Rock drag strip.

In semisleep he could see Diane and Lucy standing next to each other and there was a drift of thoughts about his own unworthiness. He should have married a Munising girl from a mill family though by the time he was in the tenth grade he had aspired to a better world and had lived a life caught in between.

As he reentered sleep he laughed remembering when their little group of outcasts including two local mixed-bloods had fired some stolen bottle rockets at the Mouton brothers' fake cowboy camp in a woodlot up the steep hill behind town. The attack came at dawn while the Moutons were asleep. When the rockets hit Sunderson and his group jumped up screaming and charged up the hill. Sunderson's terrier-Lab mix upended the biggest brother by ripping at a pant leg. Sunderson's gang got the shit beat out of them but it was worth it. Unfortunately the rocket had started a fire in the woods that spread to a few acres and his dad had to accompany him to the police station where he was threatened with reform school way down in Lansing. His laughter dampened when he recalled Diane's first visit north when they were seniors at Michigan State. He had seen her glance at the raw board floors of the dining room and the

oval braided rug his mother had made. The whole family
had immediately loved Diane and were quick to tell Sunderson he wasn't good enough for her. His dad had taken
him aside and told him that Diane had too much "class" and
was sure to ditch him.

The last bit of laughter came at dawn when Sunderson
dreamed the smell of fire and he remembered a remote
cabin that served as a meth lab over near Crystal Falls
that had burned one April. There had been a late snow
and he rode in with a new local deputy on a snowmobile.
The fire was still smoldering and right away Sunderson
smelled burned flesh but didn't mention it to the deputy,
waiting for him to make his own discovery. It was a bright
blue day and Sunderson enjoyed the growing warmth that
meant it was over freezing temperature. He watched the
deputy poking in the ruins until he heard him yell, "Jesus
Christ, a fucking burned-up body!" The deputy puked
then fainted. Sunderson rubbed snow on his face and the
deputy looked up and said, "It's my wife's birthday. I was
going to grill steaks and now I'm not."

Mona called just as Sunderson was leaving the room
short of 7:00 a.m. "I missed your peeking. It was like a
vacuum."

"Never mind. What's up?"

"I found out Dwight's origins. His mom was in the
Peace Corps in Uganda. She got knocked up by a French
civil engineer working on a dam project. She died from
various tropical diseases when Dwight was a year old.
He was raised by his grandparents. They died then it was
foster parents."

"I'm running late. Fax it along. Also go in my study and check page 300 of Judy Crichton's *America 1900*. Something about the Middle Ages from the *New York Times*. I forgot a quote I used to know by heart." It must be age he thought.

"Okay, right away. Darling, I miss your old eyes burning a hole in my butt from your peek hole."

Sunderson said thank you and rushed out.

Chapter 4

His mind flip-flopped seeing Lucy with her father. She acted like a ditzy teenager. It wasn't a chink in her armor but a whole gully. His name was Bushrod, a name Sunderson had only encountered in certain New England historical texts. He was Scots-English, a bantam sun-wizened bully with tiny tufts of gray hair coming out of his ears and eyebrows that needed a haircut.

"Ten minutes late Mister Crime Buster. I can't eat breakfast in public at this place. All those desperate old widows trying to replace the husbands they killed. I can't say I've shaken hands with a detective. You ought to look into Lucy's swindler husband," Bushrod said, offering his hand without getting up from the breakfast table in Lucy's room. The *Wall Street Journal* and *New York Times* were folded beside his plate of scrambled eggs and link sausage, which he had covered with Tabasco, also a habit of Sunderson's.

Lucy fluttered around, her face pink from embarrassment, stowing water and box lunches into a pretty canvas
satchel. "Daddy, please." She glanced furtively at Sunderson
who ate hastily because Bushrod was now up and pacing
near the door, muttering at the front page of the *Journal*.

"They ought to guillotine fifty thousand brokers in Bat-
tery Park. Can't you law people arrange it?"

"This is the first workday of my retirement," Sunderson said, amused at this antique nutcase, obviously the
source of Lucy's lifestyle. Lucy had called him a "desert
rat," someone who found the deserts of the Southwest ob-
sessively interesting.

"Find something to do full time or you'll die on the
vine," Bushrod pronounced as if he were Moses.

"I'm investigating the evil connection between religion,
money, and sex," Sunderson joked, relieved that his own
father had been a mild, kind man.

"Excellent. Send me the results."

With Bushrod at the wheel of a battered Range Rover
they drove out toward Ina and through Saguaro National
Park, with Lucy seemingly frozen in place in the center of
the backseat, leafing through a bird book without seeing
it. Bushrod explained the nature of the flora they passed,
the dozens of species of cacti while Sunderson was glum
about the relationship of adult children to their old parents.
It was a different person in the backseat and Sunderson
was inattentive to Bushrod, meditating on all the forms of
bullying in the world. He had faulted his own parents for
not letting his dog Ralph in the house. At bedtime he and
his brother Robert would lower a basket on a rope from

their second-story bedroom window. Ralph would jump in and they would pull him up to where he belonged. His dad finally caught on but it was his mother who was the prime mover of the no dogs rule. His father never mentioned their secret to her.

They reached a desert two-track and drove several miles onto the Tohono O'odham reservation with Sunderson reflecting that the scrawny cattle would have elicited calls to the Humane Society in Michigan. Bushrod pulled up near a grove of shady paloverde and when Sunderson got out his bare arm brushed painfully against a cholla cactus and he yelped.

"Nearly all the flora around here will poke a hole in you." Bushrod pulled a hemostat out of a Dopp kit and pulled a dozen slender spines from Sunderson's arm. "Keep an eye out for crotalids," he said, heading up what looked like a hundred-foot-high pile of basaltic rock.

"He means rattlesnakes," Lucy said dully, her eyes moist. Her father was already up the steep incline out of earshot. "He's driven me crazy since I could walk."

"That's not a good way to live." Sunderson supposed he was meant to follow Bushrod. Those from the upper Midwest are not born climbers except maybe when they're younger and then only conifers with lots of branches. The landscape unnerved him and having seen rattlers on television and in the movies he was not thrilled at the idea of an encounter with a snake that could possibly kill him. He calmed himself thinking that though he was intensely perceptive on his home ground because of his job, when he traveled he was a bit of a goof. Once with Diane in Chicago he had taken a solo walk and had gotten a bit lost,

remembering with difficulty their hotel for which she had
made the arrangements.

"Come along dear," Lucy said scrambling up the rocks.

His fears were leavened by her fine bottom in the khaki
shorts though there remained a bit of the "What am I doing
here?" By the time he reached the top he was breathing heavily while Bushrod and daughter had caught their breath. He
had been troubled by the many snake drawings and carvings
on the rocks. There were others but snakes were dominant.
He seated himself beneath Lucy not failing to notice the nice
underthighs beneath her loose-legged shorts.

"A lot of speculation here, possibly about the roots of
religion before sex and money came into play," Bushrod
joked. "Or maybe they all happen at once, an amusing idea.
This place is called Cocoraque Butte, not really a butte is
it? It's a little close to town for the university boys to get
interested in. They'd rather go north for the Navajo and
Hopi or maybe down to Casas Grandes. In fact I've never
seen anyone here in a dozen trips."

"Why all the renderings of snakes?" Sunderson was
uncomfortably leery that a rattler might ooze between the
boulders they were sitting on.

"Well, this kind of rockpile is habitat for rodentia and
consequently for the snakes that eat them. You have to think
that maybe primitive people were encamped here six thousand years ago and there were a prolific number of rattlers.
Say that someone from the tribe or group, probably a child,
had been killed by a rattler, which is comparatively small
but immense in the power of their venom. You naturally
would ascribe godlike powers to them. You propitiate the

snake gods by drawing or carving them, a sort of prayer.
You pray to God so that he won't kill you and in hopes he'll
give good luck to your family or group. Of course this is a
crude and speculative simplification."

"Where did the priests come in exactly? I mean I took
an anthropology course but I don't recall." Sunderson tilted
a bit for a better look at Lucy's thighs. She perceived his
intent and smiled at him, her first of the day.

"Well, these early people were nomadic and usually
had a medicine man, a shaman that stayed off to the side but
priesthoods came to people that were established as farmers or, on the northwest coast, as farmers and fishermen.
Farmers need rain and are suckers for religious leaders."

"They also offer consolation and advice," Lucy added
timidly.

"Yours should have told you long ago to get rid of your
nitwit husband."

"Please, Dad."

"Please, bullshit." He turned to Sunderson. "You ever
meet any of these people in their three-thousand-dollar suits?
They're the priests of money and pretend they have mystical knowledge about how to increase yours, which as you've
seen recently gives them a chance to swindle everyone. Me,
I'm strictly into land. You can read a realtor like a stop sign."

Sunderson immediately recognized that historically
Bushrod was from the moneyed class, which bought all the
land out of which a dime could be squeezed and even felt
virtuous about their land rape.

Lucy was in tears and began her slow descent, which
Sunderson figured was more difficult because you had your

gravity behind you. He looked off across the massive land-scape to the west and southwest and then down at Lucy who had stumbled near the bottom.

"She was a champ when young but then she became a brood mare to a fool. Early on I had him looked into. Word had it that he cheated his way through Choate and Yale."

"From this vantage point the Gadsden Purchase doesn't seem very wise." Sunderson was trying to avoid the subject of Lucy, upset by the cruelty of the father toward the daughter. He wondered at the number of parents he had known who bludgeon their children with their own ideals for them.

"I read that the part of the Mexican government that sold it to us were crooks. There's a fuss about it locally in the newspapers." Bushrod stood up and stretched with crackling bones.

"Yes, a man I'm looking for is involved." Mona's fax had said that Dwight was helping fuel this pointless controversy.

"You said you were retired."

"It's a hobby."

"For thirty years my hobby has been the desert. I don't have time to wear it out."

Bushrod descended nimbly as if in a hurry while Sunderson backed himself down, bursting into a profuse sweat when he thought he heard a rattling down in a crevasse beneath him. If you looked northeast toward Tucson the sky was discolored by the smudge pot of civilization, while to the west there were the *purple mountains majesty* in a haze of heat. He peeked down the deep crevasse praying to the snake gods to have mercy.

At the bottom Sunderson took the vehicle's medicine kit away from Lucy who was ineptly trying to patch a skinned knee.

"I've even doctored bullet wounds," Sunderson said kneeling before her and cleaning the grit from her knee. Her skin was smooth and moist with sweat. The nut twinge was not called for but was there.

"Nice legs, indeed. The only thing of value she got from her tosspot mother, whom I call Miss Absolut, were nice features to moderate my ugly ones. Did you ever shoot anyone? I bet that's not an original question."

"Just over their heads to slow them down. A couple were shot by partners. It's quite ugly." He was thinking that if Lucy's mother drank too much it was obvious who drove her there. It would be nice to slow the old fool down. "Once I entered a house south of Detroit with a partner. I knelt down to inspect a guy wheezing with a meat cleaver in his chest. He was blowing a pink bubble like a lung-shot deer. Another guy comes running out of a room with a butcher knife and my partner shot half his ass off with a .357."

"My God what an ugly story," Bushrod said.

They drove on another thirty miles to the southwest, and then on a two-track as bad as Sunderson had experienced reaching the Great Leader's longhouse. They parked at the foot of a canyon that was shaded from the early winter sun. Sunderson guessed it was nearly eighty degrees and said so.

"It gets to be one-fifteen-plus in June when we head back to Maine." Bushrod set off at a brisk pace up the canyon. Sunderson tried to help Lucy carry the lunches.

"You go ahead with Dad. I'm the squaw. He likes to lecture."

"You ever think of shooting him?" Sunderson teased.

"Many times," she replied archly.

He caught Bushrod who walked up the canyon in silence and Sunderson wondered if it was the cleaver story that battened his gob. They stopped at a place shadowed by paloverde and ironwoods and signs of a fire ring.

"I've camped here alone and been satisfied with the company. Before you showed up this morning Lucy said you were divorced?"

"Yes, for three years."

"Willingly?"

"No. It was my fault. She fled."

"You must not have much money."

"None to speak of. A pension. It's enough."

"If you're worth a lot you can't drive them away unless they can get a big cut."

"That's what I heard."

It was only beginning to occur to Sunderson that he was in the company of high rollers, hard to perceive as they weren't the least bit demonstrative like the midwestern rich. Having grown up so modestly, if not in poverty, he had done fairly well as a college graduate or so he thought. He had seen nothing enviable in the lives of richer people like Diane's parents whose peripheries seemed blinded by their possessions. His lifelong obsession with fishing for brook trout was largely free.

"She said you were from the Upper Peninsula. Way back when my family had a lot of timberland up that way and

in Wisconsin and Maine of course. We were noble predators, to be sure," he chuckled unattractively. "Later we were
mostly into paper mills. I bailed out totally in the late eighties
sensing that computers will make a lot of the paper supply
obsolete. I'd wager the *Boston Globe* will go under. My land
will always be land."

He was thinking that his suspicions were confirmed.
Now Bushrod reminded him of a big-shot banker in Marquette who yelled over to him a few weeks before when he
walked out of the Verling where he had had a fine whitefish
dinner. The banker had been parked in front of the disco
and someone had keyed his new Lexus leaving a deep five-
foot scratch along the door panels. The man was in tears of
rage and wanted immediate action. Sunderson had said that
it was out of his territory and that the banker must call the
Marquette city police, after which the man actually gasped
in rage. Sunderson had suddenly decided to be nice and
called the city police. The dispatcher had said, "That guy's
an asshole. We'll let him wait a half hour." Sunderson had
said that the city cops would arrive momentarily and had
walked off with a smile.

Deeper, though, was a rawer place, which was the
habitat of his thoughts about his father who had worked
for comparative peanuts at the paper mill in Munising for
over thirty years. His father, however, felt the job was
a big upward step from cutting pulp logs in the woods
when winter days could be thirty below zero or in June
when the blackflies were insufferably thick. Sunderson
had done it himself starting at age twelve on weekends
when he had saved enough for a used chain saw but it

was brutally hard to make fifteen bucks in a ten-hour day. Bushrod was the dictator in the faraway office who owned the timberland, the pulp mill, and tens of thousands of slaves and acres.

Lucy had laid out lunch on a sky-blue tablecloth and they sat on big rocks that someone who was very strong had dragged near the fire ring. There was an immediate wrangle because there was the wrong kind of mustard on Bushrod's roast beef sandwich.

"Dad, it's not my fault."

"Then whose fault is it?"

"You can have my chicken sandwich."

"My dear, are you crazy? You know I don't eat chicken sandwiches."

Meanwhile Sunderson felt a palpable prickling of the skin on his neck, a sign that they were being watched. When he had noted many human tracks at the base of the canyon Bushrod had said the tracks were made by illegal Mexican migrants who had crossed the border. He raised his eyes up the canyon wall and there not thirty yards away was a petroglyph of a half-man, half-lizard looking down at them. Sunderson knew that no matter what he read, no matter what was explained to him, he would never truly understand what he was looking at. The language that might do so was permanently lost. But this alone did not add up to his neck tingle. Farther up the canyon, easily a hundred yards, there was a small man, or perhaps a boy, looking at them partially concealed by a boulder and a bush. The mental jump between lizard-man and the boy was unavailable to him.

"I was wondering when you'd notice it, crime buster," Bushrod said with the self-assured voice of a bully politician.

"Quite something," Sunderson said, pleased to have diverted him from the wrong mustard.

"I have theorized it was made by the local shaman warning others away from his canyon."

Sunderson ignored him, got up with half his sandwich, a bottle of water, and an apple, and walked diagonally away from the boy up the canyon, putting the food on a solitary boulder beneath a mesquite. "Hola," he yelled, *hola* being the sum total of the Spanish he remembered from a Mexican American bunkmate in Frankfurt. He returned to quizzical glances.

"There's a boy up the canyon."

They both looked but lacked Sunderson's tough hunter vision in which you always look *through* a landscape, looking for a shape that doesn't belong.

"I don't see him," Lucy admitted.

"I think I do." Of course Bushrod was lying. "You shouldn't encourage them."

By the time they started back to Tucson Sunderson would have given an incalculable amount of money to be away from Bushrod not to speak of Lucy in her present incarnation as a dutiful daughter, which meant a piece of raw emotional roadkill. After the lizard-man the remaining singular event was a large rattlesnake crossing a two-track. They got out to look at it and Bushrod teased the viper to exhaustion with a long stick.

"I won that round," Bushrod said.

"The snake didn't have a stick," Sunderson parried.

"What's that supposed to mean, young man?"

"Try it without a stick." Sunderson loathed those television nature programs featuring people pestering frantic
animals in the name of knowledge.

"You are impudent!" Bushrod yelled.

"I hope so."

"Please," said Lucy, a frantic animal.

They drove back in silence and when they reached the
Arizona Inn Sunderson bolted from the vehicle without a
word. Safely in his room he uncapped a cheap travel pint of
Four Roses knowing it would have taken a gallon to purge
the day. There was an envelope with a fax on the coffee table.
The voice mail light on his phone was on and he listened
grimly to his mother. "Son, Berenice said the restaurant at
your hotel is wonderful. We want to come in for dinner."
He called back from his cell phone in case she had caller
ID that would read Arizona Inn.

"Mom, I'm on my way to Willcox."

"The hotel said you hadn't checked out."

"I just did."

"How sad. I had high hopes for a nice dinner."

"I'll see you in a couple of days." He called the hotel
operator and asked that all calls be blocked, then read the
fax from Mona. "This guy's a wiz. He got on to me and said,
'You'll be in real trouble if you keep tracking me.' Love, your
darling Mona who aches for her stepdaddy. P.S. the quote
you wanted from Crichton is from the *Washington Post* not
the *NY Times*."

All our progress of luxury and knowledge . . . we
have not been lifted by as much as an inch above the
level of the darkest ages . . . The last hundred years
have wrought no change in the passions, the cruelties,
and the barbarous impulses of mankind. There is no
change from the savagery of the Middle Ages. We
enter a new century equipped with every wonderful
device of science and art but the pirate, the savage,
and the tyrant still survives.

Sunderson took off his clothes and got under the sheets
after mixing a hefty second drink. Life at present called for
a professional-size nap but his mind was a whirling jangle
despite the alcohol which had failed its soporific mission. It
was 5:00 p.m. back in Marquette thus his first full workday
of retirement was finished, not that a detective was ever
truly off duty. Leisure was overrated he thought in a second
euphemism. His mind wandered among its flotsam and jet-
sam looking for a pleasant factoid that might ease him into
unconsciousness. In the 1600s thousands of Tuscan girls
starved themselves in order to get closer to Jesus according
to a forensic pathologist. No, this was too jarring. Because
of his brook trout fishing he had known for two years that
the little leopard frogs were disappearing from the landscape
before Diane had discovered the fact in an eco magazine.
She was angry he hadn't told her. So what. He had prayed
at age eight that his little brother Robert would grow a new
lower leg but when he told his dad his dad had said, "That
won't happen." Now, fifty-five years later there was a suggestion of tears. Lucy was a Diane from hell. There was a

split-second image of dropping Bushrod down a manhole
and sliding back the heavy cover. Down there with the shit
he is. This didn't work because violence causes a surge of
blood. Marion said that there were no truths only stories
and how would my story end in the desuetude of retirement?
Marion said that the computer allows people to waste end-
less hours on the novelty of their weaker interests. Just how
is flax grown and why are there so many Russian prostitutes
in Madrid? Diane's new husband is ill and is there a chance
for us to hitch up again? Doubtful. He was still the same
man she left, a man whose horizons were far lower than her
own. Early on he busted a college girl for five lids of pot
and it ruined her life. That's what her mother wrote him.
Can the brain be swollen with loneliness? Of course. The
Evangelicals largely favor enhanced torture. The years have
swallowed themselves and disappeared. Through the slit of
Slotkin's book Mona was crossways on the bed, her bare
butt aimed at him, a poignantly illegal butt if you weren't
in Mississippi or Costa Rica. His dick rose but his body
relaxed. He slept.

It was more dark than twilight with a bird fooling at the
window and sharp raps at the door. "It's me, Lucy," the
door voice said. He turned over looking for a clue to where
he might be. The rapping continued and he yelled, "Yes."
He grabbed the wrong one of the two robes hanging from
a bathrobe hook, a woman's robe that didn't quite close off
his middle. Opening the door he glanced immediately away
from Lucy's face which was swollen with weeping as if her

entire family had been wiped out in a house fire only minutes ago. In contrast she was dressed sexily in a shortish blue skirt and a white sleeveless blouse. His sleep-slowed brain computed *seduction*. She threw herself facedown on his bed muffling her voice.

"You had your phone turned off when I needed you."

"It was a tough day out on the range with your dad. I needed a nap." She looked attractive indeed but he couldn't quite make the wires of sex and tears connect.

"I have to leave early in the morning. I had this feeling you wanted me. Sadly I also had this intuition that I reminded you of your ex-wife. So it's not me you want, is it?"

"What am I supposed to say?" He was buying time what with being half tumescent.

"Never mind. I know the answer. I can't make love to you if I remind you of someone else." She began crying hard.

"I'm sorry." His brain had become a knot.

"At least hold me," she pleaded. Her voice was that of a girl, another explicit turnoff for him. Girls, unlike women, were only a turn-on at a distance, say the thirty feet between his peek hole and Mona's bedroom window.

So he did with her face against his neck which was soon wet and slippery. He questioned whether there were a limit to tears and if her ducts might eventually dry up making love possible but that was unlikely.

"Too bad you don't know how to lie," she wept.

"Jesus Christ, Lucy!" He flung himself out of bed and went to the desk, flipping through the room service menu. He had given half of his sandwich to the Mexican kid. It was 9:00 p.m. in Michigan, well past dinnertime, and he was ravenous. There was a salad with jicama whatever the hell that was. He called in an order for two cheeseburgers, a bottle of Beaujolais that he remembered Diane liked to drink in the summer, and a full bottle of Canadian whiskey for sixty bucks, the cheapest full bottle on the menu. Maybe he could drown her tears.

"We've failed each other," she wailed.

In answer he turned on the TV to Anderson Cooper who at the moment reminded him of a chipmunk. He segued to a film with a boatload of naturalists chasing a pod of killer whales off the coast of Alaska and hoped that the beasts would turn back on the boat and have a naturalist meal. He split the last of his travel pint into two drinks and she poked her head out from under a pillow at the rattle of ice.

When she finally walked out the door he looked at the whiskey bottle and was pleased that it was only half gone, which meant he wouldn't have a hangover in his top five hundred. He thought of what his dad would say if he knew his son paid sixty bucks for a bottle of whiskey. Likely nothing. Lucy had eaten only half of her cheeseburger so he took a cold bite to get full value. With the light out and chewing slowly he remembered a professor saying that carefully read history will tell us everything. This seemed not to be true. This was one of those times when he felt the utter exhaustion of not making love as if he were a teenager necking in a car. She had ended up talking so glowingly about her children he once again wished that he and Diane had had a child.

Chapter 5

Driving west at 7:00 a.m. on Interstate 10 toward Willcox into the bright headlights of oncoming commuter traffic Sunderson recalled that as a child he had devoutly wished for summer solstice all year round, when at least minimal light would tip the scales at over eighteen hours a day in the Great North. By early November it was down to about seven hours, clearly not enough to keep the soul together and one treaded the dark water in despair until after December 21, the winter solstice, when a minute or two of additional daylight helped the soul regather. Way back at Michigan State Kaplan's course on the Russian Revolution had enthralled him. One day this great professor of Russian history with his wonderful big bald head had given Sunderson a few minutes after class and Sunderson questioned the morale effect of so much darkness on far northern countries. Kaplan had said *how interesting* as he packed his briefcase and when Sunderson aced the course his skin had tingled with pride.

Not so this morning. He had barely made it out of the lobby and peeked around the corner to see Lucy coming toward the desk with a bellhop, then he had to hide in the bushes of the parking lot across the street as she got into a black sedan limo with a black driver. How much did this cost? What's wrong with a taxi?

He hit the radio OFF button when someone on NPR used the word turd *iconic*. He used to keep track of these obtuse Orwellian nuggets. A few years ago it was the relentless use of the word *closure* that raised his ire and then with Iraq the silly term *embedded*. In general Sunderson had no use for pundits. It reminded him of a recent article in the Marquette newspaper interviewing a local girl who had tried to *make it* in Hollywood who said, "Just about everyone you meet out there is a producer." Pundits reflected his idea that everyone in America gets to make themselves up whole cloth, and also the hideously mistaken idea that talking is thinking.

He had gotten up at 6:00 a.m. to call Mona before she was off to school. There had been a juvenile urge to ask her what she was wearing if anything but she beat him to it.

"Without you here I get dressed right away. Mom has the thermostat turned down to save money. Dad sent his annual note saying to keep my chin up. Can you believe that miserable cocksucker?"

Mona's father had left them when she was ten. He was the usual young realtor slicker trying to create a big development out of air. Despite the overwhelming beauty of the area it was impossible because Michigan's main population centers were at least a seven-hour drive away. Sunderson's motive in the early morning call was to get Mona off her direct hacking with Dwight which was conceivably dangerous. He diverted her by asking for specific information on contemporary cults. Sunderson had felt his focus was too narrow. After all, so much of his work had been with the minor laws made by the state legislature, the county supervisors, and the city council to pester people, not to speak of the U.S. Congress, the members of which have been so deranged by lobbyist pressure that many forget which state they come from.

"That sounds fun," she replied to the request for cult info. "Too bad you're not here. Two of my friends stayed over for a pajama party and we drank the rest of your beer. They're still here and they're naked, aren't you girls?" He heard shrieks of "naked nude."

"Please behave, Mona. I checked out of the Arizona Inn so hold any research faxes until you hear from me." He quickly hung up to the sound of more shrieks and laughter. In his own danceless life he couldn't imagine anyone laughing on a November dawn but here it was. He tried to dismiss the image of three nude girls in the same bed but it was like trying not to think of a white horse. Now there was suddenly a white horse in Mona's bedroom. It occurred to him while driving through Benson, a town that his brother-in-law Bob had bragged held thirty thousand Airstream trailers in the winter, that he hadn't seen any boys visiting Mona for a couple of years, just her goth female cabal, the nature of which was beyond him. He did not want to wander into the territory of his average male ignorance of lesbianism.

When he took the Willcox exit he began to feel pre-
sumptuous, which meant he was losing his nerve. There
was a sign saying that Willcox was the hometown of Rex
Allen, the singing cowboy, and he was way back when in
the world of the Saturday matinee when he and a hundred
other kids would watch big Rex and a dozen other cowboys
who were on horseback and would warble, "Get Along
Little Doggie," and then minutes later would be firing their
six-shooters at a group of woebegone Indians. From the
research Mona had faxed he knew there had been a scandal years ago about the Willcox cops using stray dogs for
target practice at the town dump, which was not a good
advertisement for law enforcement integrity. Another local
problem, this one of a financial nature, was an oversup-
ply of ostriches. Many people had bought breeding pairs
for fifty thousand bucks hoping to raise broods of young
ostriches for their hides, feathers, and meat to make their
inevitable fortunes. This struck Sunderson as a mini–Wall
Street scheme but too small-time to attract the likes of
Bernard Madoff, just the usual millions of suckers who
wanted to be sitting pretty.

To build his nerve back to a functional level he stopped
at a diner for the habitual heart-stopper breakfast of sausage,
eggs, and crispy hash browns his doctor had warned about.
While working at a bag of delicious local pistachios he noted
the loose wattles of all the retirees eating big breakfasts and
muttering with full mouths about the dangers presented by
Obama. It had always mystified him why so many of the
poor were right-wingers when with the Republicans the
poor went totally unacknowledged. The poor are always

betrayed by history he thought feeling both sympathy and empathy as his own interest in history seemed to be betraying him. On his coffee table he had counted nineteen volumes of an historical nature that he had bought but not yet touched. He had used reading to escape his job but as his job had withered toward his retirement party he had become less enthused. On the last day of brook trout fishing in September he had been thinking about the Etruscans while he waded a good stretch of the Chocolay River. He smelled marijuana before he rounded a bend and caught two young couples drinking beer and smoking pot on the riverbank. He flipped his badge and the girls began crying while the boys' faces turned pale. He stared at them coldly while his mind wandered to a small Etruscan museum he and Diane had visited in Italy.

"Fuck it," he said.

"Fuck what," one of the boys croaked hugging his girlfriend.

"I don't have time to take you in. I have to go fishing." Sunderson was staring at a trout rising and feeding at the edge of the eddy. How happy he and Diane had been in the Guarnacci Etruscan Museum in Volterra.

He was struggling with shelling pistachios as he drove south from Willcox past the Dos Cabezas Mountains toward the immense and ominous Chiricahuas farther south. Perhaps shelling pistachios while driving was as dangerous as talking on a cell phone in heavy traffic. His mood of unrest and a somewhat cramped tummy from his huge breakfast was matched by the weather, a strong wind from the north and a temperature in the low fifties out in the valley that was twice the altitude of sunny Tucson. He couldn't seem to keep up with the banks of clouds scudding overhead and it seemed to be snowing on the mountaintops of the Chirica-huas. His doubt came from recognizing his own hubris, the jump from busting young people for pot and meth or petty burglary to investigating the evils of religion too sizable to give him a sense of solid footing. His last burglary before retiring was an old man whose two jars of coins were stolen and Sunderson had busted the high school perps when they turned the coins in for cash at the bank the next morning. This was a decidedly nonreligious crime.

After nearly thirty miles he pulled off the blacktop at the intersection of a gravel road leading east toward the Chiricahuas. The MapQuest was fairly clear and the Google aerial showed a rather run-down ranch house with a number of corrals and ramshackle outbuildings but there was the question of whether it was a recent photo. A topographi-cal map would have been handier and so would a 4WD he thought because the seven miles of gravel led into succes-sively rougher country. He made his right turn and drove the mile toward the ranch thinking that the aerial had given no indication of the depth of the canyon on each side of the two-track, which showed signs of traffic in the dirt. He parked off to the side of a locked gate feeling a little naked without his .38, which was in a locked desk drawer back in Marquette, but then the Great Leader Dwight had always been friendly enough if somewhat distant.

He climbed the iron-bar gate with wobbly legs and headed up the road amused at the similarity of the landscape to the cowboy movies where Indians or outlaws would pop up from the uniform and phony-looking boulders and start shooting arrows or bullets at Gene Autry or Roy Rogers.

He stopped to look at a large gathering of varied birds on the bushes around a small spring, really a seep from the canyon wall, and then he was quite literally stoned. Stoned as happened in certain Middle Eastern countries like Saudi Arabia where the woebegone malefactor tries to cover his face while being pelted by fair-sized rocks.

PART II

Chapter 6

He tried to run back toward the car while covering his face and squinting out between his fingers but two large rocks hit his fingers in succession, breaking one, and then one hit the back of his head, which felled him like the trees he used to cut, with blood immediately flowing down on his shirt collar. While falling he twisted to try to see his assailants but the blood from his hand smeared his vision. He tried to grab at the bush that had been full of birds but the branches were too brittle and slight to slow his fall and he hit the ground hard facedown, which fractured his nose and knocked out his wind. He scrambled toward his blurred car on his hands and knees with the copper smell of blood gushing from his nose. Rocks continued to thud painfully against his back and the backs of his legs and another large one to the back of his head made him collapse to his stomach again. He became fairly sure he was going to die but rose again crawling

slowly toward the gate and through the bottom-most opening and then the rocks stopped coming. He heard a voice
that he was sure was Dwight's shouting, "Go away. Stay
away." He was on his knees beside the compact car and
opened the door and felt on the floor for his water bottle,
the contents of which he poured on his upturned face. He
turned and with limited vision could see Dwight standing
there between the canyon walls with a dozen or so young
people none of whose height reached his shoulders. All of
them were girls wearing skirts. They all turned and walked
back toward the ranch.

Sunderson's hands were too slippery with blood and
water to hold the car keys but he managed to open his suitcase and dry his hands on a pair of boxer shorts. He was
sure he had a concussion and wondered if he'd be able to
drive. He made it the seven miles out to the main road and
had barely pulled over when he passed out. He had noted
that it was 10:30 a.m. on the car clock and when he awoke
it was high noon with sleet beating against the windows and
now the peaks of the Chiricahuas were almost invisible. He
had the sense that the part of his brain toward the back of
his head was short-circuited. It flashed and swirled and there
were moments of intense pain. He took out his cell phone
but there was no signal so he drove south twenty miles until
he neared a dumpy ranching village named Elfrida where
he pulled off the road's shoulder and passed out again. He
awoke in fifteen minutes and now his cell phone worked and
he called his sister Berenice who was in a beauty parlor. You
always had to say things twice to Berenice and it was hard
to talk through two bloody tooth stumps and swollen lips.

He said he had fallen on his face down a canyon and needed help ASAP. He said it twice and she said she'd come over with Bob who could drive Sunderson's car. She and Bob had lived for years in Rio Rico, which was near Nogales, and she knew both a nurse and a doctor at the Nogales hospital. She said they'd reach him in two hours or less.

The lights in his brain began to dim again as he sat there with the sleet ticking off the windshield. He kept thinking, "I have no evidence," but didn't quite know what his brain meant by this sentence. He had never felt further away from his life as he had known it. He smelled the burned smell of the desert earth but that was the grit in his nose from pitching forward on his face. He figured his mind meant that there was no hard evidence for anything of value. He thought that this wouldn't help anything and was close to mumbling his childhood prayer, "Now I lay me down to sleep, I pray the Lord my soul to keep, if I should die before I wake, I pray the Lord my soul to take." He couldn't bring himself to pray but was surprised he remembered the words. He looked east at the foothills of the Chiricahuas which were disappearing with his vision. His brain could see a map in an historical text because it was just over the mountains to the east that Geronimo had surrendered in Skeleton Canyon. The Apaches were the hardest people imaginable but so were those who had stoned him.

A grizzled old man picking up roadside trash found him and was soon followed by a deputy. He was half awake when the trash man opened the compact door and yelled with breath worse than a skunk's asshole, "You look like a horse throwed you off and lit on your goddamned face." The deputy was remote and cool, apparently fresh on the job, trying to do it by the book but the book wasn't handy so he seemed unsure and frightened by Sunderson's appearance.

"I took a header down a steep canyon," he hissed through his broken teeth and swollen lips. He offered his identification including his Michigan State Police badge. He was upset that it was 2:00 p.m. Where had he been?

"Sir, we have to get you to a hospital."

At that moment Berenice and Bob showed up in their Escalade. Like her mother Berenice was a fair-sized and formidable woman. She took over.

Chapter 7

It was only in the evening of his fifth day at the Nogales hospital that Sunderson felt he had a real inkling of who he was though he was unsure it mattered. He had received a subdural hematoma from the large rock that had struck him in the back of the head, also a minimally depressed fracture that likely wouldn't require surgery. The hardest symptoms of his post-concussive state were more vague: the anxiety and depression, the inability to concentrate, and the disequilibrium when he toddled out a back door to have a cigarette. Another smoker, a Mexican orderly, pointed to the south of the hospital and told Sunderson that he was real close to the border. This was the best part of his disaster so far as nearly all of the various employees of the hospital spoke Spanish with each other, which meant he didn't have to struggle with comprehension, which was beyond him anyway. He also liked the pure music of the language. One of the only memories

he could recapture was of his Mexican friend in Frankfurt
saying "hola," so Sunderson muttered "hola" to anyone who
entered his hospital room. A slight problem was that neither
the ER doctor nor the regular doctor Berenice had secured
him believed that his injuries came from a fall. They didn't say
why and Sunderson didn't really give a shit. What could they
do, throw more rocks at him? When an attendant, a roly-poly
female, had helped him take a shower she kept whispering
"*muy malo*" as he looked at himself in a full-length mirror and
discovered that his predominant body color was blue.

Another slight problem was the visit of a plainclothes
officer on the third day. There was buzzing in Sunderson's
ear so he hadn't heard the details when the man introduced
himself. The man was short and squat, of Mexican descent,
and looked powerful and feral like some of those Detroit detectives who daily brushed against death. The man asked to
see his ID, which Sunderson said was locked in the drawer
of the nightstand beside his bed. When Sunderson struggled
with the key the man said "never mind" and that he had read
the report filed by the Cochise County deputy.

"What are you doing here?"

"Visiting my mom in Green Valley."

"What were you doing near Elfrida? No one goes to
Elfrida except for a purpose."

"I was looking the country over. I like history. I wanted
to see where Geronimo surrendered."

"Oh bullshit. The Michigan State Police said that you
retired last week. A lot of people who retire from our line
of work have someone they want to get even with. That's
not you?"

"No."

"Nothing to do with the drug or illegal migrant problems?"

"No."

"The doctor said you didn't fall down a canyon. Your palms are fine. If you had fallen they would have been torn up trying to stop your fall."

"Who gives a shit?" Sunderson watched a fine-looking vulture fly by the window.

"I do. You're in my homeland. It's easy for me to run you out of here."

"I'm looking into a religious cult. A friend's daughter lost some money to them."

"Oh fuck me!" The man laughed explosively. "Those daffy fucks are all over Arizona. They've probably blown the money on vegetables."

"I suppose so." Sunderson was relieved at the man's reaction.

"Well, take care," the man said getting up to leave. "It's obvious your cult doesn't have a sense of humor. If you shoot anyone you won't be treated like an officer. Even the cults down here are armed to the teeth. At least most of them don't do drugs. I guess religion is their drug, you know, the Marxian opiate of the people."

When he left Sunderson regretted having to explain himself even minimally but then it was a courtesy between detectives. He already felt he was too old to play for keeps and would likely back away from the Great Leader.

His biggest problem was Berenice who visited twice a day. When he told her every other day was enough she began to cry. Bob was loitering out in the hall and Sunderson added that she shouldn't bring her *asshole* husband. "Everything gives me a headache in my condition."

"I'm so sorry about you and now we think Mom had a little stroke. She's slurring her words."

"She's eighty-five and she drinks too much."

"That doesn't make it easier."

He dictated an e-mail to Mona saying, "I've been injured. I'll be okay. I'll be in touch in a few days. Don't send anything to Berenice." He didn't want Berenice to read anything Mona might send. When he got out he'd find a Kinko's store for that.

Chapter 8

In seven days and seven nights in the hospital he certainly hadn't re-created himself. Most of all he felt his age, a sensation that had previously been creeping up on him but had now fallen from the heavens like the "ton of bricks" people used to talk about. He had been warned by the doctor of certain post-concussive symptoms but had only caught the words "depression" and "forgetfulness." He had been concentrating on a nurse's aide who had just taken his temperature and blood pressure prefatory to his checking out. Her name was Melissa and he had looked forward to her visits several times a day. When she hadn't appeared the day before he had been a little teary because she was definitely his only viable contact with life. She spoke English with a heavy accent and had showed him a photo of her three-year-old daughter who wore tiny earrings, evidently a local custom or so he thought. All the staff knew he was a detective and

she told him that her husband had been a *narcotico* who had
been murdered the year before. Each day when she would
leave the room he was immediately despondent. He was too
timid to ask her for her last name or phone number. She
was friendly but he doubted she would want anything to do
with a black-and-blue geezer. They had mostly talked about
fishing and eating fish. Her father had been a schoolteacher
in Hermosillo and had taken she and her brother fishing
near Guaymas a number of times. She said she would like
to cook him some sea bass with lime, oil, and garlic but now
here he was discharged with no way to get in touch with
her. What had happened to the easy resourcefulness that
had informed his career as a detective? There didn't seem
to be an ounce of detective left in him. With great physical
or mental suffering or both simultaneously in his case comes
humility, and not virtuous humility but that of a dog who,
hit by a car, drags itself off the road into a ditch trying to
be out of more harm's way.

Berenice had found him a small garage apartment on
the northeast side of Nogales just off the road to Patagonia
for his further rehabilitation. The house was owned by an
elderly couple from Minnesota whom he readily expected
to bother him but they turned out to be bird-watchers and
nature photographers and were gone from dawn to dark
except on Sundays. His little apartment's walls were covered with too many of their photos so that the total effect
was a bit lurid and capped off with a photo of a large wild
rattlesnake with an acorn woodpecker in its mouth, the bird
staring at the camera as if to ask for an explanation, an easy
metaphor for his own situation, or so Sunderson thought.

Not very deep in his mind he knew he had no clear objective except that he couldn't simply cut and run. There was the prominent mystery of what retired people were supposed to do all day. Read and drink? Join AA? Learn to cook? Divorce had brought about the absence of Diane's good cooking which he sorely missed. He had thought about taking cooking lessons but then both Marion and Mona were good cooks and had offered to help him learn. Meanwhile he felt he should at least stay in Arizona for Thanksgiving with his mother and until his bruised mind cleared. In the miniscule part of his head he referred to as his snake brain there was a fantasy of shooting Dwight in the head from five hundred yards with a Sako target rifle. He had it coming.

Berenice took him to the dentist to have his two tooth stumps removed and in the pain-free immediate aftermath he listened to his cell phone messages. Lucy called, weeping of course and fairly drunk saying that she missed his company, which seemed unlikely. His ex-wife Diane had left a message saying that she and her ill husband were moving back to Marquette. He had a life expectancy short of a year and wanted to be in his hometown where he could be treated by doctors he knew and trusted. Marion asked if he wanted books sent from the stack of new ones and to please call. Mona's message was garbled saying that she had had a "disaster" and had sent an explanation via Kinko's with a lot of cult material. She had also prayed to Odin for his recovery. This latter fact had him stumped but then he recalled she had a lot of little statues of deities on her bedroom dresser. Many were Far Eastern and he wondered about the attraction of India and Tibet for the young.

Berenice was out in his yard looking at plants so he asked her to fetch Mona's material without snooping. Naturally tears formed and her face reddened with anger but it was all for show between a brother and sister who in their childhood had readily gotten in each other's *stuff*. There were three bedrooms in the second story of the house with his parents up front, then Berenice and Roberta, and then he and little Bobby in the back. Berenice and Roberta had a skeleton key and kept their door locked but Bobby had found a key in their dad's desk that worked, thus by reading Berenice's diary they had discovered she had lost her *cherry* the night that, as a junior, she had been crowned homecoming queen. Sunderson had been a sophomore at the time and Bobby five years younger in the fifth grade. He had questioned, "What's a cherry," but Sunderson couldn't bring himself to answer. The kids had come along in two tiers with Roberta then a year later Bobby coming along after Dad left pulp cutting and driving a log skidder for the comparative prosperity of a job at the mill. When Sunderson had teased Berenice about her lost cherry she had countered by stealing his packet of stolen Trojan condoms and putting them on their mother's plate at Sunday breakfast and an insufferable scene had followed.

Sunderson thought about his family while waiting for Berenice. A lump arose in his throat with the image of Roberta pulling Bobby up the steep hill in her red wagon in the time between when he lost his leg and when his prosthesis could be fitted.

Sunderson was sitting in a lawn chair and feigned sleep when Berenice returned with the manila envelope. He was relieved when she drove away. The packet remained un-opened for five days because of a double obsession, the first one being why he should stay so far from his native ground and in a state of severe physical and mental wreckage. He didn't have an answer least of all revenge, which was far too large and fancy a word. In the Upper Peninsula people only said "getting even." The other obsession was Melissa but then he couldn't proceed beyond her physical image and the slight lisp in her voice. She was only minimally at-tractive, handsome maybe, a little full-figured like so many of the local Chicano women. He tried to imagine being a father to her daughter but failed. Back at the office Roxie had told him that he should get married again in order to pass on his retirement benefits when he died. That was U.P. thinking. It was not a prosperous area and perhaps half the population had no health insurance. A fishing acquaintance with Lou Gehrig's disease had shot himself to save money for his wife.

Sunderson was growing a beard to hide the face he no longer understood with its yellowish-blue chin bruises. On the fifth morning of Mona's unopened package he had hung a hand towel over the bathroom cabinet mirror so he wouldn't see himself. He took his coffee out to the lawn chair in the yard surprised to find that his landlord was out weeding flowers rather than being on a nature expedition. The man explained that his wife was ill from her chemo, which she had to take for *the cancer,* as he called it, rather than for simply *cancer,* a usage Sunderson had noted in the upper Midwest as if cancer were a singular scourge and monster rather than its own multifoliate cellular nightmare.

"Despite what someone did to you, you should walk every day or you'll turn to shit," Alfred said.

"That's probably true." Sunderson was mildly pleased that he didn't feel pissed off as he usually did with advice of a personal nature.

"Out here we live up in the sky compared to the Midwest. You have to work to get your lungs acclimated. If you're in the backcountry you might think of carrying a pistol."

Sunderson nodded in agreement and Alfred walked away. If you have to carry a pistol for nearly forty years you're not enthused about continuing to do so. Maybe Marion could send his pistol with the books but it could be illegal. He couldn't remember. Sunderson had never been interested in gun control except to favor the banning of automatic weapons and having the conviction that the United States would be better off if like Canada we banned handguns. Ultimately he didn't give a shit though it was likely if he had fired a warning shot they would have stopped throwing rocks. Again he thought that there was no real conclusive evidence for much of anything.

Except hunger. He was wobbly from lack of food and went inside to heat up some lentil soup Berenice had made him. He put it on the stove and then sat down at the kitchenette table and finally opened Mona's material. On top of the stack was a brief e-mail from Lucy whom he had given Mona's e-mail to keep in touch. "Your idea was to try to screw me and forget me. You're a bad person. Love, Lucy." This message confused him because the severity of his concussion had caused memory lapses the doctor said would probably be temporary. Mona's letter about her "disaster," however, fully penetrated his bruised brain. Mona had fallen in love with a brother and sister, and her mother had made a surprise visit back home and caught the three of them *making out* in bed together. She had beat on them with a broom. The upshot was that her mother insisted she have counseling for her *perversion*. Sunderson made an effort to be shocked but instead was stimulated for the first time in two weeks. He hadn't dared think sexually about Melissa in an attempt to stay high-minded to withstand the disappointment if she turned him down for a date.

He sipped at Berenice's soup, which was without seasoning, while leafing through a pile of cult material that Mona had found on the Internet. It was bizarre indeed but didn't quite catch his interest. He impulsively called a friendly hospital orderly named Giacomo, not a Mexican name but when the orderly was babbling in the hospital room he had said that he was named after a Tucson landlord who had been kind to his parents when they came north in the 1980s. Giacomo said that he didn't have Melissa's cell phone or land line numbers, the latter unlisted because Melissa's brother was a big-time *narcotico* in one of the warring cartels and gossip had it that her brother killed her husband because of a deal gone wrong. She and her daughter were always in jeopardy of being kidnapped and the name Melissa was an alias and he had no idea what her real name was. She hadn't appeared for work today.

Sitting there with his tasteless soup Sunderson felt his confused mind becoming more liquid. The image of Mona in bed with a brother and sister floated toward Melissa and her baby daughter overlooked by Daryl, which Mona wrote was Dwight's new alias.

There was a knock at the door. It was Alfred who handed Sunderson a map saying that he had marked some places in the area for their interesting walks. Alfred then invited Sunderson to join him and his wife for dinner at their favorite Mexican restaurant. Sunderson wanted to refuse but could think of no reason to do so and accepted. After Alfred left he noted that when he pulled up his trousers the waist had become loose. He had probably lost a dozen pounds in the nearly two weeks since the stoning though part of that was because he had forgotten in his dream confusion to drink any alcohol after never missing a day since he entered college. He called Marion knowing that it was lunch hour at the school.

"I haven't had a drink in twelve days."

"Oh bullshit," Marion laughed.

"Truly. I actually forgot in what they call my post-concussive state."

"I take it you'll miss deer cabin this year?" The two of them never really hunted unless a deer approached an illegal salt block in Marion's cabin clearing.

"I can't cut and run after getting the shit kicked out of me which is a euphemism."

"If you shoot Dwight you'll spend the rest of your life in prison. I heard the food is bad."

"His name is Daryl now."

"I know. I had dinner with Mona. She's having problems with her mother."

"That's what she told me. Do you figure she's a lesbian?" Sunderson had brooded about the question for some time.

"Maybe. Who knows what you are at sixteen? At that age my music teacher was blowing me and I turned out hetero." Marion laughed hard. "He was real good at it."

"You're a man of wide experience. I was thinking you could send me some books. There are twenty-nine I haven't read on the coffee table. Send seven at random. Seven is my lucky number."

Sunderson hung up after they talked about the ramifications of Diane moving back to town. There were none except that it would be painful to run across her. He was wobbly when he got up from the table and sat down and finished the lukewarm soup, like it or not. What he really wanted was a nap but it was only a little after midmorning. A walk was in order. He spread out Alfred's map and felt good when he found his own location. There was a town called Patagonia about fifteen miles down the road, the name of which jogged his memory. The thirty-year Cochise Wars had their inception about three miles southwest of town. A low-rent rancher had claimed that the Apaches had kidnapped his child, which proved to be untrue but the war continued. It was akin to Bush thinking that the Iraq war was God's will. The utter irrationality of the human species continued to leak into Sunderson's wounded brain as he drove toward the mountain community of Patagonia.

His walk went poorly. He found a place Alfred had marked, the small road up Red Mountain, but the relatively tame incline was too much for him. He turned away, went through a cattle gate, and walked about four hundred yards, preoccupied with his thoughts, until he was on the verge of stepping into a hole covered sparsely with brush. The hole

was a pipe about three feet in diameter and led straight down
into the center of the earth or so he thought. As a citizen
of the Upper Peninsula he was accustomed to the trashed
landscape left behind a century ago by mining companies.
It was a fine place to dump the body of Dwight-Daryl if it
ever came to that. This thought shocked him into a sweat
and when he turned back toward his car he realized that he
had failed to acknowledge the depth of his anger over being
nearly stoned to death.

He stopped in Patagonia and ate a big bowl of menudo,
the tripe stew that Melissa had told him to eat daily to regain
his strength. How could he do otherwise? He wasn't sure he
liked the dish never having eaten tripe before, but that was
beside the point. The big though lovely waitress told him the
bone in the stew was a calf's foot for extra flavor. He mulled
over the idea that he was attracted to Mexican women because of his inexperience with them. You would see a few
now and then in Marquette, especially students at Northern
Michigan University, but he had never actually known any.
A Marquette bartender who had been to Mexico said that
the women down there would fuck you until your ears flew
off but bartenders were notoriously short on credibility. The
base of male fantasy life was silly indeed he thought with the
image of ears flying through the air like sparrows.

Out on the street he decided he liked this village. He
rechecked Alfred's map and decided to take a back way,
first stopping at a tavern called the Wagon Wheel Saloon. It
seemed important not to delay his reintroduction to alcohol.
There was an older man behind the bar, likely the owner,
who seemed to immediately *make* him as a cop, a beat-up

one at that. Sunderson downed his double shot of Canadian whiskey and took his beer out to the backyard smoking area. Arizona had been unable to slow down any of its public bad behavior except smoking according to Berenice who had told him not to smoke in her house. He had gone outside and his mother had bummed one. It was wonderful watching an eighty-five-year-old woman smoke a cigarette. His mother had been quitting all of her life and Berenice had said that Mom was down to a few a week.

There was a table full of construction workers, gringo and Mexican, drinking their lunch, who fell silent when Sunderson came into the yard. Was he that obvious in his ratty khaki sport coat that Diane had bought him from Orvis and he had worn until it was only a single step up from a rag? Fuck 'em he thought, taking the plastic table farthest away from them in the yard. He was busy brooding about the realities of Mexican women. He had noticed that right down to his young neighbor Mona that females had a sense of reality that no matter how widely varied was at odds with his own. Diane had bought the Sunday *New York Times* at the newsstand where it arrived on Monday. She also subscribed to the *New Yorker* and neither of these publications held any interest for him, lacking as they did the solidarity of books. The last thing he wanted in life was to be current. Despite Diane's urging he had never gone to New York City and she settled for traveling there with friends every couple of years. He could be such a stodgy prick that it amazed him. No wonder Diane had flown the coop.

The double shot of whiskey and single bottle of Mexican beer were more than enough and he walked a bit dizzily

out of the Wagon Wheel. He took a back gravel road marked
on Alfred's map past a mile-long Nature Conservancy property, slowing to watch a balding young man get on a trac-
tor, put on a slouch cowboy hat, and begin mowing a big
field of weeds. Sunderson continued on enchanted by the
road. There were fairly dense woods surrounding a creek
on the left, and on the right a series of small canyons leading to the mountains. He loved gravel roads, which were a
trademark of his youth when there were far more of them.
Gravel roads were easier in the winter because of the trac-
tion offered through the snow. He turned left to get back to
the highway but then stopped in a large pool of water when
the road forded the creek, wondering if his compact rental
could handle it. Off to the right less than fifty yards away a
man was throwing food to a group of ravens from the patio
of a small house mostly hidden in a thicket of bamboo and
trees. Sunderson was instantly homesick because he and
Marion would collect roadkill if it wasn't too rank and hoist
it up on a platform at the edge of the woods near Marion's
cabin. The ravens kept an eye out and would quickly appear.

"Just keep to the right and you can make it," the man
yelled.

"Thanks. What are you feeding them?"

"Tripe. They love it."

"Just had some myself." Sunderson waved and got
back in the compact, fording the creek slowly so the water
wouldn't surge upward and drown his engine.

Back at the apartment he took a deeply wonderful
hour's nap truncated by a call from his mother who was
very angry.

"That little bitch Berenice took my cigarettes," his mother practically yelled, her voice a little slurred by her stroke. "She also took my goddamn car keys." His mother only swore when she was very angry.

"Calm down. I'll drop some off in the morning." It was time to make a few notes in his journal.

1. There is the sudden troubling thought that my pursuit of Dwight-Daryl has a religious motive, however slight. I'd rather think that it's strictly a law enforcement matter but that is no longer my job. I'm morally pissed off, which makes it quasi-religious. This is mildly embarrassing.

2. Post-concussive state causing some new memories as if clusters of neurons were reactivated. Mother was in hospital having just given birth to Bobby. Dad went with his friend Big Frank down to Trenary to pick up a sow's head to make what they called *souse* or head cheese. I remember I was sitting in the backseat with Berenice in the old Dodge. It was a cold November day and they had just butchered at the farmer's and I stomped on a frozen pool of pig blood until the ice broke. Back at Frank's house they boiled up the huge sow's head in a scalding pot over a fire. I remember I cried because I wasn't strong enough to pick up the sow's head at the farmer's. They boiled it all afternoon then chopped it up and put it in the pan with liquid and next day it was like pig-meat Jell-O and tasted good.

Sunderson showered, heated coffee, and dressed in
fresh clothes for his upcoming dinner with Alfred and his
wife. He intended to drive to Tucson in the morning to try
to buy a pistol and would drop off cigarettes for his mother.
Why deny an eighty-five-year-old woman her pleasure?
Everyone on the continent is pestering each other not to
speak of the children and animals.

Were it not for the fact that he had looked into the bathroom's full-length mirror the good feeling of his nap would
have continued. Jesus. What did I do to be so black and
blue? Got truly stoned. He certainly didn't turn around for a
back view to see more smears of dark blue and sickly yellow.
To distract himself he leafed through Mona's big packet on
cults in the United States feeling a tremor of humility at the
job of figuring out the mess. Mona had added another note
he had missed on his first go-through of the material. She
had communicated with a disaffected member of Daryl's
(the former Dwight) new Arizona commune called Yahweh
Kwa. The woman loved "spiritual adventures" but felt that
Daryl's membership fee of twenty thousand bucks was too
stiff. The money was for a huge kiva and the stone Basque-
Apache sheepherder's huts the members would live in. Only
two hundred people would be allowed in this spiritual village. Construction had already started and the woman objected that all toilet and shower facilities were open-air as
there was no shame in being a spiritual mammal. The woman
objected to the idea of "pooping" in public and living in a
tent until her stone hut was finished. She said that Arizona
winter nights at five thousand feet could be below freezing
despite the immense mesquite log fire the tents surrounded.

The winter diet would be "natural Apache," which meant sheep and cattle and the woman was a vegan, which would be the summer diet. Another objection was Daryl's hundred levels of spiritual accomplishment. These hundred stages would remain in Daryl's care and would be unwritten. Daryl had spent years at the library of the University of California in Berkeley researching the great third-world religions to come up with the hundred levels. Each week there would be a ritual dance around an immense fire and Daryl would present that week's spiritual challenge. The Yahweh Kwa would be safe from government intervention because it was on the property of the illegal Gadsden Purchase, which Daryl was challenging in federal court.

It went on and on in this fantastic arena of cockamamie bullshit including the fact that over half the members were college graduates. Sunderson laughed aloud, his first full laugh in the two weeks since his "accident" forgetting for the moment just who had caused his nearly fatal injury. The Nogales doctor had been concerned with a specific heart fluttering called tachycardia which, after a few days, subsided on its own. The doctor had mentioned the possibility of a pacemaker, which even in his brutalized condition made him cringe further. It wasn't something to worry about in retrospect, an ugly habit of his this worrying about events that had already been resolved. He missed the calming influence of his friend Marion and wondered for the thousandth time if he would be a calmer man if he didn't drink so much, a habit that had increased in volume after Diane left. To even think about quitting made him feel that life was on the verge of cheating him.

He drew his chair up to a window that faced the south-east trying to dismiss the niggling idea that he should simply shoot Dwight-Daryl and then go back home. How tempting. His still very sore body had brought on a sense of his age like a thunderstorm. Dwight-Daryl reminded him of something he had heard about on NPR. Somewhere in South America there was a type of malevolent foot-long centipede that hung from the ceilings of bat caves and snagged innocent little bats for dinner.

Out the window a few miles to the southeast a small jet was landing at the Nogales International Airport. Why build the airport next to a mountain Sunderson wondered, but there was very little in the way of flatland in the area. Everywhere the substance of earth was rising up in the form of rocky hills and mountains, which gave Sunderson vertigo. Why did white people settle here? Why hadn't it simply been left to the indigenous Apaches? It might have been easier to digest this landscape if every plant and bush and tree weren't alien to him excepting the cottonwoods, which were obvious relatives of the popple in the U.P. Why were their so-called oaks a fake-looking green in November? He had touched a simple plant in the yard and the contact had drawn blood from a finger. Certainly he was ingenious enough as a detective of long experience to kill Dwight-Daryl and get back home scot-free. There was no hurry because it was nearly six months until the opening of brook trout season. He suddenly recalled one morning in the hospital when Melissa had pushed in a portable heart monitor on wheels. She had stooped to get something out of a cabinet and while dazed with Oxycontin he had received a clear view up her white nurse's uniform to her pubis. She sensed his gaze, blushed, and swiveled her hips so he could no longer catch the view. Now at the window this memory made him tumescent, a clear rush of life. His mind segued helplessly to the image of a nude Mona through the peek hole in his library. His hard-on twinged with pain. He was homesick. He dialed the phone.

"Hello, you big old darling. I miss you." She sounded high.

"I miss you, too. Are you high? It's illegal," he joked.

"Just an after-therapy toke. I'm told I may be bisexual."

"I'd rather not think about it." He was regretting the call.

"Don't be squeamish. Genitalia are simply genitalia. It all starts in the mind."

"Sorry. I lost my confidence when I left home." He was surprised to admit this.

"I can't imagine you without total confidence."

"Well it's true. My first trip to a foreign country has been a disaster. I mean it's technically part of the United States but I don't believe it. You wouldn't want to look at me."

"I know it. Marion said that he talked to your sister Berenice a couple of times and she said that every time she left your hospital room she sobbed."

"Thanks for all that material you sent." Sunderson was trying to get the subject away from himself.

"I've done some more poking around. Our Dwight-Daryl had an underage-sex charge in Choteau, Montana. I think he bought off the parents like big shots do. He made

another mild threat to me so now I'm doing anything touchy
through a cousin in Pittsburgh who's an ace hacker."

"That's a good idea." Sunderson had no real idea of the
technology involved but other suspicions suddenly niggled
at him. "Have you ever met anyone named Carla?" He wondered if Carla or Queenie were acting as Marquette spies
for Dwight-Daryl.

"You mean Carla the dyke?" Mona laughed. "She
made a pass at me at the tennis barn. She's a buddy of
my so-called therapist who says my root problem is my
disappearing father."

"Just avoid her at all costs." There was a knock at the
door. "Looks like I have to go to dinner. I'll call you tomorrow."

Sunderson ate like a fool at a restaurant called Las
Vigas in downtown Nogales. At first he thought the restaurant sign was misspelled but Alfred told him that *vigas* in
Spanish meant *beams* as in roof beams. Alfred walked him
through the menu and they both had *chicherones*, fried chunks
of beef intestine, a side of guacamole, and then *machaca*,
which was dry, fried jerked beef with chile and onions. Alfred's wife Molly was just finishing her second session of
chemo and had to limit herself to soup. Her wig kept slipping
and she would merrily push it back into place. She spoke
Spanish fluently with a waiter named Alphonse. They were
telling jokes about the Border Patrol and a ton of cocaine
found on a vegetable import truck the day before. When
Molly translated for him Sunderson was boggled having
never busted more than a kilo in his career and that was a
cumulative amount.

"Someone is waving at you," Alfred said, nudging him away from his food.

Sunderson looked up and about three tables away there was Melissa and her little daughter and a man. He felt his blood heating in his face and he swallowed a bite of *machaca* with difficulty. He got up slowly fearing the effects of a large margarita.

"It's so good to see you," Melissa said. "This is my brother Xavier and my daughter Josefina."

Xavier stood and Sunderson shook his left hand because his right was withdrawn. Sunderson restrained his startled reaction to Xavier's appearance. The man was dressed in a fine dark suit and red tie. His appearance was more than vaguely effeminate but his face had the pale specific edge of the ominous, the feral as if all of his schooling, his life in fact, had taken place at night.

"Are you liking our area?" Xavier asked with a cool smile.

"Yes, despite a certain unfriendliness." Sunderson wondered why he was admitting this but then Xavier was obviously no man's fool.

"Yes, Melissa said that you tripped on a vicious rock and fell off a fifty-thousand-foot cliff." He winked and clunked his gloved right hand on the table. "I tripped once myself and lost a hand." He laughed a metallic laugh. "Please sit down."

"Accidents happen," Sunderson said. Josefina was crawling on his lap and feeling the beginning of his beard with a smile the moment he was seated.

"She thinks all older men are nice grandfathers," Melissa said.

"It is a rare pleasure to sit with a detective." Xavier glanced toward the front door where two very large men were standing.

"I'm recently retired," Sunderson said with a clench in his gut.

"Someone didn't know you were retired," Xavier said, standing and dropping a hundred-dollar bill on the table. He leaned and kissed both his sister and niece. "Be kind to my sister. She likes to fish and have picnics. Call if you need help."

Sunderson watched as Xavier walked through the crowded restaurant with everyone averting their eyes including a big table of Border Patrol agents. Through the front window he saw Xavier and the two big men who had stood near the door get in the back of a black Suburban with tinted windows.

"He took a degree in the history of Spanish drama at the University of Arizona. Now he thinks of himself as a stockbroker." Melissa sighed and held her daughter close. "Let's go fishing on Patagonia Lake when you wish." She handed Sunderson a card with her cell phone number, kissed his cheek, and left.

"I know her from the hospital. Isn't she lovely," Molly said when he returned to the table.

"You're already in over your head," Alfred said gruffly. "I'd expect a visitor."

"I'm only an old man with a crush on a nurse," Sunderson said grabbing the check and noting that now the waiter Alphonse wouldn't look at him directly.

After saying good night to Alfred and Molly he wasn't in a mood that included a semblance of equilibrium. Why did fate make him infatuated with a young woman who had a brother like Xavier? He got a pint of Canadian whiskey out of his suitcase in order to calm his nerves. The only time he had run into anyone similar to Xavier was in Detroit in the early seventies when as a rookie state policeman he had been ordered to keep an eye on a cabin on the Huron River near Ann Arbor. This was back when Detroit was a vibrant, angry town with high wages in the auto industry and a residual unrest from the violent riots of 1967. All Sunderson was supposed to do was park his squad car near the driveway of the cabin to make its inhabitant, a murder-for-hire assassin from Chicago, nervous enough to go home. Sunderson had been told the man had been seen talking to a primary figure of the Detroit mafia at a Grosse Pointe horse show of all places. He only saw the man once in two days and when he drove toward him in his rental car Sunderson felt a tremor of nausea simply looking at the man's smiling face. As opposed to what is seen on television cops can become very frightened. In Detroit he had been out of his league like a cub scout with a pistol in drag.

The whiskey tasted very good and Sunderson was thinking that if the day was warm enough Melissa might wear a bathing suit when they went fishing. He very much needed a dose of life that didn't scare him. He had a dimmish recollection of an evening years before when Diane had cooked Marion's favorite pot roast dish and Marion had brought over an old movie that he said was America's best, *Touch of Evil* by Orson Welles. Sunderson had his usual too many drinks but before he fell asleep on the sofa halfway through he thought the movie was the scariest he had ever seen. And now here he was in the center of the same sort of mise-en-scène, the same ambience of dread you couldn't quite locate.

There was a sharp knock on the door and Sunderson wished he had the pistol he would buy the following day. It was the Arizona detective who had visited him in the hospital. This time he caught the man's name, Roberto Kowalski.

"Kowalski?" Sunderson smiled.

"My mom married a soldier over in Sierra Vista. He was from up in your country. Flint, Michigan, to be exact. I been there. It sucks. I'm here to ask you what the fuck you were doing having dinner with Xavier Martinez."

"I wasn't. I stopped by to say hello to his sister. I developed a crush on her in the hospital."

Roberto paused for a full minute. "I thought it had to be something else. No one is allowed to talk to Xavier. He beat her husband to death with his artificial hand. He's got a couple of heavier ones than the plastic he wears in public."

"It must have been about money," Sunderson joked.

"Of course. If I were you I'd take my affections elsewhere. If she develops a hangnail in your presence you're dead. She's a nice kid and you're a fucking geezer."

"She's twenty-five. She's a woman. Maybe a little young. You ever attracted to younger women?" Sunderson felt irritable.

"Never mind. I've tried but they can't talk. The words are the same but now they mean something different. Meanwhile

I stopped at your commune. I saw a lot of blood on the rocks. Why didn't you press charges?"

"The perps, the rock throwers, were kids, girls. Maybe around twelve years old plus or minus. Charges wouldn't work."

"Yeah. They've started a school for troubled girls. Real teachers, however Daryl had a charge for underage sex."

"Yes, in Choteau, Montana. Settled out of court. How come a guy like Xavier can cross the border?"

"His parents are Mexican but Xavier was born in Tucson when his dad was in college so he's an American citizen. He's always clean here. He's in the yellow pages as a stockbroker."

"That's funny in this economy," Sunderson suggested.

"Nothing about him is funny. Ironical maybe. We got Melissa work papers so she wouldn't get caught in the crossfire down south."

"She's safe here?" Sunderson was surprised.

"Pretty much so. It's considered bad etiquette for cartels to kill anyone north of the border."

"I'm thinking of going home. This place spooks me but then so did Detroit."

"That's a good idea."

"Maybe you could do me a favor and run Daryl out of here so he'll go back north where I feel more comfortable."

"Well, we've thought about pushing him out of Arizona. I know a local *puta* who's nineteen but looks fourteen. The charge wouldn't stick but we could scare him enough so he might run."

Roberto stood up looking very tired. Sunderson offered him a drink and poured big.

"Delicious," he said, downing it in two gulps. "I've lost two wives to this job."

"I lost one. Every day you come home with shit on your shoes." Sunderson paused trying to recapture his thoughts. "You know up in Marquette Daryl was named Dwight and was known as the Great Leader. What I've been thinking about is that it couldn't simply be a con for money. He has to believe somewhat in what he's doing."

"Maybe every other day." He pushed his glass across the table and Sunderson split the rest of the pint. Roberto's face was slack with puzzlement. "I only talked to him for a few minutes but he reminded me of a schoolteacher, you know, the hottest teacher at a local school. His followers were staring at him as if he glowed."

Sunderson was exhausted when Roberto left at midnight but was pleased at the ordinary aspects of the conversation. They were just a couple of law and order stiffs though Roberto had hunted for larger game in a far more violent area.

"I hope you feel better than you look," Roberto had said when he left.

"I'll get there," Sunderson responded without conviction.

He fell asleep in his clothes on the sofa and awoke at nearly 3:00 a.m. thinking in his haze that he heard birds. The sound was coming from the area of the concussion in the back of his head. The birds continued when he turned on the lamp then slowly subsided. He considered this a message from a decade before when he had fished in the evening on the west branch of the Fox and when it became dark started a small fire, ate a sandwich Diane had made for him, and curled up in a sleeping bag in the open air after a single sip from his flask. It was near the summer solstice and he awoke a little after 4 a.m. to the first faint light that far north. There was a dense profusion of birdsong on the liquid dawn air and he had the illusion that he could understand what the birds were talking about in their songs. The lyrics were of ordinary content about food, home, trees, water, watching out for ravens and hawks. It didn't seem extraordinary and the ability to understand the birds lasted right up until he stirred the coals and made his coffee. A day later when he told Marion after failing to figure it out Marion told him that he was lucky to have this religious experience.

Now in Nogales a decade later his homesickness was lessened by the fact that it was deer season in Michigan and a full five months from trout season. He got into bed naked and when he turned out the lights the birds resumed in the concussion sector of his head. He hoped he wouldn't wake up as a baby. He certainly didn't want to reenact his life. Where could such an idea come from? Anything that would purge the *copness* out of his brain would be welcome. There was a man at Northern Michigan University that taught a course in Middle Eastern history that would be good to audit, and another prof who taught human geography wherein one might learn why people lived in this particular hellhole of the world. Marion had said that he would qualify as a substitute teacher and it might be pleasant to correct widespread misapprehensions about American history. Anything to escape the copness that had driven his wife away.

Chapter 9

He awoke so cold that momentarily he couldn't imagine being in Arizona but there through the window wide open to the north wind was Alfred and Molly's cactus garden. The effort it took to close the window made him a little dizzy but his most negative thought was that if he went fishing with Melissa the next day she certainly wouldn't be wearing a skimpy bathing suit. His bedroom couldn't be more than fifty degrees and the blanket he was rolled up in was insufficient. He began to laugh, which was definitely not one of his morning habits. The fantasy of Melissa sitting in the backseat of the rowboat in a skimpy bathing suit in this weather pattern became comic, if a bit self-lacerating. There was a mere forty years' age difference between them, the kind of thing that normally only worked if the man was wealthy. Why would a lovely Mexican girl have anything to do with a black-and-blue geezer whose bruises were turning yellow here and there?

Thinking about Roxie on his throbbing clothes dryer didn't work. It was Carla against the woodpile at his retirement party that set him off. It was parodic like an old retired plumber he knew who bought a convertible and lime-green jump suit thinking that with these accoutrements he would become attractive to young women. That and five hundred bucks as a starter might get you a taste, Sunderson had advised. So what in God's name am I doing chasing this girl he thought, making his coffee and taking a glug of cranberry juice that was supposed to help his gout and kidney stones. American boys have this absurd carryover when they get older, as exemplified by three old men he had overheard at the Ford garage waiting for their cars to be repaired told sex jokes as if they were still in the game. Or retirees watching porn films at their deer cabin when they couldn't get it up for a waitress at gunpoint. It was likely that Carla had allowed him to back scuttle her because she was spying for Daryl-Dwight or perhaps she'd had a moment of sheer wantonness like many humans experience.

He cautioned himself against self-ridicule. It was part of the comedy of trying to maintain his Upper Peninsula sensibilities in this alien place that had him continually off-balance. Part of it might be the *post-concussive instability* the doctors had warned him about.

He leafed through the Tucson Yellow Pages that Alfred had loaned him, trying to match a gun store location with a city map. He felt untraveled because, simply enough, he was. He knew an approximately 300-by-100-mile area of the Upper Peninsula but nowhere else. The spring before he had picked up a prisoner in Grand Rapids and managed to get a little lost. He had volunteered for this early joyride saying to his colleagues that he knew Grand Rapids but he hadn't been there in thirty years. The prisoner had said, "Hey man, you're fucked up. You're supposed to be on 131 North and you're headed for Muskegon." The prisoner was pissed off in the heavily screened backseat because no smoking was allowed in state police squad cars.

Sunderson took the long way to Tucson so as not to miss his health regimen of a bowl of menudo and a morning walk in Patagonia. Despite the cold north wind the mountainous landscape had a resplendent clarity. He had read that human mules carried fifty-pound bales of marijuana across this rugged landscape and thought that these mules must be in good shape. What a way to lose weight. He caught himself thinking of what was wrong in this beautiful area. It was really why Diane had left him. She had said, "Your profession is to find out what is wrong and you've done it so long you can no longer see what is right about life." This was what the media called a *crying indictment* and it was right on the money. He had no argument to counter it.

He pulled off the road near a picnic table thinking that he had to stop this unprofitable way of thinking if he was ever going to lock up Dwight-Daryl. He was softening when he should have been hardening. He immediately thought that part of the problem came with being a bachelor and no longer having to monitor his moods, which you had to do in marriage to maintain civility, the day-to-day etiquette that makes marriages last. He had become too easily diverted by rather inane moods, which were fueled by overdrinking and the general sloppiness of his household. Life without a woman to temper your stupidities was difficult indeed. Even something so banal as grocery shopping could throw him into a skewed loop of anger. During his marriage Diane would always shop for dinner impulsively on her walk home from the hospital and then cook with pleasure, actually singing silly show tunes. By contrast he could blow fifty bucks in the supermarket during a quick shop and come home to discover that he didn't really have anything for dinner. He had quarreled with the store manager over prices because he hadn't yet caught up with the idea that prices hadn't actually gone up that much but packaged quantities had been reduced from sixteen ounces to twelve. The manager had patiently explained that he was a vendor of the food not the manufacturer.

Sitting there on the roadside viewing the vast mountainous landscape and the cloak of snow far up Mount Wrightson he vowed the cold clarity of a simpler chase. A few years before the divorce he had met with the game wardens of a half dozen Upper Peninsula counties to help map strategies to catch two poachers up from Tennessee who were involved in the not so uncommon crime of killing numerous bears for their paws and gallbladders, which were precious and extremely valuable items in Chinese pharmacopeia. These bear body parts were dropped off in Chicago and made their way to Beijing on a Northwest flight. Customs in Chicago had picked up on it in the post-9/11 X-raying of random luggage and backtracked through United States Fish and Wildlife Service to a Chinese restaurant owner in Evanston and thence to the two hunters in Tennessee who needed to be caught red-handed hunting and in possession of bear parts in the U.P. of Michigan. It was two weeks of wonderful October pursuit with Sunderson masquerading as an alcoholic bow hunter, not a far reach in sailing terms.

He used his dozens of informants and snitches in taverns across the U.P. and after two weeks or so of fruitless searching it was an informant at a country bar in Wolf Junction north of Newberry in Luce County that panned out. He had called around midnight and was mildly drunk but then so was Sunderson.

"They were headed north toward Superior so they're likely going over to Crisp Point or Grand Marais. I would have followed to see if they turned left or right south of Deer Park but they was a bit scary and mean looking. One chews a big gob of bubble gum and they're driving a crew-cab black Ford and they got hounds."

Sunderson couldn't sleep so left for Grand Marais about three a.m. in a snowstorm that he knew wouldn't last because the wind was turning south. He felt silly with his camo archer's outfit and his compound bow in the backseat because he couldn't hit a barn at gunpoint. On a hunch, at daylight he decided on the Barfield Lakes area. He had alerted by phone the two game wardens in contiguous counties but the trouble in the U.P. is that poaching was low on the totem pole of seriousness and taking a deer out of season was fairly popular after the bars closed, and after July Fourth when the deer would lose the cedar taste after yarding up in swamps during the winter.

It was barely daylight and he was driving south on a small county road up Pull Up Hill when the three-quarter-ton pickup passed him going the other way. His cell phone worked on the hill and he called a game warden who had positioned himself in Seney. He waited a few minutes before turning around on the off chance that they would "make" his pickup if he was close on their trail.

His luck held when they turned off on a no-exit two-track near Seney where Sunderson had fished the Driggs River. He and the game warden reconnoitered and after an hour they heard hounds baying and a rifle shot and they called in reinforcements. Within a half hour another game warden and two state police arrived. Bingo, Sunderson thought. When the pickup approached it tried to turn around and Sunderson shot out the back tires with his .38. In a cooler full of ice in a hidden compartment of the pickup there were sixteen gallbladders, one of them still warm, and sixty-four paws. The bust was big in the news but Sunderson declined all credit passing it on to the game wardens. The last thing he wanted was to become too visible. He did, however, relish the pleasure of an ultraclean bust. The perps got five years.

Outside of Patagonia his cell phone rang with the *William Tell Overture,* music that he hated but he didn't know how to change. He answered because he saw it was Mona on the caller ID.

"Good morning dear."

"You can't believe what's happening as we speak. You know how dark it is here in November at seven a.m.? Well Marion pulls up in his car on the way to work. He goes in your house and then he pulls a book in your study and I can see the crack of light. He's been peeking at me for about ten

minutes. I thought it was our special secret. It pisses me off
that you told him, darling."

"I didn't tell him," Sunderson laughed. "He's picking
up some books to FedEx me. It was his own discovery."

"I did some nude yoga so he wouldn't be disappointed.
I think I believe you. I mean it's a silly thing but I like the
idea that it's just between us."

"Well, he's not going to pick up books to send me every
day. Here's a nifty thing to do. When you hang up with me
call his cell and say, Caught you, you shitheel pervert."

"I want to write my own lines," she laughed. "Maybe
I'll say, Come on over, big boy."

"Please don't."

"Are you jealous, darling?"

Sunderson hung up on her and when he ate his menudo
the labial texture made him horny. The freedom of retirement was distressing. Normally at this time back home he
would be driving to work and mentally rehearsing the cases
at hand. Why was the little old widow whose husband left
her a nice pension embezzling from the dry goods store
where she worked twenty hours a week? A tiny video
camera caught her. She wept. She was helping a niece
with cancer but it turned out she didn't have a niece. She
was addicted to hitting the slots at the Indian casino east
of town. A month after the judge gave her probation she
was caught on video stealing change from other players'
coin cups and stealing tips from tables in the lunchroom.
Sunderson disliked interrogating her because despite his
innovative questioning he couldn't make a dent. She said
she was aiming at winning the hundred-thousand-dollar

jackpot and giving it to her church because the pastor's wife had cancer. A phone call revealed that the pastor's wife didn't have cancer. Dealing with this senior citizen ditz gave Sunderson heartburn and a deep need for more alcohol. In his last week of work she had been caught at midnight rifling parking meters using a technique she refused to describe. When Sunderson met with the prosecutor they went to the bar at the Ramada Inn where he received a cell call from Snowbound Books. The owner had caught the woman jamming three copies of the new Danielle Steel in her underpants in the back room. "Shoot her," Sunderson had said then closed the phone. This was clearly not a life.

When he finished his last piece of tripe which raised the image of Mona he thought that a serious man can't be pussy struck at breakfast. What a fool he had become in his loneliness, a fungoid teenage boy. He pondered the idea that he should be over this nonsense at age sixty-five but he wasn't. He couldn't very well ask Melissa to wear a miniskirt while fishing. Now that he was recovering, however slowly, it was time to up the ante on the Great Leader. His dad used to say that idle hands are the devil's work tools. He didn't want to be idle but the true mystery was how to proceed so far from home ground. He needed to somehow daily carbonate his brain to become less sodden and more attentive.

He walked a route in the Nature Conservancy property for an hour without his usual attentiveness in natural surroundings because he remembered what an abrasive Detroit detective had told him forty years before, "Paranoia is healthy for a cop." Maybe Roberto Kowalski wasn't straight and suspected Sunderson of being a fed, maybe a DEA guy from out of state snooping into crooked locals? Maybe two weeks before Melissa had told her brother Xavier about a beat-up detective in the Nogales hospital and Xavier had told her to check him out? The question was whether or not this paranoia was healthy or delusional.

There was a slight rustle and movement of leaves and he jumped back as far as a man his age could jump back. He had a preconception that the area was chock-full of rattlers though in truth it would take an expert and hard looking to find one and the morning was far too cold at fifty degrees for a rattler to be active. He knelt down feeling the pain of his bruised legs and examined a large black beetle making its way slowly through the leaf detritus. Such large beetles were unknown in the north and he wondered how it made its way through life, where it ate and slept, and how it mated.

The beetle took him out of his head and into the world and he backtracked a few hundred yards to the path along the creek. He had barely noticed the creek when he was pondering the subject of paranoia but now he sat down on a cottonwood log and stared at the moving water. It would have been a good brook trout creek had there been any brook trout this far south though he had read that there were rainbow trout in the mountains farther north in Arizona. He spotted some minnows swirling in unison in a deeper hole and then watched a blue heron fly over above him looking smaller than the great blues of the north.

He studied the thicket of mesquite trees across the creek. There was also a number of large green bushes that looked like the elderberry back home, and a number of vast cottonwoods. He heard only bird sounds and the sound of moving water, his two favorites beginning in his childhood. He noticed that he was more relaxed and breathing more deeply than he had since he left home. He smiled remembering a slightly religious experience on a small river down near Steuben south of Shingleton the summer before. It was a hot August morning and he had been trying to catch brookies under logjams with a short line and his preferred fly, a small olive woolly bugger. The fly had snagged under the logjam and he was in despair because it was his last one and he had forgotten to tie up anymore. He was also hungover, which he had noted dozens of times made him a little inattentive. He threw in the towel as it were, pulled himself up on the riverbank, and stripped off his waders and clothes down to his undies. He carelessly plunged under the logjam with a hand, following the fly line until he could detach the fly hooked on the slippery log, not quite a victory as he had to struggle violently to back himself out against the current thinking how odd it would be to drown while saving an olive woolly bugger. He emerged breathing hard and grabbing a branch to hold himself in the current, tossing the fly up near his rod on the bank. For no reason he let go of the branch and floated downstream rolling over and over in the water, then simply floating on his back looking up at the hot blue sky and the trees that bordered the stream. About a hundred yards downstream he crawled up on a sandbar and lay there, happier than he had been in the three years since Diane left.

The Tucson gun store was a mud bath, festooned with patriotic and anti-Obama signs, including the usual LIVE FREE OR DIE. The clerk was plump, florid, and middle-aged smug.

"I need a .38 Smith and Wesson revolver," Sunderson said.

"You look like you need a pistol," the clerk chortled.

"Thanks." Sunderson was impatient to get out of the place and pointed at the pistol he wanted under the glass.

It turned out that despite his expired detective license and still current Michigan concealed weapons permit he couldn't buy a pistol because he was a nonresident. He was pissed off enough to feel his temples pounding. The clerk waited for the bad news to sink in, chortled again, and gave Sunderson directions to a public library.

"You get a library card and that's proper Arizona ID and then I sell you the pistol."

Sunderson was jangled at the insanity of it all but calmed down sweetly at the library because the desk clerk girl, though homely, smelled like lilac, a fatally sexy scent for him. He felt like a daffy old fuck as he proudly showed his library card from back home but she frowned at the Nogales address he gave.

"I love the next town, Patagonia," she said.

"I do too. I eat menudo there every morning."

"I can't eat tripe."

"It restores your strength."

When he walked out after the second pass at the gun store he felt the unpleasant heft of the .38 in a shoulder holster thinking that the .38 had been following him around for nearly forty years like the longest-term tumor possible. Back in the car and heading to Miss Saigon for a *pho* fix he pulled over near the University of Arizona to make a cell call. Grungy young men and beautiful young women were passing on the sidewalk in such profusion that he thought about the failure of birth control in the world at large. He called a colleague back in Marquette.

"Sunderson! Gett'n much?"

"More ass than a toilet seat. I need information on an Arizona detective by the name of Roberto Kowalski."

"Hold on, I'll do it as we speak."

The colleague, divorced twice, always gave the staff the impression that he was a prime pussy chaser but this was unlikely.

"No one by that name in Arizona law enforcement," was the answer.

"Thanks for the favor."

"You're missing deer hunting."

Sunderson couldn't think of a thing to say so he pushed the END button. He sat outside again at Miss Saigon smoking two cigarettes in a row and realizing that he had been a little suspicious of Kowalski, not at the first bruised meeting in the hospital, but the second time, at his apartment. The guy lacked a certain tinge of the genuine because he didn't speak the shorthand that detectives use with each other. His cell rang just as the waitress was bringing a variety *pho* that included tripe, also pork meatballs. It was Lucy.

"I'm not crying anymore darling but I've been thinking of our questionable night."

"I was worried about your Kleenex budget. Look, I'm in a meeting. I'll call you back." He quickly turned the phone off before she could respond, wondering about the faulty aspects of memory. Why didn't she say that the night had been rotten rather than the euphemism of "questionable"? If you're lonely any contact is better than none.

Two hours later he had found another small temporary apartment on a hillside in Patagonia. It was a room and half, a bit tight, but there were chickens in the backyard and a couple of rabbit hutches. His parents had supplemented their protein budget with a lot of fried rabbit. On the way to Nogales to pick up his meager belongings he reluctantly passed the Wagon Wheel Saloon. It would have to wait for later.

Alfred was in the yard and told Sunderson that soon after he had left Mr. Kowalski had stopped by to fetch his precious cigarette lighter.

"Did you ID him?" Sunderson asked, alarmed.

"Well, no. I mean you guys were together an hour last night. I admit I glanced in the window and he was on the phone at the kitchen table."

Sunderson didn't bother telling Alfred that Kowalski was a phony. Alfred was upset that he was leaving but pleased when Sunderson told him to keep the rest of the month's rent.

"Where are you going?"

"It would be unsafe for you to know."

"I get it. You're undercover?"

"Obviously not far enough."

He packed his suitcase and papers from Mona. Nothing in the apartment looked *tossed* though the papers appeared in less disarray than he had left them. The Great Leader must have been poor reading for Kowalski but now he had Mona's e-mail. He rang her up.

"Don't respond to anyone in this area except me."

"Okay darling but why?"

"I'm being tailed and he'll try to find me through your e-mail."

"That's impossible but it sounds exciting. I have to write a paper on Emily Dickinson and she sucks."

"No she doesn't. She's wonderful." Sunderson had been fond of Emily Dickinson ever since he was a sophomore in an American literature class at Michigan State.

"That joke really worked with Marion. I did a little nude dance then I called him. I heard his cell phone hit the floor."

"Good job."

"Your fucking friend Carla wants me to come over for dinner. My therapist will be there. Just us three girls. Maybe they'll try to gang bang me."

"Don't go. But if you do, snoop around. Keep your clothes on."

"Of course Daddy."

He hung up and called Melissa. She had been going to pick him up for fishing in the morning but as a precaution he didn't want her to have his new address and told her he would meet her at Patagonia Lake. She was flirtatious on the phone, which made him suspicious though he cautioned himself about letting his paranoia ruin the fishing trip and its remote sexual possibilities. He was on the way out of the apartment and bidding good-bye to Alfred's wife Molly who was dusting her roses for aphids when a FedEx truck pulled up. He had nearly missed the books Marion was sending.

"My second cycle of chemo isn't working," Molly said. "So this is good-bye."

"I'm sorry," Sunderson said, feeling paralyzed.

"Do you believe in the afterlife?"

"I haven't figured it out. I guess I'm not very religious."

"I don't think anyone has. Someone said, I forgot who, that if nothing happens we won't know it. I'll miss flowers, birds, and lemonade."

He gave her a hug and got in the car itching for a double whiskey and thinking that there wasn't much left of her. She was made up of Tinkertoys, fragile sticks out of which you could make little buildings and bridges but not human bodies. He recalled that he and his brother Robert had found a recently dead fawn, it didn't stink yet, and they had given it what they had thought to be a proper burial. Molly couldn't weigh much more than the fawn that Sunderson had dropped in the shallow hole he had dug. There wasn't much of a thunk when the fawn hit the bottom of its grave.

The consolation, however slight, was the heft of the package of books Marion had sent. He opened the package in the parking lot and selected *Playing Indian* by Philip Deloria, which Marion had loaned him a couple of years before, rather than one of the new ones like Jeffrey Johnson's *They*

Are All Red Out Here: Socialist Politics in the Pacific Northwest, 1895-1925, or Kyle Wilkison's *Yeomen, Sharecroppers, and Socialists: Plain Folk Protest in Texas, 1870-1914*, and certainly not the new edition of Reinhold Niebuhr's *The Irony of American History*, which he had skimmed through years before and which had precipitated a deep funk.

Over his first double and beer chaser at the bar he read Marion's letter, the first half of which advised him to read the Deloria, which would help him understand the Great Leader's use of faux Indian "rigmarole." Marion said that many non–Indian Americans had used their fantasies about Indians to acquire a "hokum" spirituality. The second half of the letter was a comic recounting of Marion pulling the Deloria book out from above Sunderson's desk and seeing the nude Mona at her morning rituals. "Don't even try it, friend. It's very upsetting and she caught me red-handed. I drove off to work shamefaced and with a hard-on like a toothache. I thought of a scholarly article by a psychoanalyst named Sullivan that said that at their best poetry and religion push back the boundaries of the ineffable. Well, so can a woman's body."

The barmaid Amanda brought him his second double. He had caught a nice breast view when she had bent over to get ice for a margarita.

"What are you staring at, asshole?"

"I'm staring into my mind. I can't see it very well," he said.

"That's cute but a little evasive," she laughed.

Sunderson felt a trace of fear. Two doubles were enough when bad people might very well be tracking you. It was

five in the afternoon and he knew he should eat an early
dinner, do some reading, and embrace sobriety. From want
of good sense he went to the Mexican restaurant and ate
yet another bowl of menudo, sprinkling it liberally with
the blistering hot and flavorful chiltepins. He was proud of
becoming acclimated though it was easiest when he was in
Italy with Diane and liked everything he ate.

   In his new digs he laid out his books including White's
*"It's Your Misfortune and None of My Own": A New History of the
American West* and Mackay's *Extraordinary Popular Delusions
and the Madness of Crowds* from his suitcase. History books
were his central solace in life along with brook trout fishing
but on this night history had abruptly fled. He figured the
problem was that the sense of his own peril forced him to
consider only life in the present tense. He tried the television
news but his mistrust of the instant history of the media was
jangling. He couldn't find a movie suited to his mood and
had to settle on a cop film only because it featured Robert
Duvall, his doppelganger, who was uniformly credible in
movies. Sunderson almost never watched cop movies because they lacked the visceral aspects of actuality. Once
while in training in Detroit he had visited a downriver dope
house with two cops and they had found two severed heads
on a kitchen table, both with bulging purple tongues and lots
of flies because the heads had been there a couple of days.

   He was thirsty but stupidly didn't drink water because
he didn't want to get up to pee with his geezer's overactive
kidneys. The gout struck at midnight, an easy self-diagnosis
because it felt like a rat was chewing on his right big toe. He
hobbled to the bathroom and took two colchicine pills plus

an Oxycontin for the pain. His daily allopurinol had lost the battle with gout and now the crystallized purines in his toe were grating against the nerve endings. It had obviously been the tripe because he remembered tripe had been on the gout list his doctor had given him. It was usually doe liver during deer season. Like his father before him Sunderson simply couldn't resist deer liver.

Sleep was fitful at best. To Sunderson the only reliable drugs were alcohol and tobacco and even ibuprofen and aspirin were suspicious, varying as they did the dream life that amused and fascinated him. His main worry was whether he'd be able to screw Melissa on the long shot of an opportunity. Toe anguish isn't sexy and a rowboat isn't a hospitable place for intercourse. Early in their marriage when camping he and Diane had tried it on Lake Gogebic but they had given up, laughing at the awkwardness. If he were religious, he thought, he could at least pray for warm weather so he could see a little skin. He finally slept because luckily for once he was old and with aging you gave up trying to account for everything that might happen, the hopeless attempt to balance the hundreds of variables with your brain's billion-roomed house between which there are not nearly enough doors. Once again he realized that life had too many moving parts.

He was at the Patagonia Lake marina a half hour before Melissa was due. By Michigan standards the lake was dinky indeed but made up for it by its beautiful mountain setting. He had to half drag his aching foot but was eager to row while Melissa fished. He reached the dock from the parking lot with difficulty, his big toe and to a lesser extent the whole front part of his foot feeling like the pulse of a toothache at the root of a loose tooth, certainly better than the grueling pain at the beginning of an attack. At least gout didn't entail an emotional hangover. Gout was something you did to yourself usually by willful inattention. The list of prohibited foods was taped in clear sight above his desk. The problem was that pain is abstract until it arrives and couldn't compete with a skillet of quick-fried doe liver that had been sliced thin. His father had told him that liver was the healthiest of meats for building strong bodies but then liver was also the cheapest meat a relatively poor family could afford. He had so wanted to be strong like his father who could easily lift one of cousin Charlie's boxes of whitefish that weighed three hundred pounds.

Sunderson sat there on the dock near rowboat number seven that the marina clerk advised was the best of the dozen or so. It was clearly a piece of shit in the long line of rowboats in his life. The mythology of liver and rowboats faded when he thought of the pungency of Deloria's *Playing Indian,* which he had leafed through in the midst of his pain. Most academic history books he read were real prose clunkers and sometimes Diane would read aloud a sentence or two from them and laugh. Diane liked to listen to Leonard Cohen while reading her favorite author Loren Eiseley. He liked both but not at the same time. He began to doze from his drug combo of colchicine and Oxycontin to which he had added Imodium. Colchicine could be a violent purge. When Melissa had called earlier in the morning to ask what kind of juice he wanted with lunch he had said, "A pint of vodka," another questionable ingredient.

She finally pulled up in a newish Toyota 4Runner
Sport, a vehicle he had yearned for but could scarcely afford on his pension, and definitely not affordable on her
nurse's aide salary. Likely it came from her faux stockbroker
brother.

They quickly loaded her small tackle box, two spinning
rods, and the picnic hamper. She was so effervescent that it
verged on playacting and he cautioned himself in his haze
against looking for something wrong rather than right. She
wore a light-blue jacket and jeans rather than the skimpy
clothes of his fantasies. He rowed the gunk boat, sipped
vodka, and hummed, "You Can't Always Get What You
Want." He had always preferred the edgy Rolling Stones
to the frivolous white canticles of the Beatles. She finally
caught a decent smallmouth bass on a Rapala she was casting
but released it saying that she preferred to eat saltwater fish.
It had become warm enough for her to take off her jacket
and her braless breasts in the light sleeveless pullover jiggled
pleasantly when she cast the lure. The sight penetrated his
drug haze and he felt a specific nut twitch. She was trolling
a worm and heavy sinker with her other rod and hooked a
little catfish, which he detached because it was too ugly for
her to touch. He had brought Alfred's map and was rowing
toward an estuary area where Sonoita Creek, which he had
walked along in the Nature Conservancy land, emptied into
the lake. He had skipped breakfast and was hungry for the
picnic.

The creek was braided near the lake but he found an inlet
deep enough to pull in the boat. He watched as she laid out
the picnic on her hands and knees, a fetching sight. He took

a solid gulp of vodka to ease a foot tinge. There was a fruit salad and a dozen huge shrimp that she said she got through Hector who owned Las Vigas. He knew shrimp was on his proscribed gout list but said *fuck it* to himself, dipping a shrimp in a blistering hot salsa verde. She laughed at his tears.

"What are you really doing down here?"

This caught him off guard and he knew the question was meant to, but after a near lifetime of interrogating perps, more recently designated "persons of interest," he was an expert at cat and mouse.

"I'm checking out a cult leader. Seeing my iron mother. Anything more I'm not at liberty to say." He immediately realized that he should have put the subject to rest but he wanted to tease her. He put on a cool, impassive face when what he was really thinking about is that he should have brought along an Oxycontin.

"You don't trust me!" She took his coolness as truth, and got up and walked away wandering in the bushes nearly out of sight.

He was sitting back against a small tree he wished he could identify. He intended to call Alfred and take a walk with him so he could learn some of the mysterious flora. Meanwhile he was watching her through barely open lids and wondering at her next move now that it had become clear to him that she was spying for her brother. He was pleased she was upset that he was cooling toward her, thus failing in her mission. It was then that he saw her in the gap between the bushes give a fake little shriek and intentionally plop herself down in a boggy hole. He begrudgingly got up from his resting place then sat back down when he saw she was walking toward him with muddy jeans and tears in her eyes. He had always been puzzled by the emotional volatility that allowed women to cry on demand.

"I'm a mess. I have to clean up. Shut your eyes."

With eyes wide open he watched as she stripped off her jeans with her back turned. She sat and pulled the jeans off her feet and then knelt on her hands and knees rinsing the jeans in the clear water of the inlet near the boat. She wore white thong undies and had the prettiest, most perfect ass he had ever seen and it was easy to crawl over, pull down the thong, and start lapping, errantly thinking, *I am a dog who accepts food from strangers.*

"Oh you pig, you fucking pig," she said laughing.

He didn't have much more than a half-master because of his numbed condition but he managed to get it in where it properly grew in the wet heat. The drug numbness also helped him last longer as did the oddly melodramatic mountain landscape. His hard strokes had pushed them down the grassy bank so that she was grabbing the gunnel of the rowboat to keep them from sliding in the water.

"You are a fucking pig," she said turning back to look at him.

"No, I'm a dog wondering if I'm going to have a heart attack."

They struggled back to the blue tablecloth she had spread for the picnic. She slipped into the thong and clumsily tried to wring out her jeans but he stopped her from putting them on.

"I need to study your beautiful ass."

"You don't get my ass unless you cook me a fine meal."

If this was meant to lead him by eyes, nose, and pecker further into the void it worked. While rowing back to the marina she asked him to come to dinner at her place the following evening. He accepted, ignoring the idea that Xavier might be there. She said that now she had to go home, make Josefina some flan she'd promised, take a shower to wash off the "pigginess," and then work the 4:00 p.m. to midnight shift at the hospital.

On the drive back toward his humble digs in the village of Patagonia he pondered his postcoital slump. In a more distinctly natural world he was the male spider who flops over after ejaculation to provide a meal for the female. He was mildly resentful that sex could still wield this sort of power over him, that a geezer could be so strongly hooked by the biological imperative. His little male dog, now in heaven, used to jump up hopelessly at the high rear end of the female collie down the street. His mother used to say, "God works in mysterious ways, his wonders to perform," but that was when a local hockey team had beaten the thugs from Iron Mountain.

He forced himself to drive past the Wagon Wheel. The two shrimp he had managed to eat before rutting weren't enough cushion for a couple of double whiskeys. A nap and something to eat would help prepare him for the usual cocktail hour. He avoided the pathetic temptation to stop at the restaurant and have yet another bowl of menudo, opting for the grocery store and a few frozen dinners, which normally repelled him but he lacked the verve to cook a real meal. He also treated himself to a fifth of Absolut vodka although he normally only drank the cheapest brands.

He sat down at the kitchen table because memory was prodding him and he needed to make a journal entry.

1. Melissa reminds me of Sonia when I was nineteen and an unconfident sophomore at Michigan State. It's more than their mutual raspberry scent or their fine butts. Sonia was a hippie graduate student in history and we met at the bookstore when we started talking about the failure of the White Russian Army. We had coffee and then agreed to meet now and then and talk about Russian history about which she was obsessed far beyond me. She was a genuine kook and wore orange and black clothing because she believed in evil and her favorite holiday was Halloween. Sad to say I only met her in May a few weeks before the end of the school year after which she was going to Leningrad for the summer on a travel scholarship. She spoke fluent Russian because her parents were refugees from World War II when they lived in Kiev. They were Jews but not religious so it was easy to understand why her belief in evil was so firm.

2. When I was six my mother slapped me real hard. I haven't remembered this for years as if it were a small visual splotch. (This was a time when school-teachers were still allowed corporal punishment.) I was in the first grade and having trouble learning to read. I was sitting with Mom in an easy chair while she read aloud to me from a story called *The Water Babies* from the Book House and I was attempting

to follow the text with a forefinger. I was upset because I thought the story was a big lie. I had fished
brook trout with my dad and there was no way
that a group of human babies could live underwater
in a river swimming around through water weeds
without coming up for air. Meanwhile Berenice was
prancing back and forth through the room yelling
"dumby" at me. It was a rainy Saturday afternoon
and Mom smelled like the rhubarb wine a neighbor made every year. Berenice came too close and
I grabbed her by a pigtail and called her a "bitch."
Mom reared back and slapped me very hard. I had
no idea what the word "bitch" meant.

3. This area reminds me of the collection of DVDs
   called *The Blue Planet* Diane gave me for a birthday. Much of the underwater life was alien with
   no possible human reference point. Some of it was
   troublesome and repellent. There were clusters of
   two-inch-wide, six-foot-long worms living a mile
   deep in perfect darkness. I certainly didn't want
   to go there.

4. An image of Melissa's ass in the broad daylight of
   the estuary. There should be a legion of pollsters
   asking all the men in the world what an ass means
   to them.

5. I keep thinking of a photo in an old *Life* magazine of
   monkeys bathing in a hot spring in northern Japan.
   It's snowing but they're quite warm though wet.
   How do they get out and dry off without freezing
   their asses off? That's the question.

He undressed totally for his nap trying to dismiss the power of his negative thinking. After forty years as a janitor trying to clean up the culture's dirt, here he was in a decidedly alien locale trying to chase down someone who had committed no readily provable crime. He had been stoned by mostly female preteens or so he thought from the few glances before trying to shield his eyes. This seemed to be causing a murderous edge back there in his mind. He perforce had an edge he had developed in order to function at his job but then the edge had become an organic part of his character. A goodly number of people, some unconsciously, sensed this edge and avoided any more than nominal contact with him. It reminded him of the way people in social contact with a doctor would wedge in a medical question, usually ineptly. With Sunderson the brave ones would ask a peripheral question about law enforcement because it was the rare male who hadn't committed a felony, unwittingly or consciously. In bars and on social occasions Sunderson tended to be reassuring saying that strictly speaking the entire population of the United States should be imprisoned but then who would take care of the innocent children? Law enforcement was merely the manhole cover on the human sewer. People within earshot would laugh a bit nervously.

He napped solidly for three hours by grace of an Oxycontin and a gulp of vodka, dreaming of church bells on wintry Sunday mornings in Munising. The bells turned out to be his cell phone with Mona on the other end.

"I've called five times. Where the fuck were you?"

"Taking a health nap. I've had a gout attack."

"You're always having gout attacks, darling."

"I can't seem to learn from experience. What's up?"

"I had dinner with Carla and my therapist and found out some nifty stuff. First of all they fed me this cheap California chardonnay that tasted like rancid butter. Then they wanted to rub my body with Apache lotion, can you believe it?"

"I wasn't aware that Apaches were into cosmetics."

"Carla gave me the bottle. It was made in Boulder, Colorado. Well, we smoked a joint and I got a little drunk and dozed off on the sofa and the next thing you know when I opened my eyes Carla was taking a raised skirt photo of me."

"Pardon?"

"She was on her knees before me and taking a raised skirt photo with a flash. I said 'What the fuck are you doing?' and she said that her boyfriend likes raised skirt photos of young girls. Guess who her boyfriend is?"

"That's easy. It's the Great Leader. I'm sure she's one of many."

"Carla says if you don't lay off she's going to accuse you of sodomy, you know, at your retirement party. She's got Queenie as a witness."

"How interesting." Sunderson's mind whirled with the permutations, which were easy to dismiss. "It would be embarrassing but it wouldn't work. There were a number of cops there plus friends from the prosecutor's office. There are also photos of her going sixty-nine with Queenie. I've got more and better witnesses."

"Should I tell her that?"

"No. Of course not. We don't want a pissing contest. Just don't go to her place."

"I miss you, darling."

"I miss you, too."

He was only able to eat one of the wretched frozen chicken dinners before he felt gaggy. It was time to drive to a supermarket and set up a proper kitchen. He had planned to spend a quiet evening reading Deloria's *Playing Indian* and making some written notes on his situation. He knew he felt a certain misplaced pride, a questionable hubris that he could deal with this new territory when there was no evidence so far that he was actually capable of doing so. He had let down his guard after being freed from forty years of work habits and the results of this slippage had been poor indeed. Before answering Mona's call he had had a confused dream that had his favorite brook trout creek becoming round, a perfect circle in the meadow, woods, and marsh that was its path. Toward the end it had become coiled and serpentine, which reminded him of some of Marion's favorite ideas. The aging process was linear with the inevitability of gravity but our thinking and behavior tended to occur in clusters, knots that wound and unwound themselves. His current central problem was comparable to the poorly remembered Gospel parable: when you clean out the room of your life via retirement you have to be careful what you let back in. Since it was five months until brook trout season he had only his obsession with the Great Leader, which was not something to pleasantly fill a life. He had an image of a lovely old basilica he had walked in to on a side street in Florence while Diane napped at their room at the Brunelleschi. He

had sat on a bench in the basilica calmed by the utter loveli-
ness of the place, the wonderful simple lines compared to
the rococo monstrosity of the Duomo. An old lady and a
pretty girl of about twelve entered, lit candles, and knelt
and prayed. The question was why not destroy the Great
Leader who so grotesquely diminished what everyone must
sense, however remotely, as the divinity of existence. To be
sure, Sunderson only felt this in the natural world distant
from the collective human puke that drowned so much of
what was good in life.

Berenice called and he answered out of guilt. She wanted
him to come to dinner the following evening because their
sister Roberta was passing through town. He said he was
booked and they settled for lunch. He was chain smoking
and noted with irritation that he was down to five cigarettes, not nearly enough for an evening's reading. Was
he capable of walking to the Wagon Wheel for cigarettes
without getting stewed? Time would tell. Another more
irritating thought occurred. What would his mother think
if he was charged with sodomy? Not good.

He poured a modest drink not bothering with ice and
called a former colleague in Marquette explaining Carla's
supposed intentions. The friend explained that the prosecutor would never bring such a pathetic case but to make sure
they would bring Carla to complete "attention." An informant had told him that Carla sold not only the occasional
lid of pot but also totally untaxed cartons of cigarettes a
Chippewa member of Daryl-Dwight's cult brought in from
the smugglers in the Sault Ste. Marie area. The latter would
be a federal charge and the threat would "bunch her undies,"

or so the man said. The little cigarette sideline gave Carla a profit of twenty bucks a carton.

Sunderson was nearly cheery walking the few blocks to the bar. The thought of pissing off his iron mother had been a powerful corrective ever since his youth. Near the motel he saw a young man wearing a turban above his bliss ninny face and asked Amanda at the Wagon Wheel about it. She said he was from the vegan cult up Harshaw Creek Road. Sunderson pondered the possible spiritual content of raw vegetables remembering the rubbery carrot and celery sticks on the grade school hot lunch program.

"Maybe the raw vegetables release their secret powers," he suggested polishing off his first double in a single long gulp.

"Got me by the ass. I do know that when they get too pure the medevac chopper from Tucson has to pick them up," Amanda laughed.

By lucky coincidence an older, Mexican woman came into the bar selling fresh tamales for a buck apiece. Sunderson bought six, eating three immediately with a cold Pacifico beer. They beat any bar food he had ever had in the Great North. They were so good he didn't feel up to another drink. He looked forward to eating the other three tamales for breakfast. On the walk home he idly thought of becoming a Mexican knowing a lot of Americans retired far to the south of the border where life was less dicey. Just before he reached his place down a dark alley he saw two men loading something in a pickup. They glanced his way and he pretended he hadn't noticed them with his eyes straight ahead.

"You're looking for someone?" Amanda had asked when he left the bar.

"I better not say," he replied with an urge for mystery.

Dawn, which is late in November, found him carving his first mango, sexual to the touch, but he didn't care for it so maybe he wouldn't become a Mexican after all. With his coffee he had read a chapter in Deloria titled, "Hobby Indians, Authenticity, and Race in Cold War America" and recalled a number of powwows he had been to in the U.P. while looking for perps, persons of interest. Once at the big winter powwow in Escanaba he had seen the renowned fancy dancer Jonathan Windy Boy and had gotten unwilling goose bumps at the man's inconceivable grace. There were a few white dancers, usually awkward.

Pushing the book aside he decided to start logging what he was doing in order to bring focus. He had logged notes in journals his entire career to prepare for the obnoxious reports he was obligated to write for the official record. Sunderson recognized good prose despite being unable to write it. Reading so many clunkers in the field of history didn't help. Like scholars he tended to multiple qualifiers in order to be right without ambiguity. "Are we to believe, unlikely as it seems, that the perp only recently, perhaps in the month since his return from Milwaukee, came into possession of illegal ammunition, usable, mostly in illegal full-automatic weaponry," that sort of thing. By contrast, Diane had written beautifully, publishing a memoir with Michigan State University of her father's family adventures in the logging business. She wrote daily in a diary and only read fine nonfiction and literary fiction. He enjoyed Hemingway's fishing pieces but failed to finish *The Sun Also Rises*, which was about a bunch of layabouts getting drunk and going to bullfights in Spain.

He sat staring at an empty page of his journal, ballpoint poised, but couldn't move a mental sentence. The most singular entry since his arrival in Arizona was, "I hurt all over," written on the last full day in the hospital. It was true. A large rock had hit the crack of his ass while he was in a crouched position so that even around his asshole there was a big bruise.

He took an hour's walk up Harshaw nodding to an altruistic group of young vegan cult women. Marion had said that vegetarian women tasted better but Sunderson had never had an experience with a vegetarian woman.

He left early for Green Valley wanting to get his grocery shopping out of the way before lunch at his mother's. Afterward he knew he would want a drink and a long nap before going to Melissa's. The highway went right past Alfred's house and Alfred was in the yard so he stopped to say hello, a bad choice because Alfred was pissed off. Someone had broken into Sunderson's apartment when he and Molly were out for dinner. No damage had been done except to the door's lock. Sunderson offered him fifty bucks, which he pocketed.

"A cop came but he didn't take prints like on TV. Anyway, I saw a painted redstart this morning."

"Lucky you," Sunderson said, knowing that the redstart was a bird.

The Green Valley supermarket was a melancholy experience. Everyone in there was his age or older. Admittedly they looked better than retirees in the U.P. whose only exercise tended to be pressing the clicker for the television set. The women especially were tanned and sprightly while the men obviously spent too much time on their golf carts. There was a magnificent display of vegetables compared to back home where the pièce de résistance was always the pasty. To Sunderson vegetables were an obligation rather than a pleasure since Diane with her cooking skills had left. The coup was finding a package of frozen rabbit pieces, to make one of his favorite meals.

His mother, Roberta, and Berenice were sitting on the front porch luckily without Berenice's dipshit husband. The Escalade was gone but there was a gray Prius with an Obama sticker, obviously Roberta's car.

"Nice car. A little pricey," Sunderson said accepting a glass of nasty California rosé that Berenice poured.

"She's a real success not an alcoholic sex fiend," his mother said, her voice slurred.

"All I wanted to be was a Podunk gumshoe," Sunderson said with an edge to his laugh.

"And you lost the world's finest woman," his mother continued.

"Oh for Christ's sake Mom, lighten up and stop bullying him." Roberta had had a hot temper since she was a baby and was the only one of the four children that their mother had never been able to push around. Sunderson was four years older than Roberta with her having arrived a scant year before Bobby in a birth control error. Those two had been a tight little unit and had been good at defending themselves against the rest of the family who were always considered by them to be possible enemies. Sunderson had thought of them as from another generation.

His mother launched into a fresh caterwaul about her lack of grandchildren.

"You have to learn a new song, Mom," Roberta said, then suggested that she and Sunderson take a walk. They weren't a half block down the street when they turned melancholy.

"How is it with you?" she asked.

"So-so at best."

"You got the shit kicked out of you. Nobody told me why."

"I'm not sure why. I'll find out pretty soon."

"You won't back away, will you? You're a bit long in the tooth for physical bravery."

"That's why God made guns," he tried to joke but it was lame.

"You know I keep in touch with Diane. You also know her new husband is dying. Any chance of you two getting back together?"

"None whatsoever. What's wrong with me then is still wrong."

Roberta suddenly stopped and looked around in puzzlement at the uniform beige stucco homes and absurdly uniform lawns.

"I'd rather retire to the south side of Chicago," she spit out.

"Me too," he agreed.

"Think how Bobby would have hated this place. He was always using the word *bourgeois*. Think of it. The only man I could ever love was my brother."

Sunderson's feet became glued to the sidewalk. She walked ahead for a few steps then turned shaking her head with tears in her eyes. Looking at her he felt his own tears well up uncontrollably. He moved toward her and they embraced, his heart thumping with this inconsolable love.

He was too overwrought when he got back to Patagonia for either a drink or a nap. He swerved off a side road, forded Sonoita Creek, and walked out around the Conservancy property again. His mind was swollen by his sister and the evidently vast quantity of love that was beyond sexuality and its simpleminded merging of genitalia. He wondered if religion was partly the love for an imaginary parent and whether any steps to make contact with this parent were justifiable. People sought out an intermediary like Daryl-Dwight or any sort of priest, preacher, swami, or guru in order to shortcut the search. As questionable luck would have it about halfway through the loop path he ran into a rather eerie young woman he guessed to be in her early thirties studying a bird book. Her skin was too translucent for his taste as if there was a danger of seeing her skull underneath the skin. He could see the blood of life pulsing lightly in her temples. She pointed out a bird in a mesquite tree about twenty yards away. It was disconcertingly colorful as if it had been painted by numbers.

"Elegant trogan."

"Yes it is," he agreed.

"No, that's its name. It's a male and it's a new life lister for me."

"Congratulations." He had an urge to escape but she put a hand on his arm.

"You look like you're having a hard time," she said, staring at the bird through her binoculars.

"You're right on the money." He was becoming frantic.

"Me, too. That's why I look at birds instead of inside my head. Good luck."

She walked off in the opposite direction and for once the idea that this woman had a nice butt was irrelevant. She obviously possessed information that he needed. His brain began to perk with exterior landscape rather than interior.

He was driving down the alley to his quarters when he saw Kowalski, the fake cop, driving hurriedly out of the driveway. Sunderson didn't give a shit unless the man had left a bomb behind. Kowalski had put a note on top of the folder of Daryl-Dwight research that Mona had sent. The note read, "Why don't you just go over there and shoot the cocksucker?"

Sunderson couldn't nap and a drink still seemed inappropriate. He felt that his concerns were levitating him an inch above his bed. The primary result was homesickness. He thought of the bird woman he had met in terms of something that Marion had said about his own obsession with paying attention to the natural world that already was, rather than himself. Marion was totally without self-concern, thinking that as a human he was essentially a comic figure.

When it was time to get ready to go to Melissa's for dinner he checked his cell phone, which had been turned off, for messages. Mona had called, sounding effervescent, to say that Carla had been busted for a pound of weed in her apartment and a dozen cartons of unstamped cigarettes. Out on bail Carla had screamed at Mona on the phone detecting the trail of her bust. Sunderson grinned. Something had worked. He also felt a trace of rejuvenation in the shower but was less than enthused about the upcoming dinner. Typical of his age he had not yet regenerated from the previous day's sex. This was a case where the tired fountain does not overflow.

Melissa had a smallish stucco house in a semigated community that wasn't guarded. There was, however, a very large man sitting on her porch whom Sunderson recognized as being near the front door that evening at Las Vigas. The man's heavy eyelids made it look as if his eyes were closed.

"Señor Sunderson, of course," he said not getting up from his chair.

Sunderson sat with Melissa in a wildly flowered backyard drinking a margarita she had made fresh with tiny limes and a tequila that cost fifty bucks he had seen in the liquor store. She seemed scattered and a little cool, glancing at Josefina in the corner of the yard playing on a swing set with a nanny. He was wondering if she regretted making love to him the day before. When she had welcomed him at the door and guided him through the utterly elegant living room with its burnished copper walls and antique furniture he had thought again that nothing down here is what it seems to be.

"What are you going to do?" She wasn't looking at him.

"I don't know for sure. I'm thinking about moving over to Willcox or the Dos Cabezas to be closer to my enemy."

"If you don't have a pistol I have an extra." Now she was looking at him as if he were incompetent.

"I have one."

"But I can tell you're not wearing it. What good is a pistol if you don't have it with you?" She kept checking her watch and then led him into the house. They sat down at the dining room table and Sunderson was disappointed to note that the table was set for four. Looking at her in her short green skirt had warmed him up after all. She explained the platter of ceviche, a Mexican fish dish pickled with lime juice and hot chilies. He loved the ceviche because it reminded him of the pickled herring of home.

"You're very nice but I worry that you will be killed like my husband," she said furtively as the front door opened and Xavier arrived with an attractive young thing who looked 99 percent female but her Adam's apple told Sunderson that she was likely a transvestite. Will wonders never cease? Melissa rose to kiss her brother but refused to acknowledge his girlfriend, or boyfriend, or whatever. Xavier was ebullient and placed three cell phones near his plate.

"I keep one for Melissa but I have two new cell phones every day for my business. Sorry we're late but I must make love after work every day to remind me that I'm human."

"Please," Melissa said, blushing.

"I have solved your mystery," Xavier said, looking at Sunderson and pouring a white wine that Sunderson recognized as Diane's favorite, Meursault. "My problem was that I said to myself, what are two men from Marquette, Michigan,

doing in my area? One has the other nearly killed. They must
be quarreling about money. Then I learned a lot of information about you. You are studying this man's cult. I know you
have a pension of thirty-two thousand a year, which is not
enough. I know you take Norvasc for high blood pressure
and Levoxyl for a deficient thyroid and your wife left you
three years ago. And now you have moved to Patagonia. I
thought you were snooping about me through my sister but
now I think you are just another horny old man. Your enemy
is camped on what I think of as my land with a hundred of
his followers. Today I had him brought to me in Nogales for
a conversation. He wasn't very happy. I have been forced to
tell him that he and his people must leave by Christmas. Why,
I must ask you, are you fascinated by this lunatic?"

Sunderson was unnerved by Xavier's high metallic
laughter. Melissa stared at Sunderson harshly as if to say,
"You are imperiled. Be honest."

"My hobby has always been history," Sunderson began
slowly. "I became interested in the relationship between
religion, money, and sex."

"Well, you are a fool or a scholar or both. They are one.
They can't be separated," Xavier interrupted.

"Perhaps, but this enemy was in my area, as you say.
I didn't like what he was doing to people." Sunderson was
developing a case of ice cubes in the guts.

"I mean you can't think of sex, religion, and money as
individual building blocks. They have bled into each other
until they are a huge unruly animal, quite vicious, really."
Xavier was enthused about the conversation as if he were
taking part in a college debate.

"My job until a few weeks ago was to protect the citi-
zenry from those with criminal intent," Sunderson said lamely,
biding for time. He remembered reading William Blake way
back in college who had said something to the effect of brothels
being built with the bricks of religion.

"You people haven't protected shit. You've built little
dams here and there. People are natural children of the beast."

They stopped talking for a few minutes and ate what
Melissa called *carne adovada,* which was little chunks of pork
cooked with hot chili. Sunderson was beginning to sweat
and felt in his pocket to make sure he had his Gas-X.

"I didn't realize you were ranching in the area of the
man who calls himself the Great Leader," Sunderson teased,
knowing full well that individual cartels control specific
routes of import all along the nearly two-thousand-mile
border.

"You are becoming impolite," Xavier said petulantly.
"We are speaking as educated gentlemen. You may stay in
the area through Christmas Day so you can have Christmas
with your mother and sister in Green Valley. After that, go
home."

"And if I don't?" Sunderson's heart swelled in anger.

"You will become menudo for the vultures and ravens,"
Xavier laughed.

"How inhospitable." Sunderson's ice cubes had become
a solid block.

"And don't see my sister again. I can't have you fucking
her like a dog in broad daylight."

"Xavier!" Melissa screamed, getting up and going as
far as the kitchen door.

Xavier smiled and pointed a forefinger at Sunderson as if it were a gun. Sunderson got up slowly and walked to the front door, summoning his courage for a backward glance at Melissa but she was staring down at her feet. Now on the front porch there were three men that Sunderson supposed were there in case he presented a problem. He didn't intend to.

PART III

Chapter 10

Sunderson was dumbfounded by his fragility. He walked. And walked and walked, the only thing he could think of to do to leave what he had become behind him. He wrote a single entry in his journal, cryptic but on the money. "I am a very short man in tall grass."

After leaving Melissa's he had stopped at the Wagon Wheel for seven double whiskeys, his favorite number. The whiskey had none of the desired effect. The barmaid Amanda wasn't there and her replacement was clearly frightened of him as if he were one of the spate of vampires who had descended on the land compliments of television. A soused tourist lady had approached.

"Are you Robert Duvall?"

"No, I'm not," he had responded gruffly.

"Prove it. I know you're Robert Duvall."

"Go fuck yourself."

She had shrieked and he left the bar. This Robert Duvall misidentification happened a couple of times a year. This
used to amuse Diane who thought he should learn how to
tango because Robert Duvall tangoed.

Reaching the apartment he vomited in the backyard, the
whiskey vomit stinging his nasal passages. This was clearly
one of those rare times that alcohol was unable to do its job.
His brain was fluttery rather than dulled. He spent a wretched
night within a recurring dream of when at age twelve he had
cut pulp during winter vacation to earn money for Christmas.
His dad had dropped him off at daylight but it was ten below
zero and he had skipped breakfast. He couldn't get warm
except for his hands which he pressed against the cowl of
his Stihl chain saw, his proudest possession along with his
green Schwinn bicycle. At midmorning he was still shaking
and carried the saw out to the section road where after half
an hour he had been picked up by a county snowplow driver
who was a friend of his dad's. The man said, "You got to eat
breakfast if you're going to work in the woods." They stopped
at a diner and Sunderson ate a hot roast beef sandwich with
potatoes and gravy and then fell asleep in his chair. In the
dream he had never gotten out of the woods but had grasped
a beech tree to avoid shaking into pieces of frozen meat.

He got up at 4:00 a.m. and drank coffee for an hour
until he could call Marion at five, which was seven Michigan time.

"You sound pretty rough."

"That's a fair thing to say."

"Maybe it's because you had the necessary habit of
work for forty years and now you don't."

"That must be part of it. I'm going to take a powder for a week or so. If Berenice or Mona call tell them I'll be fine."

"Are you sure? I could come down for Thanksgiving and we could talk it through."

"No. I'm just going to walk and knock off the sauce and then maybe come home."

"Sounds wise. Here's a thought re: our Great Leader. I read a piece by this historian named Carter who claims religion is biological."

"Jesus Christ. Why not? Give my love to Mona."

"That's not hard. She and this brother and sister have started wearing identical clothes. It's upsetting the school authorities." Marion laughed.

Despite repeated rinsing the whiskey puke odor was still in his nose. He turned off his cell phone and put it in the refrigerator for no particular reason. He strapped on his shoulder holster and revolver thinking that it would be fun to shoot Daryl-Dwight in the head but then the problem wasn't the Great Leader's but the world's and the only real solution was to shoot himself.

He drove to the Tucson airport and exchanged his compact for an SUV. He remembered to have breakfast because he was going to the woods of sorts. A burly brown waitress in Birkenstocks saw his copy of Alfred's map spread on the table and gave suggestions for camping places. She was the typical eco-ninny but pleasant. Her green shorts and brown legs indicated that she was an experienced hiker.

"I don't want to see anyone for a week including myself."

"You're in a bad way," she laughed. "Try the east end of Aravaipa Creek up near Klondyke. It's north of Bonita

between the Pinaleños and the Galiuros. Take the fork up
Turkey Creek so the Conservancy assholes don't hassle you."

"Thank you and God bless." Sunderson had never said
"God Bless" before but Roxie used to after he screwed her
on the clothes dryer.

"Drop by and let me know how it works," she said
going off to wait on other customers. She smelled wonderful like a hay field and Sunderson felt a touch of life. He
went into a huge sporting goods store and bought a cheap
sleeping bag, a tarpaulin, a primus stove, a bunch of trail
mix and freeze-dried food, coffee packets and a pot, and a
canteen. On the way out he looked at a display of bowling
balls, which reminded him of Xavier saying that religion,
sex, and money aren't separable. He was likely right. A
human is as indivisible as a bowling ball, a biological knot
like any other creature, a distressing notion but then so
was much of life.

Three hours later he was camped on a flat up Turkey
Creek a half mile from his car. The beauty of the mountain
landscape made him feel insignificant, which was the feeling
he was after. The heavy weight of his personality needed to
disappear for a while. Properly and openly perceiving the
landscape made his currently dismal self vanish. He had
been confused since leaving home in Marquette to a degree
that daily seemed impossible at his age when he should have
had things figured out.

He walked and walked. Turkey and Aravaipa Creeks
were obviously without brook trout but he realized that
was missing the point. The truly important idea is where
creeks were, often in the most ignored and neglected parts

of the landscapes including marshes, swamps, and deep gulleys, landscapes from which the human race couldn't extract money and therefore they were mostly left to simply be themselves. Marion had said that we have eaten the world and puked it up and except in isolated locations what we have left is mostly puke. This idea was an unpleasant reminder of the tinge of whiskey odor still in his nose so he knelt and snorted some creek water then rubbed some juniper on his upper lip.

The first late afternoon and evening were hard without his habitual alcohol. He simply never missed drinking every day except when he had the flu and then he felt virtuous about not drinking. He had walked so far his legs trembled so whiskey would have been nice and sitting near his campfire he was fearful over how long the nights were in late November, close to fourteen hours at least at this latitude, and worse far north in Marquette. He and Marion always celebrated on winter solstice, December 21, when it turned around and the light began to increase in increments of a minute or so per day.

He slept well from his walking fatigue from eight in the evening until midnight. The dinner of freeze-dried beef stroganoff had been wretched and his irritation over forgetting a bottle of Tabasco or a jar of dill pickles was outsized without the calming influence of a little whiskey. It was a feeling similar to losing all of your favorite marbles in a schoolyard contest. This was miniscule compared to the haunting feeling at midnight when he awoke and fed the fire. Alcohol had always worked fairly well in ameliorating or subduing his hair-shirt memories but now without a trace of it in his body he was struck dumb by the little movie his mind made of the morning after Thanksgiving when the Mayflower van had come and moved out Diane's collection of fine antique furniture and her many boxes of art books. She was in Naples, Florida, with her parents and her stuff was being moved to a bungalow near the hospital from where she could walk to work. He had opened a bottle of cheap Early Times when the movers had left and it was gone by dinnertime when rather than dinner he had opened another bottle of whiskey. This had gone on a couple of days and when he didn't show up for work Monday morning or answer the phone a colleague had checked up and found him facedown and comatose on the floor of the unheated enclosed back porch after a ten-degree night. There was a trip to the ER in an ambulance and two days in the hospital where Marion had visited.

"You should have called," Marion had said.

"I didn't have anything to say."

That had been the longest winter of his life though from force of will he slowed down his drinking to a point short of passing out. Toward the end of April and the beginning of trout season he found that his fingers trembled so that he couldn't tie a fly to his leader at which point he was able to cut back to his traditional two drinks after work and two in the evening. This would not have been possible had he not fished a hundred evenings and weekend days in a row. Moving water was the only workable tranquilizer for the central error of his life, the divorce.

The fire flared nicely after he added a large piece of juniper stump. He wondered at how the totally sober mind's tongue reached the rawest spots. He should have known that

Melissa was spying for her brother and not truly drawn to him, the Lone Geezer from the north. He still had the lovely memory of her crouched all nude and moist in the small clearing of the thicket in the estuarine area of the lake's end. Part of him had known she was a spy but the stronger part chose to ignore it, led by vanity and the biological ring through his nose until the inevitable falling smack on his foolish face. A fool for love and lust or something like that. How absurd. As he drifted off he heard the howling of coyotes up the canyon break into yips, which meant they were closing in on the kill. He thought that the sex game must be about over for him but then it had never been much of a game, more like a mortal intrusion.

At dawn he shivered from the cold, the dew on his sleeping bag crisply frozen. Why hadn't he set up the tent, where a single candle or two would have kept him warmish? He could just barely reach his pile of wood from the bag and flipped a few pieces on the coals. Ever the detective he had awakened thinking that if the Great Leader could be caught with the raised-skirt photo that his girlfriend Carla had taken of Mona he could be charged with possession of child pornography. That would put the sucker away for a while even though it was definitely pushing the envelope to think of Mona as a child except in the eyes of the law. He lay there brooding over the matter until the sun peeked through the Pinaleño Mountains to the east. Of course it had been okay for him to peek at Mona through his bookcase. It was easy in stray moments to forgive yourself.

He arose, his muscles creaking painfully, and made coffee and then scrambled eggs by adding water to the egg

powder in the pan. How nasty and poorly planned. Why
hadn't he brought along a stack of the fine local tortillas?
Why hadn't he brought along a cooler full of steaks, chicken,
pork chops, bacon, eggs, and cheese? This dried shit was
for hikers who needed to travel light. He could easily have
walked the half a mile back to the car once a day to pick
up supplies. He had clearly lost his wits in this alien place
called Arizona. He had to figure out how to pick up his new
life from the ground where he had merely been walking on
it and reshape it into a tolerable form.

Lucky for him he gave up thinking when he walked.
His recent thinking always arrived at a pile of the same old
compromised shit wherein the mistakes of the past readily
suffocated the present. When he walked his level of attention
was spread thinly but intensely over the entire landscape
as it likely had been for walkers a million years before. His
thoughts were idle little slips such as trees stay in one place
and that even the smallest creeks or trickles follow declining
altitude. His mistakes were those of a relative flatlander. If
you climb a steep hill it doesn't mean that like Michigan you
can get down the other side. It took him a couple of days
to figure out that there was no way to reach the top of the
butte that capped the steep cliffs along Aravaipa Creek. He
resented this then concluded that no one had ever been up
there except birds.

As the days passed his sack of dried food diminished.
On the fourth day he ate only two granola bars and he felt
how far his trousers were loosening. He had worn holes in
his only pair of heavy socks and instead put on two pairs
of his cheap thin office socks. His feet became so sore he

soaked them an hour each day in a pool of the cold creek.
He snuck around a small Nature Conservancy cabin at dawn
because you needed a permit to enter their land and he didn't
want to wake anyone up. He proceeded west increasingly
intimidated by the steep canyon walls and wondering how
the conifers, oaks, and mesquite seemed able to grow out
of rock. There was certainly nothing comfortable about the
heraldic land of the Apaches who in many ways seemed the
tribe least like the white intruders. We made much of their
savagery though indeed we cut off the head of their leader
Mangas Coloradas and shipped it east to the Smithson-
ian in the name of science, a fact that made the Apaches
improbably difficult to subdue. They wanted to enter the
spirit world with their dead bodies intact. The West wasn't
settled by nice people.

He was fatigued by midmorning and forced himself to
eat one of the two pathetic so-called *energy* bars he had carried along. He thought that just because you're older doesn't
mean that death is imminent every day. There's generally
a tip-off when it's coming. He sat by the creek chewing his
food thinking that we'll never understand anything. Here he
was unable to name the hundreds of varied plants and birds
he was seeing that had the solace of taking him away from
the miserable world of men, his life in fact. He abruptly felt
that even his habitual study of history was parasitic. Like
the small leech his was a perfect parasite because he didn't
kill his host, merely attached himself and fed.

He had fed on history and sometimes the food nauseated
him. For instance, several months studying the Indian Wars
were disastrous. It reminded him of how Diane loved Mahler

but Mahler severely jangled him. Composers attached clusters
of musical notes to their large emotions but Sunderson didn't
want big emotions so he had truncated his study of the Indian
Wars. He often wondered if this emotional timidity was part
of the male ethic of the far north, that is, aim low and you
won't be disappointed. In retrospect his being the first college graduate on either side of his family seemed puny. He
was amazed after sitting by the creek for fifteen minutes to
finally notice the tracks of a big feline in the damp sand near
his own feet, obviously a mountain lion. His skin prickled
thinking that the beast might be watching him from any of
a hundred hiding places along the canyon walls or from the
verdant thickets. He didn't carry his pistol on his walks but
then decided he was likely too large to be easy prey. The
many small hoof prints also in the damp sand were those of
the small pig-like creature the javelina that he had read were
the central food of the lion in the Southwest. His ex-landlord
Alfred had said that a small number of jaguars, a much more
ominous creature, had been migrating north from Mexico.

   On the long walk back to the campsite he passed openly
on the trail through the Conservancy property and was ac-
costed by a young man and a woman who were hanging up
clothes in the yard of the cabin. To avoid any problem he
blithered out pidgin Italian he remembered from the trip he
and Diane had taken to Italy. The young man was embarrassed and merely pointed the way east off the property.
The young woman grinned as if catching on to his ploy.
Her brown legs emerging from her blue shorts gave him a
nut buzz. When you don't see a female in five days a plain
Jane can be striking. As he walked on down a two-track

she nagged on him in unison with his need for a cigarette.
He only had seven cigarettes left and wanted to stay for
a full week, which meant two more days in his somewhat
helpless addictive purgatory.

On the sixth day his feet were so sore he mostly sat
at the campsite staring at the creek and pondering his next
move. He checked the small calendar card in his wallet and
noted it was two days until Thanksgiving when he would
force himself to grace his mom's dining table. His mind kept
raising the image of Melissa's bare butt wagging near the
lake. He wanted to see her again but he also wanted not to
be dead.

The day had become warmish and he had a disturbing
nap with a brief dream wherein the natural world became
too vivid to become tolerated. This mood continued on waking. The untitled birds around him had the eyes of snakes,
their ancient relatives, and the surrounding foliage became
livid. He smoked several of his remaining small cache of
cigarettes and decided his mental distortions were due to
hunger and loneliness. He cooked up an insipid freeze-dried
concoction called Spanish rice but only managed to eat half
before his gag reflex began to tickle. He saw a slight movement among the rocks about fifteen feet across the creek. It
was a small rattlesnake, perhaps a foot and a half long. He
aimed his revolver but couldn't pull the trigger because he
didn't want to hear the noise. He would zip up his floor tent
partway tonight. For the first time in nearly six days he felt
an urge to read a book. When darkness fell he made a plan,
a map of war, before a roaring fire. He had been offered at
least temporarily the clarity of breaking a habit.

Chapter 11

Before dawn he sat waiting impatiently for enough light to reach his car. He was packed up and studying the single cigarette he had left, which he held in the palm of his hand. He felt pretty clearheaded about his intentions and was amused wondering what level of enlightenment the Great Leader might consider him. He thought that in some otherwise intelligent people there must be an improbable religious yearning that would make them give up their savings and livelihood to the Great Leader. Again, did he actually believe in what he was preaching? Maybe on alternate days. Sunderson recalled that when he was thirteen and his father had a minimal heart attack he had prayed in the Lutheran church with his mother. His prayers were diverted in their intensity by the sight of a girl named Daisy across the aisle. A friend had heard that she had given a blow job to a guy from Shingleton for two beers and a joint. Meanwhile his family cut back on their comparatively meager expenses so that Dad didn't have to work twelve hours a day six days a week. There it was, Sunderson thought while dousing his campfire, sex and religion and money.

It took an hour to reach Willcox. He bought cigarettes and gas, and had a bowl of red chili and beef at the truck stop, then headed south to see the Great Leader, his revolver unbuckled in the shoulder holster.

To his surprise the gate was open and there was a pile of sleeping bags, packs, pads, and several garbage bags full of trash and belongings. He sorted through the pile that they probably planned to come back for as some of the sleeping bags were expensive models. He was tempted to swipe a smallish day pack that was full of papers and magazines but decided it would be wise to wait until his way out. He was pleased to note that a batch of magazines were issues of a soft-core porn rag called *Barely Eighteen* that he had seen in convenience stores and truck stops in the Upper Peninsula. He had watched hunters and fishermen buy this magazine along with the old standards *Hustler* and *Penthouse* on the way out to their camps.

He was alarmed to hear a vehicle coming down the canyon toward him and felt for his unbuckled revolver but it was a green-suited Forest Service ranger at the wheel, swerving to a halt.

"May I help you?" He was clearly pissed.

"Looking for a possible felon." Sunderson flipped his expired badge from a half dozen feet away.

"Those jerks flew the coop for Tucson. They leased forty acres here from a rancher but didn't comprehend their

boundaries and built a permanent structure on federal land.
They're cleaning up the site to avoid charges."

"We're contemplating serious charges in Michigan,"
Sunderson said, diffidently looking around and wishing the
guy would go away. "How many are in there?"

"Just two. What charges?"

"I'm not at liberty to say."

The man drove off with a conspiratorial wave. Sunderson headed down the road on foot hoping for unde-
tected surveillance. He took his cheap binoculars along,
pausing at the place he had been stoned and noting the
dark markings of his blood on the rocks here and there.
He felt a newfound energy from having had something
real to eat. He peeked around a boulder and saw two men
disassembling a small stone hut, their newish blue Ford
pickup nearby blasting loud rock music. Through the binoculars he could see one was a sallow young man who
wasn't working very hard but then there was also Clayton,
a mixed-blood Chippewa he had met at the longhouse in
Ontonagon County. He had checked Clayton out: he had
had a few minor scrapes with the law and was evidently
on the payroll, not being a religious type. Clayton was a
renowned brawler with a thick chest and big arms so Sunderson approached with his revolver drawn. The young
man saw him first and took off running up a hill toward
a thicket. Clayton grinned leaning on the pickax he was
using to dislodge the stones of the hut walls.

"Hey, boss. Good to see someone from home. I didn't
throw stones at you."

"What's up?" Sunderson put the revolver back in his holster and looked toward the hill where the young man had run. "Who was that?"

"He's the Leader's main pussy scout. It's a legally sensitive job." Clayton laughed. "The Leader's name is Daryl now. He's into shape changing, you know, playing Indian."

"I figured that. You get paid in cash?"

"Why?" Clayton was nervous.

"You don't want the IRS after you. Give me Daryl's address."

"Of course." Clayton was relieved that so little was being asked of him. There was more than a trace of despair in his face. "The money is the best of my life but I'm getting the fuck out of here. I'm going home. This area is too fucking weird and violent. When I was at a lumberyard in Douglas getting supplies this Apache told me he was going to cut off my big nose. And then these big Mexican guys come along and tell us to move on. This is a drug route, you know. I've seen groups of guys carrying bales of pot and whatever over that way." He pointed in the direction the young man had run.

"I know." Sunderson sniffed the air smelling something painfully familiar. He walked around the stone hut and in the back there was a Dutch oven iron pot on a small bed of coals. It was a venison stew.

"The deer meat down here ain't as good as back home. Want some?"

It became absurdly like old home week with the two men sitting on boulders and eating bowls of venison stew, reminiscing about the U.P., mostly fishing and hunting and eating fried whitefish and lake trout.

"This is a foreign country down here," Sunderson said, helping himself to another tortilla wrapped in aluminum foil and another portion of stew.

"No shit. That's why I can't wait to get home. I went into a grocery store and they'd never heard of rutabagas."

Sunderson headed for Tucson, stopping at the airport to exchange the SUV for a less expensive compact. He stopped at the diner hoping to see the girl who had directed him to the fire camping site. She wasn't there and he felt a specific pang of disappointment. He left her a thank-you note that included his cell number. Back in his car he suddenly realized that the address Clayton had given him for the Great Leader was a street near the Arizona Inn. It wouldn't do to let his immediate presence be known but he gambled on a drive past. Dwight-Daryl was in the side yard of an expensive house playing doubles badminton with three girls well under eighteen. On the way out of the cult site he had grabbed the day pack he'd eyed and was eager to look at the contents. He mulled over the whole, deep mud bath of human sexuality admitting to himself that you surely didn't see the best as a cop. Returning to Tucson his thinking had been confused by the sheer number of attractive women walking around, especially near the university, after a week in the wilds in which he had only seen the one female at the Conservancy cabin. The fresh look reminded him of the nondirectional yearning he had felt toward females in high school when the excitement of simply hugging a girl had made him dizzy. In the expensive market he stopped in before leaving the city he lamely pushed his cart around behind a knockout in her thirties but then she caught on, turned, and frowned and he reddened. He bought steak, shrimp, and a pile of fruit and vegetables. Everything looked delicious after his week of stupid privation. At the checkout register the woman he had stalked pulled her cart in behind his and he raised his hands in a mime of apology. She smiled shyly which relieved him of his immediate sense of being a fool.

Back in Patagonia it wasn't quite drink time so he made a cup of instant coffee and thought over some plans he had made. He was thinking about calling Lucy in New York and trying to get her to come to Tucson and infiltrate the cult in the guise of a wealthy woman. The drawback was that she was a tad unstable. He tried to dismiss the question of how long his ex-wife would follow him like a ghost and whether there were other Diane doppelgangers like Lucy? Probably.

He slowly unpacked the contents of the cult bag. There were a half dozen issues of *Barely Eighteen,* which he leafed through with no particular interest, not being turned on by photos. A spiral notebook with Dwight-Daryl's handwriting was a severe disappointment. The first page was titled, *I Am Many,* but the following pages were in code which he would have to FedEx to Mona, or maybe just take back home as he was thinking of hightailing it after Thanksgiving. Comically there were a number of small bottles of Viagra, Levitra, and Cialis to keep the Leader's pecker up. It added up to not much but then he shook the magazines to make sure and eureka the third contained a printed-out e-mail and digital photo in between the pages featuring Candy the High School Dropout. The photo was an electrifying

one of Mona on a sofa with her skirt raised and no undies.
Sunderson blushed and turned the photo over on the table.
The e-mail was from Carla and read, "Dearest, here's a photo
of the creep, which might turn you on though she's a bit old
for your taste. I went down on her for an hour which you
would have liked watching. Love, Carla"

Sunderson began to sweat and reached for the absent whiskey bottle. How could he have forgotten to buy
whiskey or wine? Mona had said nothing had *happened* that
evening. One of them was lying and he hoped it was Carla.
In any event he had a fine piece of evidence, perhaps not
enough to convict but plenty to cause a heap of trouble.
He brooded as he made a salad not wanting to fry a rib
steak without having a bottle of wine to go with it. The
loaf of French bread was fair and he was inclined to feel
virtuous even though he had simply forgotten the whiskey.
He finally stored his groceries and was amused to see his
cell phone in the refrigerator. He had assumed it wouldn't
work in there but he was of course wrong. What the fuck,
he thought, being electronically ignorant. He took out his
notebook and jotted down messages from Berenice for
the Thanksgiving dinner, one from his mother telling him
that he was, as always, a disappointment, a cheery one
from Marion, and three from Mona saying that someone
had broken into her house and stolen her computer. To
his surprise there were five messages from Melissa, which
frightened him because of Xavier's threat at dinner. He
called anyway feeling a memory-driven nut itch.

"I want to see you," she said.

"I don't want to die."

"Xavier is at his apartment in New York City because there's a war between everyone. His people are hiding out down in Obregon. Anyway it causes too many problems to kill an American."

"How nice. Why do you want to see me?"

"Companionship. Everyone else is afraid of me."

"The Wagon Wheel bar ASAP," he said, pressing the OFF button then calling Mona.

"I'm sorry about your computer. I'll buy you a new one."

"Everything's in there. I feel like I lost my past."

"I can't do anything about that."

"No shit. Can you still turn a doorknob? Where the hell were you?"

"Camping in the wilderness without my cell. Cooling off. I found that raised-skirt photo of you in the Leader's day pack. He can be nailed for possession of child pornography."

"I'm a child? I better tell the guy that fucked me an hour ago." She laughed.

"That's not funny," he said lamely.

"It was fun. Why should I be faithful to you? You won't touch me no matter how much I tease you. I don't really like to do yoga at dawn. Everything was for you, darling."

He hung up. Now he really needed a drink. He called Berenice and said he'd be there for Thanksgiving dinner and turned off the phone before she could get started on his week's disappearance.

The first double shot and Pacifico at the bar made him glow. Alcohol beat the shit out of the Shroud of Turin as a miracle though the fair-sized crowd of drinkers didn't look merry.

"Where you been, cutie?" Amanda asked.

"Camping."

"Oh bullshit. A pretty Latino named Melissa is look-ing for you. Also a guy named Kowalski although he didn't look like a Kowalski. He wondered if you had left town. He doesn't know that I know his name but he's a low-rent P.D. from Rio Rico. Mostly divorce cases."

"Thanks." Hearing Kowalski's name made him glad he had the photo and Carla's e-mail in his sport coat pocket. It occurred to him that Kowalski must have been retained by Dwight-Daryl. He decided to kick his ass if he saw him again.

All of the men in the bar had turned to the door while Sunderson was rehearsing violence and refusing to recog-nize the abrupt limitations of his age, the way the years drew closer daily, and the fact that Kowalski, being much younger, might very well kick his ass. Where is the consid-erable strength of yesteryear? Mostly gone.

He finally turned and saw Melissa at the door, im-patient to be acknowledged, wearing a blonde wig and a waist-length fur jacket. The outfit didn't work but he still felt a tingle. What's with blonde hair and black eyebrows? It looked silly and vulgar. He beckoned her toward the side table farthest from the jukebox, which was playing a Latino lament. He had been avoiding gringo stations on the car radio in favor of the Latino, finding it remarkable how often the word *corazon* was used. Amanda brought him another double and a beer and Melissa a predictable white wine.

"What's a *corazon*?" he asked.

"It's the heart, stupid. I'm taking you to Spain on Xavier's dime."

"I couldn't accept that."

"Of course you could. We'd meet in Barcelona. I lived there a year when I was nineteen. Xavier keeps saying that he's lost a lot of hard-earned money on the market. Isn't that funny?"

"I suppose so. I need you to do me a favor."

"Then let's go to your place."

"I don't want you to know where it is. I don't want my severed head found in the toilet bowl."

He went on to ask her to stop at the Leader's address and pretend she was interested in the cult. She was fascinated and agreed saying that she would try it tomorrow if he'd keep his cell on. She said she and Josefina had to move to Tucson anyway because Xavier felt that Nogales was too vulnerable a place for his sister while the drug wars raged.

"Tomorrow is Thanksgiving," he said idly.

"I grew up without your pilgrims," she laughed.

He bought a pint of whiskey from the bar and they took a ride down past the Conservancy and up Salero Canyon Road, pulling off on a two-track, behind a mesquite thicket. He was mortally disappointed when she said she had the monthlies and couldn't screw. He felt like a teenager sucking her breasts in the car. She began to blow him and then stopped.

"Do you want my back door?" She was laughing.

"Of course." He had paused not quite comprehending. Other than feverish incidents late in high school and in college he hadn't had wide experience, what with his

faithfulness in forty years of marriage to Diane. He felt
tremulous and daring as they got out of the car and she
leaned over the front seat, turning out the dome light and
handing him a bottle of lotion from her purse. There was
enough moon that her trim buttocks fairly glowed.

"Take it easy, kiddo."

"I don't think I'm going to last long." And he didn't
mostly because a dog growled loudly behind them. He
pulled out instantly and she shrieked and crawled across
the seat. He scrambled in after her. Now she was laughing
and he turned to see through the car window a big black
dog not a dozen feet away. The dog jumped up against
the car and started snarling in at Sunderson. Still laughing Melissa started the car and backed around throwing
gravel as she drove out the two-track. Now the dog was
chasing the car and roaring.

"It's the ghost of my father," she hissed. "When I was
twelve he caught Xavier doing that to me and beat him
nearly to death. Do you think that's why Xavier became
gay?"

"I have no idea." Sunderson didn't want to digest what
he was hearing. There was the discordant mental image of
pilgrims fucking in their funny pilgrim hats. He unscrewed
the pint and took a long, choking drink.

"You shouldn't drink so much," she said. "I worry about
your drinking."

"I worry about your brother having me killed."

"He won't do that. I asked him not to. He likes to say
such things. Though of course he killed my husband with

his plastic hand then complained about the expense of getting a new hand."

Sunderson had looked forward to a real bed but later when trying to sleep found he missed the sweet outdoor night air, the sounds of nocturnal creatures, and even the lumpy pad under his cheap sleeping bag. And at dawn never had bad instant coffee tasted as good, as he planned his walking. He had opened the windows wide but there was still the slight smell of cleaning fluid in the room. All in all he was glad to not be dead and that the big black dog hadn't bitten him in the ass.

For twenty years he had been trying to dismiss a haunting night image. Back in March 1989 he had investigated a wife beating a few miles from Sault Ste. Marie. A diminutive woman who weighed less than a hundred pounds had been slugged by her husband with such massive force that it had driven her nose bone into her brain and she had died instantly. On the gurney her face looked like a plum from the subcutaneous bleeding. Her husband kept saying, "I only hit her once." When Sunderson finally got home to Marquette that night he had wept over a glass of whiskey in the kitchen and Diane had gotten out of bed and comforted him. For twenty years he had to face this nightly plum image and after trying to dismiss it for a long time he'd finally given up. But now the little woman's face appeared normal and she was smiling. He was so startled he turned on the bed lamp. Had he gone daft? Nothing was amiss except that the nightcap he had poured sat untouched on the kitchen table. He wanted to feel good in the morning.

A rooster awoke him before daylight and he was pleased to be in a village that allowed chickens. Roosters were the sound of his childhood when he would awake early for his miserable paper route from which he made five bucks a week. He made coffee and quickly fried half a strip steak and two eggs that he put on toast. It was all uncommonly delicious. He was feeling positive for the first time in the month since his retirement and attributed it to the week far from the world of men. He had no expectations that it would last long but it fueled his walk nearly to the top of Red Mountain from which he could see over the top of a range to the south and far into Mexico. The landscape was too vast for a flatlander and seeing seventy miles or so unnerved him. He descended so hastily his shins ached. He had become quite abruptly homesick. He would go home as soon as possible and do something reasonable like shovel snow off his sidewalk and out of the driveway.

Back in his temporary apartment he noted that a fly had drowned in the glass of whiskey and that there was a message on his cell phone from his ex-wife. He felt lightheaded when he called her back.

"Your mother is worried you won't show up for Thanksgiving. Please do so."

"I'm heading over in a half hour for her special oven-dried turkey. How have you been?"

"I've mostly been a nurse. My husband is on hyper-aggressive chemo. How about you?"

"I went camping alone for a week. You would have loved the place."

"I can't believe this," she laughed.

"It's true. I was recovering. At this late date I'm becoming a boy again by camping."

"Did it work?"

"Somewhat, except that getting away makes you want more getting away. I'm going to come home and spend some time at Marion's cabin to think over my pursuit of the Great Leader."

"It's not a cabin, it's barely a shack. You'll spend your time cutting wood."

"All the better."

"Have you found companionship?"

"Of sorts. There's this young Mexican woman but she's a tad daffy. It seems nearly all women are daffy except you."

After he concluded their chat he found he had a lump of grief in his throat. Life moment by moment is so unforgiving and I'm a slow study, he thought. It's hard to repair a boat after it's sunk. As he prepared to leave wishing he had some good wine to take along he was amused at his dread of the upcoming meal before which his mother, Hulda, would say a lengthy grace. Her annual Thanksgiving grace was traditionally a summing up of her spiritual fiscal year, more similar to driving nails than the polite "Thank you, Big Guy."

Sunderson's peripheral consciousness had expanded and on the way out of town he guessed that a man sitting at the head of an alley in a white sedan reading a newspaper was Kowalski. In the rearview mirror he saw the white sedan pick

up his tail as he crested the first hill out of town. He stepped
on it and was well ahead by the Salero Road turnoff and
then the serpentine turns through the canyon before Circle
Z Ranch slowed him down. His compact was a slow dog
indeed compared to his old Crown Victoria with which he
got up to 150 miles per hour chasing down a car thief in the
Seney stretch. For no reason except impulse and the fact that
the gate was open which it never was he turned left at Three
R, a narrow gravel road leading south into the mountains.
Kowalski followed a quarter mile behind and Sunderson took
out his *pistola* as it was known locally. He parked off to the
side and Kowalski pulled up behind him and got out grinning.
When Kowalski reached him and leaned against the compact
Sunderson pointed the pistol.

"Your cell phone, please."

Sunderson opened his car door violently, catching
Kowalski's shins with the bottom of the door and dropping
him like a tub of shit.

"You're annoying me," Sunderson said. He turned the
compact around and on the way past shot out both of Kowalski's front tires. Kowalski was sitting in the road with his
eyes closed hugging his shins.

On the way to the freeway to Green Valley he stopped
at the Safeway on Mariposa to buy a couple bottles of the
cheapish champagne his mother favored on special occasions. He was surprised the store was open but then Melissa had said that Latinos didn't grow up with pilgrims and
they could scarcely celebrate the conquistadors who were
butchers at best. He didn't worry about her infiltrating the
Leader's compound. She was a tough cookie.

Bob's glistening Escalade was parked out front and Sunderson wondered if he washed and polished it every morning, certainly a possibility. Expensive cars had always seemed loathsome. Those from the U.P., often called Yoopers, who had gone downstate and made good money would return in the summer and expect the locals to admire their new cars. They were largely out of luck.

Mom, Berenice, and Bob were sitting on the front porch and Hulda's lap was covered by the hideous family album. She had been extraordinarily handsome as a young woman and a lifetime later she had become a cranky crone.

"My remaining son," she announced. She had been calling him this for thirty years because the death of his brother was still current news to her.

"Surprise!" Sunderson said, holding up the two bottles of faux-champagne that had cost ten bucks apiece.

"Cool it off Mister Bigshot. And make the brown stuff." She was referring to a roux that Diane used to make to give the turkey gravy an appealing color. Diane had taught him and he found the process tedious.

"The Detroit Lions are playing the Chicago Bears in eighteen minutes," Bob said.

"I'm a Packers fan," Sunderson said.

"That's not patriotic. You should root for your home state." Bob was in a huff. "I like my gravy dark brown. I always was a gravy man. Valerie will help you. She's my niece."

"I'm cooking a twenty-two pounder. I put it on at daylight. We'll be eatin' on that sucker for a week. Put some juice on ice for me, son," Mom cackled.

Sunderson dutifully kissed Hulda and Berenice on the forehead and shook Bob's clammy hand. He went inside and was pleased to see that a fairly chubby young woman had already started the roux and was setting the table. She looked good bending over the table in her short skirt. She introduced herself and said she was going to cooking school in Santa Monica.

"This fucking turkey's going to be dead as a doornail. And what's this?" She opened the refrigerator and pointed at a tomato aspic dotted with ripe olives and tiny marshmallows.

"That's Hulda's secret recipe from the Great North," Sunderson laughed. He noted that the roux was a darker brown than he had ever achieved. "Nice roux," he said wanting to pat her on her plump ass but thinking better of it.

"I'm here interviewing for jobs in Tucson restaurants but the economy is tits up. Uncle Bob said I could be an assistant manager at his trailer park in Benson. I drove over there and it's a suckhole. He says you're on the track of top-rung criminals."

"He's on the money. I'm daily imperiled." This was sort of true. He opened his sport coat flap so she could see the shoulder holster hoping to improve her questionable dank mood which was everywhere present in America.

"Oh bullshit, everyone's carrying in this state," she said raising her eyebrows as he poured his mom a full glass of champagne on the rocks.

"It's the message not the delivery," he said.

They finally arranged themselves at the table. He had meant to tell Valerie not to carve until after grace as the food would lose its heat. He knew that his mother got her ornate prayer language via the King James version of the Bible plus her bug-eyed little minister back home.

"Let us bow our heads and close our eyes in prayer. Our heavenly father we thank thee for our ample foodstuffs on this gladsome day. Whilst thou art in heaven with my husband and son sitting on your right hand we thank thee that we are still alive and kicking. As thou knowest it was a tough year with my stroke putting me on the fritz for a while. We thank thee for curing Berenice's sprained ankle which she got tripping over the hose Bob left on the front steps after he washed her car. We thank thee for Bob's prosperity which keeps our hides and hair together in these troubled times. We thank thee for getting Simon back on his feet after he got beat up by a Mexican gang. Lord, protect the borders of our country. We pray that niece Valerie finds a job and keeps her body pure for the hubby in her future . . ."

Sunderson opened his eyes a squint and saw the startled look on Valerie's face. Next to him Bob was text messaging on his cell in his lap. Berenice was staring up at a fly on the ceiling. The torpor was in full flood. Hulda paused to take a gulp of her iced champagne. He was bored enough to childishly drop his fork on the floor in order to catch a view up Valerie's legs. He leaned over and the view was dizzying what with Valerie abruptly giving her legs an extra spread. There was the fabled little muffin contained in blue undies. When he popped back up he blushed when she gave him a silly grin. Why was he such a fool? "To thine own self be true," said Polonius but then his Shakespeare professor at Michigan State forty-five years before had said that Polonius was a parodic character blathering the street wisdom of the day.

"And Lord, we are in thine hands for better or worse," Hulda continued with a champagne burp, "and of late it's been worse for my little retirement fund which as you know is handled by the Lutheran Brotherhood. It sure would be nice if you could see fit to let the market fly high like a balloon."

And so on. Luckily Valerie reheated the turkey gravy in the microwave. Sunderson left as soon as it was vaguely polite to do so after Berenice's medley of pies, which apparently came from a bakery as they were without her vaunted lard crust. He was barely in the car when he got a cell call from Melissa.

"It was unpleasant," she began, then paused. "He was wearing a red robe and we were alone in a den."

"Yes. Go ahead."

"He was like, you know, a slick fraternity guy at U of A. He wanted to see my butt and I said no. That put a stop to things so for you I quickly showed him my butt which because of you is sore today. So then he got friendlier. The ticket for me to enter the group would be fifty grand which would get me complete spiritual satisfaction and a transcendent mind whatever that is. I asked him why he needed so much money and he said he and his people were moving to Nebraska in the spring."

"Where in Nebraska?" Sunderson asked.

"How should I know? Nebraska is Nebraska. Anyway, he got real friendly when I let on that I was rich and the fifty grand wasn't out of the question. He said that it appeared I was already on level twenty-three of the hundred levels of spirituality. Then he shocked me and suggested that I give him a blow job. He wouldn't come in my mouth because he had to save his fluids for younger women who needed them more. He said that sperm is the most powerful fluid in the world. I thought fast because I can't blow a man unless I actually like him so I told him I couldn't because I had a tooth pulled yesterday. So that's that."

"Thanks. You did a fine job."

"A little bad news. Xavier is coming home tonight and he's real pissed that we met at the Wagon Wheel so be careful."

Sunderson's heart dropped in temperature and he pushed the OFF button. Jesus Christ. He called Mona and asked her to book him a flight home via Minneapolis or Chicago, whichever was soonest. She said that he sounded scared and that he had to pony up fourteen hundred bucks for her new Apple. Within a minute she had him on the dawn plane for Minneapolis with a two-hour wait for Marquette. He said fine and she said she'd call Marion and make them a nice dinner.

He wasn't thinking clearly and stopped at the Wagon Wheel for a pick-me-up. He couldn't help himself and asked Amanda how Xavier could have known that Melissa met him at the bar. She was evasive.

"She needs a lot of looking after. He's a good stockbroker and a good brother though he's up to no good in Mexico. She just lost her volunteer job at the hospital for stealing drugs. Last summer she got busted twice for leaving her kid in the hot car. In July she ran off with some motorcyclists from the Aryan Brotherhood in Idaho and

Xavier retrieved her in bad shape. Last winter she tried to
board a plane for Hermosillo with a pistol in her purse and
had to be restrained. She had to go to a clinic for a month
to stay out of jail. There's more. I was thinking of warning
you but I figured that you were just another horny old fool."

"Thanks." He bought a travel pint and sped home to
pack. Kowalski had tossed his apartment again, which bored
him, leaving a note saying "Where's my cell?" Sunderson
had dropped it out of the car at the Nogales interchange
hoping that some kid would find it and call China. He had
wondered idly how Melissa was acceptable to the Aryan
Brotherhood but then an attractive woman has a passport
to anywhere.

He was packed in fifteen minutes and on his way to the
Tucson airport where he intended to sleep in the car in a parking lot. Mona had shocked him with the price of a first-class
ticket, the only seating available. He was sorely overspending
his retirement income but then it would be cheap again when
he got home. The mountain road between Sonoita and Interstate 10 that led to Tucson spooked him in the moonlight. All
of his life he had been drawn reverentially to the moon but
down here it could look malevolent. This was of course part
of the United States but it was considerably more alien in
some respects than the northern Italy he had traveled through
with Diane. Descending Sonoita pass he saw a group of illegal migrants huddled in a ditch and they reminded him of
drawings of the starving Irish during the potato famine who
were not considered human by their English landlords.

The parking lot as a sleeping place didn't pan out. It
was a cool night in Tucson, around freezing, and he had to

keep cranking up the car heater for warmth. It reminded him of parking on a country road with a girl in the winter when he was in high school. He had paid a hard-earned hundred bucks for his '47 Dodge but the interior was large and airy and the heater worked poorly. He recalled his cold hands on hot thighs, which was a pleasanter image than his head in a bloody toilet. He had no real idea of what to think about the relationship between Melissa and her brother. She had said that Xavier loved Mozart but then so did Goering and Goebbels. Anything was possible. A priest had doubtless said mass minutes after buggering a ten-year-old boy. He had also noted that Melissa didn't seem upset that Xavier had beat her husband to death.

At midnight he bit the bullet and checked into one of the dozens of motels surrounding the airport, eighty-eight bucks for a single with the usual print of a sad-eyed donkey wearing a garland of flowers, plus another of a pretty senorita drawing water from a well in old Mexico. Marion and his wife had traveled to Mexico a number of times during Christmas vacations to avoid questionable family gatherings, and loved Michoacán and Oaxaca which were obviously without border problems. Marion had seen sad-eyed donkeys but none wearing flowers.

He set up the desk pot for morning coffee and allowed himself a single nightcap from his whiskey pint desperately not wanting to miss his dawn departure. He put his revolver in his suitcase to be checked but his niggling paranoia about Xavier delayed unloading it until morning. When he was lying in Nogales hospital as a big lump of bruises Melissa had been a vision of delight. In the bookcase in her house in

Nogales he had noted a number of well-thumbed volumes
of Marquis de Sade, which had seemed quirkish. He surfed
through the TV channels watching ads for both Scientol-
ogy and a new, revolutionary pill that would extend your
dick. He thought that there was a will to power in both
religion and sex that seemed transparently biological, and
then money had always been the sole ticket to the future in
the culture, with education trailing off far behind. Xavier
had belittled the smallness of his pension but then the richer
people of Marquette, and more so wealthy tourists, had
never excited envy in him. The woods and creeks were free
and cheap whiskey and plonk, Diane's word, were sufficient.
The closest he came to the delight of dancing was when he
was walking along a creek looking for brook trout pools. For
the first time he felt deeply that life might be good after retirement. He might even return to the Southwest for winter
walking and camping though far out of range of Xavier and
Melissa, say on the east side of the Chiricahuas where the
Apaches once rode like the wind. Camping was cheap. Just
before the divorce when Diane had received her inheritance
he had been embarrassed by the large amount. Given his
background it seemed unnatural.

Chapter 12

He only fully exhaled when the plane was in the air. He was beside the window and as the plane curved he could see Nogales, Lake Patagonia, and the road to Patagonia. There was no apparent reason for taking southern Arizona from the Apaches except to raise skinny cows and mine unproductive mines but then much the same could be said for the Upper Peninsula where all the virgin timber had been cut and the earth hoovered of its wealth. Both Apaches and Ojibway had lost out to invading armies and the postwar economy had razed the landscape.

There was a certain indecipherable smugness in first class that he was trying to ignore. He had heard that drinks were free but then 7:00 a.m. was a tad early. He relented and had a Bloody Mary out of relief, he supposed, from escaping Xavier and his murderous thugs not to speak of his daffy sister. The expensively dressed matron next to him was tittering over the new *Vogue* with its ornately dressed stick girls. Diane had been a subscriber.

"I'm not going to get a boner from this," he had said to Diane leafing through the pages. Occasionally he liked irritating her with vulgarity.

"That's scarcely the purpose of the magazine," she had said.

When his seatmate seemed to frown at his dawn drink he wished he could fart but he was not a fart-on-demand kind of guy. Breakfast was an omelet of aerated faux eggs with two tiny sausages that had no pork flavor. He noted that his neighbor was wisely eating Cheerios with kiwi, a fruit he considered fraudulent.

"We winter in Tucson but I have to go back to Minneapolis to see my ill sister. Have you been vacationing?"

"Yes. In Nogales and Patagonia. Lovely places."

"Really? I've heard they're quite dangerous."

"That's nonsense. They're both safer than Minneapolis. The violence is in the drug cartel wars across the border. Americans are always afraid of being mugged even after being scammed out of trillions by the financial community."

"My husband is a banker," she said in a mild huff abandoning her Cheerios for an article on two-thousand-dollar handbags.

That ended the conversation. He fell into a deep sleep in which he dreamed music, mostly a Scriabin piano piece that Diane loved that was played only with the left hand. He had studied the Russian Revolution so deeply in college and after that he sometimes dreamt of Russia though the idea of actually visiting the country seemed to be too large an undertaking.

Though groggy with sleep he felt at home in the Minneapolis airport, which was filled with the thickish, whey-faced
citizens of the Great North, so many of whom he thought
must be Scandinavian, or Germans from farm country. They
all seemed to have a pork-and-potatoes businesslike sad-
ness about them. Doubtless they chuckled now and then
rather than laughing. His spirits rose further when he had
a pot roast sandwich, the food of his childhood, along with
a Bloody Mary and a beer. He managed to sleep again
between Minneapolis and Marquette despite a bad-weather
advisory that normally would have worried him. Dying in
a plane crash had always seemed inappropriately modern
to him whereas drowning in Lake Superior, like so many
relatives who were commercial fishermen, was a logical conclusion to their profession.

Marquette was admirably bleak with a few feet of snow
and a pleasant early-winter temperature of ten degrees and it
began to get dark at four in the afternoon. He felt the hopeless sentimentality of the familiar driving up the snowy alley
to the back porch of his house. He stood looking straight
up at the snowflakes heading downward at his face. There
was a sense of belonging, of being where he was supposed
to be, that had been absurdly absent in the Southwest. He
inhaled the cold air deeply and coughed waving at Mona
who was waving from his brightly lit kitchen window. When
he opened the door from the porch to the kitchen the smell
of the roast pork shoulder and mashed rutabaga was won-
derfully strong. They embraced and she slid his hand down
onto her bottom and he quickly removed it. They kissed
and he backed his tongue away from her emerging tongue.

"Mona, for Christ's sake."

"My analyst says it's all obvious. I mean my crush on you. My dad cuts and runs when I'm seven and I think it's at least partly my fault. You're sort of my stepdad. I'm trying to hold on to you so I act sexy. I almost didn't wear undies so I could give you a peek when I sat on the sofa."

"It's unhealthy." He knew this was weak as he poured himself a strong whiskey.

"Don't be such a silly fuck. What's *unhealthy* mean? It's harmless and I know you're not going to touch me so what's the problem with flirting and a little touch? I'd already be an old lady in India and Africa."

"Well, civil authorities have established a law that you're underage . . ." His mind ground to a halt. He may as well have been saying blah, blah, blah, blah. She was wearing a short-sleeved black sweater and a short black skirt. When she leaned way over to check the pork roast he looked out the window at the gathering dark. Her legs were smoothly muscled from running the eight hundred meters for the track team.

"Spare me the legal shit, darling." She sat down and took a sip of his whiskey.

"I have an unpleasant question before Marion arrives." He took Carla's e-mail and the photo from a jacket pocket and passed it to her. "Here Carla says she went down on you and you told me nothing happened. Who's telling the truth?"

"Who cares?" She was blushing ever so slightly.

"I care. If you'll testify we can send Carla to prison for years."

"No chance. Maybe a night in jail but not prison. You said yourself when you and Marion were talking about the Catholic priest sex scandal that a priest giving a sixteen-year-old hundred-seventy-pound young man a blow job wasn't worth ten million bucks. Why didn't he run for it?"

"Boys are different," he said, pausing to glance into his studio den with relief. He intended to put a NO sign up on his peek hole. Enough was enough. It seemed that his thinking was becoming less muddy. "Boys can be polymorphously perverse into their teens. Of course I'm unsure about girls. In the last three decades or so the culture has been prolonging childhood so it's altogether natural that the age of consent be moved up to eighteen. Apparently the young are more sexually active than ever but the law is there to appropriately protect them from older predators of which there are many, like Dwight-Daryl."

"Carla told me that as of this morning he's changed his name to King David," she laughed.

"Jesus Christ! What next?" He finished his whiskey but stopped himself from pouring another.

"I'm different. I'm old for my age. I cooperated so it would be unjust to send Carla to prison. We're the world record holder for sending people to prison. Skip Carla, concentrate on the Great Leader."

"For the time being maybe." He was remembering that he had been expected to be a man at fourteen. And his sisters were hard cases at that age. He certainly had no clear idea why the societal change had occurred. His own family had been matriarchal with his mother holding the iron hand and his dad mostly bringing home the bacon. Mona's mother was a mostly absent ditz.

"Can I sit on your lap for a minute?"

"If you behave."

His knee felt the heat of her butt. What would happen to this waif? Did he have guidance to offer?

"You're under arrest," Marion said, standing at the open door in an orange coat and orange overalls. There was snow on the front porch which had muffled his approach. Sunderson was busy diverting his thoughts away from Mona's warm ass with errant thoughts of the history of the Panama Canal, his dislike of college communities and their mental tourism, and the obvious fact that the human body should have been designed so that you only needed to pee once a day. He was sure his knee was beginning to sweat. How many BTUs does a vulva generate?

"I'm wearing my hunting clothes because I'm tired of my school principal clothes. Tomorrow's the last day of deer season. We should give it a try."

"You look truly ugly," Mona said, getting up and reheating the mashed rutabaga and adding more cream and butter.

"It's defensive, dear, the most visible color, which will save me from getting shot. Most hunting accidents are alcohol related."

"I'll tag along. I'm not saying I'll fire a shot." Sunderson felt dullish from his dawn plane ride though part of the fatigue might have come from being away from Xavier's gun sights.

"Just before dark I saw a doe dragging a leg. She'd never make it through winter. You'd love doe liver."

"I'll count my gout pills."

By nine the next morning, a clear glittery day of ten degrees with the snow glistening, Sunderson was frying the doe liver in too much butter, salivating and watching Marion carry in a load of split beech. The evening before, despite having had only two whiskeys, he began to nod off after two servings of the pork roast and mashed rutabaga and a bare nibble of salad. Mona and Marion had scarcely left when the phone rang and it was Queenie's father, the big-shot Bloomfield Hills businessman who had earlier tried to get Sunderson to retrieve his daughter's money from the Leader. Queenie had come up missing in Tucson and the man wanted him to look for her, an easy request to decline rather rudely. He gave the man Kowalski's Nogales number. They deserved each other. Mona had winked at him when she left and he wandered into his den studio for the soft-core porn peep show but found himself unable to remove the book that would give him the view. He went directly to bed not wanting a case of what Satchel Paige had called the "agitations." He poured a nightcap but didn't drink it thinking that since touching Mona was unthinkable he had to transcend the remote lecher in himself. Before Marion left he had repeated his advice to Sunderson to closely read Philip Deloria's *Playing Indian* for an insight into the behavior of the Great Leader, currently called King David, a hard to swallow name change, but then Sunderson had already begun the book.

At 6:00 a.m. he was up drinking coffee, looking for the shells for his .30-30 deer rifle, making a hash of leftover pork and potatoes, and trying to find where he had put the

Deloria book and, not incidentally, D. H. Lawrence's *Studies in Classic American Literature,* the latter impulse coming
from the shred of a dream. As a college sophomore in a basic
literature course the teacher had been a youngish hotshot
directly out of Princeton, already an author of a book about
Cotton Mather. Sunderson found them both suffocatingly
dreary. This young professor loathed D. H. Lawrence which
served to make Sunderson curious and he had had a brief
Lawrence period that spring before coming to his senses and
returning to history for relief. The dream had only included
the professor's feet, which were far too large in his English
brogans for his body. It was time to run a tighter ship, which
included not taking a dawn peek.

Halfway out to Marion's shack on the snowy two-
track at daylight Marion braked and jumped out of his
ancient, boxy Toyota Land Cruiser with his .30-06 and
shot the doe, which was down a slope between a grove
of small white pines and alders beside a tiny creek. Sunderson could barely see the deer, which dropped in its
tracks. Marion said, "Poor girl" while he gutted it with
Sunderson holding the hind legs splayed to make it easier
for Marion's knife to avoid the anal sack. She was fairly
healthy he thought examining her shattered knee, which he
deduced came from a shot earlier in the two-week season.
While Marion skinned the doe Sunderson had stoked the
woodstove until it reddened. He guessed that he had gotten the cabin up to fifty degrees by the time they ate the
liver off warmed tin plates.

"You have totally fucked up my schedule with your
pursuit of this nitwit," Marion laughed.

"I'm sorry."

"No, you're not. I've done a fair load of research while you were in Arizona possibly drinking and chasing pussy not to leave out getting the shit kicked out of you. Yours is the first American case of stoning I can recall."

Marion had been helping his wife Sonia who, though lily white, had been a crack tribal administrator until she had taken a long leave to aid in the research in the nation-wide lawsuit against the Bureau of Indian Affairs to recover billions of lost royalties coming to the tribes. A few years before, after Sunderson dealt with a particularly gory case of spousal abuse, he had been deeply puzzled how Marion had come up with a thick pile of articles on the subject along with a lengthy bibliography. Sunderson was still married to Diane at the time and she had hidden the material fearing another of his March depressions. A good deal of his puzzlement on the matter came from his father teaching him that it was forbidden to ever strike a female even if she hit you first.

"I think I'd have a much better grasp of the Leader, now King David, if I had his hundred stages of spiritual development in writing." Sunderson swabbed up his butter and liver juices with a piece of mediocre white bread.

"No, that's the wrong track. They probably don't exist in writing. Maybe a number of them in his noggin. His power comes from the idea that he's the only one in the know. He's the judge. His followers must be kept off balance in their strain to prove their spiritual accomplishment."

"But then what is he offering for their time and money for Christ's sake?"

"The ecstasy of belief. That's what we want from religion. Something we can count on as helpless children in the face of ninety billion galaxies. In a despondent culture he is telling them how to live, how to get out of their very limited bodies into an arena of spiritual confidence." Marion was grinning as he turned down the damper of the stove which was now putting out too much heat.

"But how do you tie in the sexual thing?"

"That's an attractive come-on. Remember that guru in Oregon, the Baghwan what's his name? His followers had absolute sexual freedom for a while then out of fear of disease he promulgated that they had to wrap themselves in plastic for sex. He went downhill after that and lost his thirty-two Rolls-Royces. I think our government shipped him back to India."

"He's certainly an effective predator. I'm a bit mystified by his interest in females that are too young." Sunderson took Carla's e-mail and the photo of Mona from his jacket and slid it across the table to Marion who was startled.

"This is hot stuff. I'd make copies. The young girl stuff is at least partly biological, you know, like Warren Jeffs and those apostate Mormons. Without knowing it men want to continue their own genetic line so they try to get there first by even getting rid of the young men. With mammals as varied as antelope and mountain lions the alpha male chases off the competition. It's quite a battle in the so-called natural world. Male bears kill the cubs fathered by other male bears to further their own line. With humans some stepfathers are notably unkind to children sired by previous husbands."

"What a fucking mess."

"Not at all. It's just us. Certain scientists are now positing the biological origins of religion. We're perfect parasites when we maintain order in society and maintain the host that feeds us, and religion is an essential way of maintaining order."

"The Lutheran church is a biological organism?" Sunderson laughed.

"At least partly. Bring it all home. Look at yourself. Consider what either of us do to conduct our lives in terms of sex, finance, and religion. We've been friends for more than twenty years. We talk about everything. You've said that after your divorce you felt sexually deprived scurrying around looking for a good piece of ass. You've said that money has always made you nervous and you try to ignore it because you've made five times as much as your poor father did without even trying hard. You've never said much about your religion, though you've inquired about mine a lot."

"I thought it over quite a bit in the Nogales hospital when I was trying to organize an interest in continuing my life. Of course the drugs helped but they're mostly a lid over the pain like a manhole cover and you remain aware of the surge of pain underneath. Anyway I'd keep making a list of my favorite brook trout creeks, nine of them in fact. Also my favorite landscapes, maybe a half dozen, two of them from boyhood on Grand Island, and also that long gully you showed me west of here. I'd go over these places in my memory for hours and was surprised how well I remembered them right down to the minutest detail. The day I left the hospital it occurred to me that these places were the location of whatever religion I had. This started when I was a boy. In these places I never think of anything except where I am, sometimes for hours. I remembered that Mother said that when you pray you're not supposed to think about anything else, which was a trick I never could manage but can in these places. I found another one when I camped out for a week in Arizona."

They walked for two hours on this rare windless day, normally a period when northwest winds off Lake Superior pound the locals senseless with their fury. It was a little odd not to find any wolf prints in the fresh snow but Marion said that here on the eastern edge of the Huron Mountains the wolves retreated far into roadless areas at the first shot of deer season.

Back at the cabin Sunderson fried up the sliced doe heart for a snack and then they dozed in their chairs after a few exhausting sentences about Mona's future.

Chapter 13

After their nap Marion and Sunderson took Mona to the Verling for supper. Sunderson was frantic for a mess of fried whitefish. A "mess of fish" was a localism. People would say that they "fried up a mess of brook trout" they had caught. Sunderson was in a peculiar mental state not having totally awakened from his nap and a dream in which he was a god in the sky but hadn't done anything with his godhead except wander around the heavens. He had returned to earth in his mortal body and was relieved.

Mona was stunning in a black pantsuit she said a "friend" had given her. She was pouty because her father had called from Cleveland for the first time in months and had said he was buying her a car. She had told him "I don't want your fucking car" and had hung up. She changed the mood by taking out a page she had ripped from *Vanity Fair* to which her mother subscribed. She read aloud to them an item that said that at an auction of the belongings of the deceased fashion designer Yves Saint Laurent, a single chair had gone for twenty-four million dollars. Marion had laughed so explosively that he alarmed the adjoining tables while Sunderson was merely puzzled to the point of melancholy and also irked that his whitefish and glass of beer had arrived and he had forgotten to order his habitual double whiskey. He thought he was losing his grip and corrected his error. Meanwhile Mona was thrilled at Marion's laughter and asked him why he thought the chair's price was so funny.

"Money would be great if we didn't die but since we do it's an absurd obsession."

Sunderson was struck by Marion's answer to the point of hypnosis. He couldn't seem to move the forkful of fish halfway to his mouth. Mona tapped his arm and nodded toward the door. Carla and Queenie were self-consciously flouncing in wearing twin sheepskin coats. They took off their coats and shook out their short hair that didn't move all that much and headed toward the table to say hello as if everyone were lifelong friends. Sunderson was startled to see Queenie and puzzled by her native dress and the pounds of turquoise jewelry hanging from her neck.

"Your dad is having you looked for in Tucson."

"So I heard. I'm going back tomorrow. He wants to borrow money from my trust. He and some friends want to buy the Lions to save Detroit from further shame. I'm not loaning the asshole a single cent."

Sunderson nodded thinking about girls and their daddies. He was relieved when his whiskey arrived because

Carla was causing him discomfort. How could this nasty twerp be so ferally sexual dressed nearly as a boy?

"Lunch tomorrow at noon at the Landmark Inn?" Carla asked.

"Of course, darling." They left for their table and Sunderson downed his whiskey as if it were water.

"Why is she wearing that absurd Indian costume?" Mona laughed.

"I've met a number of American women who think they were Pocahontas or Sacajawea in their past lives. They're never a miserable squaw shot in a tent by advancing United States Cavalry." Marion loved this sort of irony. He was a speed eater and signaled the waitress for more fish.

Sunderson was so pleased to reach home and sit at his desk with a stack of books, relatively sober because it was quite a struggle for the single double whiskey to work its way through his belly full of food. Intending to stay up late he made a small pot of coffee and surveyed the glory of his home though in truth the carpet needed to be replaced. After Diane had left he had stopped wiping his feet properly and there was a lot of scuzz on the wall around the stove and sink in the kitchen. Also, all of the windows in the house needed washing. He and a friend had set up a window washing business for fifty cents an hour when they were fourteen and it had been horribly boring work. He reduced the stack of books to three: Deloria's *Playing Indian,* D. H. Lawrence's *Studies in Classic American Literature,* and the Bible, King James version. He needed to go through the New Testament to remind himself of the gist of Christianity, which had garnered countless billions of dollars over the years. When on their trip to Italy he had stood with Diane in Saint Peter's Square, he had been mightily impressed but had also wondered about the top-dollar cost of the project and how the construction workers had wended their weary ways home for a simple bowl of spaghetti. He took out his journal.

1. I read that in the 1940s we made fifty phone calls a year. Now we make five thousand. Reminds me of the cacophony of blackbirds in spring or wild geese who will honk for hours at a time. Actually I think I heard this on NPR.

2. All of the *lachryma Christi* in Italy. Why is Jesus always weeping?

3. At Marion's shack I had this feeling of just how ordinary I was. I simply have to nail the Great Leader but the group is so intact I must somehow catch him red-handed. I talked to Roxie briefly and she said the cult father who filed the early complaint and then went off to Flint had now withdrawn the complaint. Possibly paid off.

4. The bitterness of history. At the Sand Creek Massacre our cavalry shot low into the tents at dawn but the warriors were off hunting so we only killed women and children.

5. The childish attempt to tie oneself to history. I used to say while drinking in bars that I was born during the Blitzkrieg in World War II but only three old men even knew what I was talking about.

The phone rang and the caller ID said it was Mona. It was unthinkable not to answer.

"I just danced naked to 'Wild Thing' and you weren't even watching. The dance was in thanks for dinner. Is your peeking period over?"

"Yes, it's over. I intend to become a white Christian gentleman."

"Aren't you worrying about losing your manhood?"

"I hope so."

"A couple of items. My friend Freddy was looking into universities. He's a senior. Anyway, at Tufts in the Boston area they have a course called 'Sex, Religion, and Money.' Maybe you should fly out there and enroll. I could go along and sleep on the sofa."

"Thank you but no. I've proven myself ill-suited to leave Marquette."

"I forgot to tell you at dinner but I talked on the phone to Carla when she was stoned and this spring the Great Leader aka King David is going to move his followers to Choteau, Montana, or Chadron, Nebraska, or Channing in Michigan. He insists that there's mystical power in the letters 'ch.' Myself, I have doubts."

"Good night, darling. I'm doing my homework. I have to read the New Testament." He was thinking that the G.L. would know that the Hebrew "chai" held mystical powers.

It turned out that the New Testament was hard going. Reading Matthew brought on a specific memory of being wedged between his mother and Berenice in the Lutheran church so that he couldn't escape. He had been a rawboned troublesome boy with difficulties trying to connect religion to his own life in a small town surrounded by forest and Lake Superior. Struggling with Matthew he began to think of Marion's insistence that it is easily forgotten that character also emerges from the landscape of our early years. If your antennae are educated by following your dog through the woods all day and your major preoccupations are hunting and fishing you don't lose this molding of your character by merely going to college, falling in love and getting married, or becoming a detective in an area with very little viable crime. No wonder he couldn't deal with Nogales.

He pushed the Bible aside and fetched the proper volume of a 1920s edition of the Britannica, back when the writing was better and without the cruelty of the Warsaw Pact and atomic power, a fine place to check out the essence of Christianity. His eyelids immediately began to droop but then he was saved by the phone, this time a call from Mona's mother in Lansing. A representative from University of Michigan would be in Marquette on Monday to talk to talented students and their parents. Would he mind showing up at 2:00 p.m. at Marquette High School and acting as a guardian? He'd be glad to. Unfortunately Mona's mother was named Gidget, a product of her own mother's fascination with the 1961 film *Gidget Goes Hawaiian*. Sunderson felt there was something to be said for biblical names.

He was suddenly fatigued with his feeble attempts at reading, poured a nightcap, and watched the 11:00 p.m. news in which he noted again that car bombs were much smarter than smart bombs. The weather forecast was pleasantly awful with an Alberta clipper, a vast storm coming down from the northwest across Lake Superior to bury

them in an early blizzard. Splendid, he thought. Well back
in his brain, a naughty place, he thought his noon lunch
might lead to a sexual encounter. Their woodpile fusion
had been electric indeed. Now the possible encounter was
sullied by the fact that he had to be at the high school at
two. He brooded about this as he poured a second nightcap
to cure the coffee jangles, took the clicker, and segued to a
satellite channel playing a non–Oscar winning movie called
Ninja Cheerleaders. Marion had said that a central fact of our
time was the triumph of process over content. In the movie
these nubile but powerful girls would leap high in the air
and viciously kick bad guys in the face in an explosion of
blood and lost teeth. Despite some marvelous butt shots
he dozed, waking in a couple of hours to one of those save
the whales movies where a crew in a rubber boat cruised
through bumpy waters pestering the marine mammals. Back
at camp a geek in a black turtleneck said that male whales of
different generations keep in touch with their moms. On the
way to bed Sunderson imagined a mother whale introducing
her newborn daughter to a forty-year-old brother, "Sarah,
this is your brother Leviathan."

PART IV

Chapter 14

He awoke just before daylight feeling rather good and vow-
ing to turn his life around. He had the firm idea that the
loop he had been thrown for by Diane leaving him had been
waiting for him a long time and he had been too densely
wrapped up in his habits to see it coming. There was an
urge to list these habits many of which were involved in
his wrongheaded perceptions of the nature of life but he
was eager to bundle up and walk down to the beach. Ever
since childhood he had been addicted to the beauty of severe
storms and had been raised in and lived in the right place
to appreciate them. He had heard the storm and despite
being frightened by Lake Superior gathering in strength
when he woke to pee at five a.m. he hurried through a bowl
of tasteless oatmeal without milk and reheated coffee without cream in eagerness to see the mounting seas. He hadn't
been to the grocer's since arriving home because he was an

absentminded dipshit, or so he thought. He listened carefully to the weather on the local NPR station disappointed that it wouldn't be a full gale though by evening the wind would gust to sixty knots, enough to raise the seas high indeed.

He headed out into the teeth of the northwest wind, his eyes tearing and his wool watch cap pulled over his ears, consoling himself that the wind would be at his back on the way home. Well before he finished the seven-block walk he regretted not putting on long underwear. His dick was turning into an ice cube. He tried very hard to remember the dream that had made him feel so good on waking but failed other than to see in his head the middle branch of the Escanaba River south of Gwinn, normally a fearful place because he had once stumbled in his waders and gone under in a swift stretch of the river. Anyone who didn't think waterboarding was torture had never come close to the ultimate horror of nearly drowning wherein you're wallowing, sucking water rather than air.

Turning from the beach and the loose sand and snow blasting into his face with the thunder of the waves in his ears he resented the frailty of his age. He felt that the cold was his heritage and now it was betraying him, a bit dramatic for the simple fact that he had forgotten to put on his wool long underwear.

It was nearly pleasant walking back toward home with the north wind helping to push him up the long hill. He stopped at the grocer's on Fourth, amused at a woman getting out of her car and standing in the full force of the blizzard talking on her cell phone. Nothing will stop the addiction to this instrument he thought. The spring before while searching for a perp on the campus of the local university he figured that of the hundreds of students crisscrossing the campus between classes a full 90 percent were on their cell phones.

His breath shortened a bit when the woman on the phone followed him into the grocer's. He held the door and she walked right past him jabbering away without recognizing him. "Fred's been quite a disappointment," she said. It was Debbie Anne, his girlfriend when they were both sophomores at Munising High School. Age had not been kind to her and it was her voice rather than her appearance that immediately gave her away. They used to drive into the country and get in the back of his '47 Dodge to make out. She was sexually precocious and popular with the school athletes. She would help his trembling hands pull on a Trojan-Enz condom and then say, "You can park your car in my garage and throw the key in the grass," a line from a dirty joke. She would hoot and chirrup when they screwed. He quickly dodged through the aisles foreshortening his shopping for fear she would recognize him. She was still talking while she sorted through the big family packs of pork chops when he escaped.

Back home he hastily took out a notebook before the heat of the house could make him drowsy. He turned to a fresh page avoiding any notes he had made about Melissa and Xavier in Nogales. He wrote:

1. My job as a janitor trying to sweep up the detritus of society is over. My grand finale will be to get the Great Leader in prison but this might not be possible.

2. My divorce has blown a three-year-long bomb cra-
   ter in my life. I have to get over this before it de-
   stroys me at which it is presently doing a good job.
3. I have to control my habits. In the glory days of
   marriage I'd have two drinks after work, then a glass
   of wine with Diane at dinner, and then a nightcap
   while reading in the late evening. Any more than this
   has come to depress me. I want to feel good like I
   did when I camped for a week in Aravaipa Canyon.
   I have to drive over to Shingleton and buy a new
   pair of snowshoes. It occurs to me that no matter
   that he's a lunatic the Great Leader is a pretty smart
   guy with a lot of resources and if I'm going to catch
   him with blood on his hands I better go into training.

Lunch with Carla at the Landmark Inn was confusing. She
had come into the restaurant with Queenie who was seated
across the room with two elegantly dressed men who, Sunderson decided, couldn't possibly come from the state of
Michigan. Carla told him blithely that the two men were
friends of Queenie's from Los Angeles. After Brown University Queenie had gone to film school at UCLA and the
men were *producers,* a mysterious term to Sunderson. The
men struck him as a new kind of tooth decay in the mouth of
the room. He was impatient to get on with the denouement
but couldn't repress his curiosity about these interlopers.
    "So they came to Marquette for the blizzard?"
    "Effective people don't hang around watching the
weather channel like locals do. Queenie has the idea that

Dwight's life would make a great movie. These guys are also interested in the idea that if you create a viable new religion you got a real moneymaker on your hands."

"No shit?" Sunderson's mind whirled with the idea.

"We stayed up most of the night partying and talking about both the movie and religion-for-profit idea. Oral Roberts, Jerry Falwell, and Pat Robertson took in billions."

"But they were ostensibly Christian," Sunderson countered.

"It doesn't matter. We're starting from scratch like the Mormons. They're a worldwide powerhouse. We're also using the recruitment techniques of the Scientologists. They're a bright bunch."

Sunderson sat there looking around the familiar room to make sure he hadn't been transported to an asylum. He had ordered a bowl of chili and very much wanted a beer, which was verboten because of his upcoming appointment at the high school. Carla did look like she had been rode hard and put away wet. Her eyes were bleary as she sipped her second glass of sauvignon blanc and played with her Caesar salad (without anchovies).

"It sounds utterly deranged."

"That's because you're trapped in your tiny ex-detective box. You don't have a clue what the world has become. The real movers and shakers are out there on the peripheries discovering new forms. Think of Bill Gates thirty years ago, damn it. Dwight's basic tenet is that semen is the most powerful fluid in the world. It's been totally overlooked. I mean that the Bible said you're not supposed to spill it on the ground, you know jerk off, but that's not what he's doing."

"Pardon?" Sunderson felt his neck redden because four ladies at the next table had turned hearing the magic world *semen*.

"Jizz. Cum, for Christ's sake. It's the stuff of life," Carla said loudly.

"Of course." Sunderson felt this was the moment of truth. He reached into his sport coat and took out the folded e-mail and raised-skirt photo of Mona he had found on the cult site in Arizona.

"Where did you get this?" Carla asked looking over-long at the photo of Mona. She wadded up the material and dropped it into her Caesar salad, looking pale and staring at the ceiling.

"I have twenty copies. Perhaps we should talk in private." He had, in fact, forgotten to make copies. He reached for the wadded paper and dabbed the salad dressing off with his napkin, glancing at Carla's face which had hardened and become hateful.

"Fuck you!" she screamed with alarming volume. She grabbed for her coat and fled toward the door. He stood, deciding not to look around for reactions, dropped two twenties on the table, and followed. Outside the wind had subsided but thick snow was falling straight down and there was a half foot of fresh snow on the recently plowed parking lot. He tracked her easily to Queenie's Range Rover, which she had started. He wiped away fluffy snow and got in the passenger side hoping the heater was fast because he had left his coat in the restaurant. She was curled up fetally on the driver's seat sniffling with her back turned to him and her skirt pulled up the undersides of her thighs. Here we

go again, he thought coldly, staring at the marvelous rump
he had banged away at against the woodpile.

"What are you going to do?" she asked in a hushed
voice.

"I don't know. Maybe put you away for a few years.
Maybe not. Mona's not excited about testifying."

"What's that mean?" She curled up tighter, more fully
exposing her butt in pale blue panties.

"For the time being it means it's your duty to stay in
close touch with me via cell and e-mail. Any dereliction of
duty on your part and I meet with my friend the prosecutor.
You are my slave informant. Agreed?"

"Yes. Get a card out of my wallet."

When he leaned to retrieve the wallet from her purse
he got a better view of her bottom, which all in all was the
best in his experience. His feelings were mixed but he was
becoming tumescent. His general disgust for her didn't seem
to include his dick, which was an independent compass.

"Marion said you could easily start a religion with the
world's shortest man or the world's tallest woman. She's
seven foot eight and Chinese."

"Fuck Marion," she squawked. "You can play with my
ass if you want."

"I'll pass for now."

He was nearly to the high school, shivering and feeling virtuous. His mind, such as it was, had been diverted.
He didn't want to go back into the restaurant and face the
stares which, though after the fact, were a consideration.

Mona and the gentleman were already in a small office
at a desk when a secretary showed him in.

"Hey Daddy. This is Mr. Schmidt."

"Your daughter is top-notch!" Mr. Schmidt barked. "I'm sure we can make things easy for you financially."

"She always was smart as a whip and cute as a button," Sunderson said stupidly.

"I find her interest in both musicology and botany fascinating. What universities is she looking at?" Mona was sitting too close to Schmidt, which seemed to be making him uncomfortable in front of her putative father.

"I've checked out Harvard, Tufts, and Macalester on the Web. Also the University of Puget Sound in Tacoma. The trouble is that a wadded Kleenex can look like a white rose and a white rose can look like a wadded Kleenex," Mona said thoughtfully.

"Really?" Schmidt raised his eyebrows.

Sunderson was wondering about this tangent, feeling crummy possibly because he was crummy. The work at hand was to de-crummy himself.

"Make me an offer I can't refuse. Ann Arbor is attractive because of all the music in the area. I'd like to meet my heroine Aretha Franklin in person. Music soothes the savage beast inside me."

"Really?" Schmidt said again.

Afterward Mona took the rest of the afternoon off from school and they drove to the hotel so she could run in and pick up his coat and then they went to the New York Delicatessen down the street so he could order chicken soup and a massive corned beef sandwich. "Don't trim the fat please." Real life wasn't exactly panning out and a very long nap was always a primary solution. He toted

up the figure and realized that he had only been retired
for thirty-three days.

"My parents are so worthless you wonder why they
bothered having me," Mona said plaintively, then dug into
her sandwich with a grin.

"People don't think far ahead."

"Diane called me this morning. I'm sure you know
they're moving back up here from Florida because her husband wants to be treated by doctors he can trust."

"I heard that. I'm not sure I can bear to see her."

"Of course you can. She's going to be my surrogate
mother. I could use one."

"Me too," Sunderson laughed. He was tired of swimming in a cold swamp of ideologies hopelessly connected to
money. He had never thought of Mona as a semidaughter
like Diane did. When Mona's mother was absent Diane had
been extremely attentive to her, becoming a combination big
sister and parent in absentia.

"I never made you your homemade birthday pizza. I'll
do it tonight."

"Make it later," he said, already drowsy from the soup
and massive sandwich. Marion made his own corned beef
in order to get the Jewish flavor he remembered from going
to college in Chicago.

"I feel rejected that you don't peek at me anymore."

"You'll have to get used to it. How can I get after King
David for his penchant for underage girls if I'm peeking at
you?"

"The Great Leader goes real young to catch them at
the right formative time with his semen, the mightiest fluid

in the world. That's what Carla told me. I'm not really that young. I easily pass for eighteen."

"That's what I heard." Sunderson ignored her comments wondering where the Great Leader got his semen theories.

Sunderson had a four-hour nap waking at eight, made fresh coffee, and smelled his stack of books. Why smell books? A habit. He waved from his kitchen window to Mona's kitchen window where she and Marion were rolling dough and getting ready to assemble the pizzas. He was on page 37 of Deloria's *Playing Indian*, feeling the usual dread. To Sunderson the Indians were the monstrous skeleton in the American closet. He always imagined stretching a white sheet across the United States and historically seeing all of the hundreds of locations where the Indian blood seeped through. At Michigan State he had felt nauseous when a professor had explained the Sand Creek Massacre. As the Russians said, consciousness can be a disease.

He impulsively called Carla and was surprised that she was in Los Angeles and sounding stoned.

"We left by private jet right after our lovely lunch. You didn't eat your chili. We picked up Dwight and tomorrow we're heading for Maui to discuss the movie and the future of our religion. Satisfied?"

"Not quite. I need to know how much he's bilked out of his followers so far."

"Don't say *bilked*. They've freely given contributions. About four million but he spends money fast. I can't wait to hit the beach."

Chapter 15

At midnight he was sitting in his dark upstairs bedroom looking out at the snow falling softly and straight down under
the streetlight, thinking of winter as a vast dormant god of
sorts. He had been in bed a mere fifteen minutes or so when
he began to weep. The weeping was unacceptable so he had
gotten out of bed and gone downstairs to pour the nightcap
he had forgotten which now sat on the windowsill reflecting
the streetlight in an odd way as if the light were drowning in
amber whiskey. He occasionally had wondered if his pillow
was haunted though he readily admitted that the notion was
goofy. It was his childhood pillow and Diane had teased him
about how ratty and lumpy it was even in a fresh pillowcase.
He suspected that he was weeping because his brain was
melting into a kind of clarity that unnerved him. Since the
divorce he had become quite lucid right down to the burying
of his dog Walter which had felt like burying his marriage.

The evening had gone well until 10:30 when they finished Mona's gorgeous pizzas and she had left with friends who picked her up for a dance.

He and Marion had been a bit melancholy after Mona's departure as if a certain life force had left. Sunderson told him about the encounter with Carla and the preposterous ideology of semen. Marion guffawed and said that no religion could explain itself clearly. The need to feel ecstasy, the capacity to get out of ourselves was so great a need that we would buy the most ornately simpleminded beliefs. He said that Sunderson wouldn't take in the idea until he gave up the concept of *evidence* that so pervaded his detective profession.

"It's a hard habit to break," Sunderson had said. "If only you could track gods in the snow. The Greeks and Romans tended to identify exact locations where the gods were thought to live."

"Before I quit drinking, saloons were the home of my gods. They were the only place I felt good. Once on a Saturday in Iron Mountain I spent fourteen hours in a bar playing euchre and watching football. At closing time the bar owner told me that I had gone through two fifths of whiskey. That seemed too much even though I was a pretty big boy back then, which was in my midtwenties. I was a road man for a snowmobile company and driving, say, from Superior, Wisconsin, to Escanaba I'd stop at a dozen roadhouses as if they were chapels you'd stop at on a pilgrimage way back when."

"Some of you skins would drink until just short of death and sometimes you made it all the way. Once on the way back from the Soo I got a call on my radio that a frozen Indian had been found near Rudyard. There was no evidence of foul play but the autopsy revealed blood alcohol of .44 which was a record. Dead Indians were always the toughest part of my job, probably a tinge of guilt like investigating a lynching down south."

"There are many forms of Emmett Till. And maybe you folks would call Wounded Knee a still-open case a hundred and twenty years later."

"Murder is never a closed case."

When Marion left and he hurriedly cleaned up in the kitchen he remembered how much his dog had loved pizza crusts. This memory probably helped precipitate the weeping upstairs. Back at the window with his nightcap he watched Mona arrive home from the dance. If only she was ten years older but then she wasn't. How fatuous. The fatality of time struck him suitably dumb. He had heard on Garrison Keillor's *The Writer's Almanac* on NPR how the famed German writer Goethe had fallen into a depression when at age seventy-three an eighteen-year-old girl had refused to marry him. There was evidence here that great writers could be the same variety of dickheads as ex-detectives. He slipped into a pleasant thought of a canyon near Aravaipa Creek he hadn't had time to walk to the end of, only discovering it the last day. He had made his way fearfully down the sides where he had seen cattails at the bottom through his binoculars. There was a small spring with five species of birds he didn't recognize flitting around. When he looked west where the canyon began in the mountains a few miles distant it was so enticing. Maybe he would go back someday and walk it out. Eureka, he thought, picking up his nightcap from the windowsill. He had never seen Au Sable

Falls near Grand Marais in the winter. He would walk for a week. It had worked once, why not again? He had made real progress today on his case of the Great Leader what with getting Carla as a Judas spy. These pleasant thoughts, however temporary, put him into a tearless sleep.

He left at daylight, about 7:30, in a mild sweat from having uprooted so much junk in the rear of the garage to find his Bushwacker cross-country skis, relatively short and wide, to get through the trees in the woods. He only found one ski pole, which would be awkward but then the skis were only a substitute for conditions not suitable for snowshoes. While rummaging around and making a lot of noise he turned to see Mona watching from the open garage door. She was bundled up and when they embraced he smelled the incendiary odor, for him, of lilac from her hair damp from the shower. He was disappointed when his nuts clutched because he wanted his thoughts to be pure as the plenitude of fluffy snow not the product of the tub of guts that is the human body.

"Don't go so far that you have trouble getting back," she said, heading off for school at a walking pace that far exceeded his own. Diane's comfortable pace had also been faster than his own. He recalled one of those PBS nature films that showed a huge shaggy-maned male lion pacing around slowly, almost lazily, protecting the territory while the females stalked and raced through the veldt snagging all of the food. When mating time came he couldn't begin to catch them but had to wait for them to be ready and willing. Sunderson had always known that he wasn't built for speed but a plodding steadiness. He was a tugboat not a Yankee Clipper.

On the way east on Route 28 along Lake Superior he
turned off NPR in order to avoid the world's plentiful bad
news, and turned away from the state police building near
the prison in order to enjoy the huge dark green Lake Superior where the swells from the storm were subsiding. Passing
through Munising he had a sudden poignant memory of his
mother's best friend, their neighbor Mrs. Amarone, who
had died in her fifties from breast cancer. She had taught
his mother how to make a spaghetti sauce out of canned
tomatoes and the local Italian sausage called *cudighi*. They
had it every Saturday night and it was the family's favorite
meal. He would make the same sauce for camping trips with
Diane, drenching a container of cooked pasta with olive oil
so it wouldn't stick. He and Diane would get out of work on
a Friday summer afternoon, head out, and he would heat up
the dish in a skillet over the campfire in the twilight. One
summer they had camped a half dozen times near a small
uninhabited lake, really a pond, near the west edge of the
Kingston Plains between Melstrand and Grand Marais. The
area wasn't especially striking but they had counted at least
a hundred sandhill cranes in the open field and if you were
careful you could approach the young ones closely. On a
warm evening they had listened to the raucous crane chorus
and bathed nude in the pond. Diane had said, "We are naked
apes," and laughed. They made love without drying off, and
drank a bottle of Barolo with dinner. She had always said
the sauce with the pasta turned her on having grown up in
a WASP family where the condiments tended to be limited
to salt and pepper. They had made love again at first light
when the cranes wakened them with their primitive yawp.

He pulled into the Township Park in Grand Marais and set off on his new snowshoes west down the shores of Lake Superior on the fairly hard-packed snow, stopping to stare at the latticed ice on the rocks at the water's edge and the thirty-story precipitously high dunes in their light caramel color. He felt strangely blessed because the air was still and the mist was lifting off the lake, revealing blue water which had been greenish in Marquette and which he immediately gave up trying to figure out. He reached the mouth of the creek in a little more than an hour and headed up the trail along the creek floundering in the deep soft snow. Now the world was all blackish trees and white snow and it was much cooler in the shade of the deep gulley. He was sweating hard when he reached the waterfall and was amazed at the delight the thunderous falling water brought to his mind. He had always been aware how brutish his aesthetic sense was compared to his wife's but at times rose to the occasion. He had admitted to her that when she played a certain Villa-Lobos composition on the stereo his skin invariably prickled.

He sat on a stump for a half hour watching the water until his sweat dried and he was chilled wondering idly how the Ojibway, or Anishinabe as they called themselves, the first citizens here, the aboriginals, the true natives, regarded the falls and decided it had to be a sacred place to them, an idea fairly alien to our own culture. He was startled when he arose from the stump to see that a group of a dozen or so northern ravens had gathered soundlessly high in the trees behind him. One of them squawked and he squawked back. The squawking back and forth continued on his way back down the creek gulley to the lake. His dad had taught him early on to talk to ravens because they enjoyed it and would keep him company on walks. Perhaps these avian creatures besides being themselves contained the ghost of his ancient predecessors. He shivered at the idea on his way back partly because the notion was untypical and partly because he had neglected to eat breakfast in Shingleton. Marion had insisted that religion tends to emerge from the landscape and given the austere nature of Anishinabe beliefs this appeared as a sound concept. Christianity could spruce up its message by including bears, ravens, and other animals, or so he thought, but then the desert country out of which Christianity emerged was without these glorious creatures. Maybe he should look up what religions came out of jungles.

By the time he reached his car his limbs were leaden and his breath short and gasping. This aging thing was a real pain in the ass, he thought, resolving to continue hiking every day of the week. Why not? He could read afternoons and evenings within the deep puzzlement of retirement. He stopped at the Dunes Saloon for a burger and a cup of chili and talked to a big man named Mike who once owned the bar and whom Sunderson had to bust twice for throwing men out through the window of the bar and also the hardware store. The judge liked Mike and the sentence had been a course in "anger management," which Mike had said "pissed me off." They talked about their mutual passion for brook trout fishing and grouse hunting.

"I quit grouse hunting when my dog died," Sunderson said.

"What the hell do you do in September when trout season ends?"

A good question Sunderson thought. His dog would trot through the woods well ahead and bark when it flushed and treed a grouse. He'd make the easy shot out of the tree, the bird would fall and the dog prance with joy. Diane, who was not much taken by wild game, loved roasted wild grouse. This wasn't close to the classic version of grouse hunting but a successful peasant version of man and dog teaming up to get dinner.

The sun beat in the car windshield and he stopped at the rest stop on Route 28 near the Driggs River, the upper reaches of which were good brook trout fishing. Down the highway there was a small road leading into a five-mile-long pond on the Seney Wildlife Preserve, a good destination for the following day. He put his seat back and was immediately asleep for an hour, finally awakening to a rapping on the window. There was the state police cruiser parked next to his own car and Corporal Berks was staring in the window.

"Just making sure you're alive, sir."

"I think I am. I took a long hike. How are you Berks?"

"Fine. We miss you at the Post. The new guy's from Mount Pleasant and doesn't catch on to the U.P. How are you doing?"

"Just fucking, dancing, and fighting. Tell the new guy to give me a call if he gets especially puzzled."

Berks drove off and Sunderson was amused by having said "fucking, dancing, fighting." It was one of the things Diane liked least about the U.P., the male braggadocio she called "macho." Marion, a frequent visitor to Mexico, corrected her on this saying macho meant a man who was gratuitously vicious. U.P. men were often intelligent louts,

strutting and growling like their logging and mining grandfathers. It wasn't really about manliness, a word not much
in use until the recent decade and one that in former times
would have been embarrassing. He couldn't recall men ever
talking about manhood when he was growing up. It was a
more recent, absurd development.

Back home Sunderson was pleased by a note from Marion saying that he had put about twenty pounds of venison
from the doe in the fridge, then Mona burst in the porch
door glowing with excitement.

"Carla tried to call you from Hawaii. Where's your
cell?"

"I have no idea." He fixed himself a whiskey.

"You're not going to fucking believe this. It looks like
King David might do ninety days in jail. You know those
two fancy L.A. guys that were with Queenie you told me
about? Well in this high-class lounge in the hotel in Maui,
Dwight, I mean King David, wiped up the floor with them.
I mean Carla said he beat the shit out of them. He exploded
because they were trying to defile his religion. Carla said
he went totally apeshit and trashed the place after he beat
them to a pulp."

"Will wonders never cease?" Sunderson smiled. He
had observed when he met Dwight that he was in fine shape
and in fact put his followers through an hour of rigorous
exercise a day plus their manual work load. This was part
of the *warrior* nonsense, the faux Indian part of the cult.

"I guess you're going to have to take a break," Mona
said.

Chapter 16

And that's what he did. He planned on walking in the mornings and reading a book a day in the afternoons and evenings. Of course it didn't work out that way with human willpower more than occasionally a weak item. He was making a New Year's resolution a few weeks short of the actual new year and there was a traditional problem with retirees in the Great North that they tend to come close to hibernation in the deep winter months of December, January, and February. A week after Mona had made her startling announcement about King David Sunderson was sitting at his desk sleepily reading about the Whiskey Rebellion in Pennsylvania in the 1790s when Carla called.

"Dwight got ninety days," she sobbed.

"I'm not surprised."

"What the fuck do you know about Hawaii?" Her voice was shrill with anger.

"Everywhere public mayhem is punished." It was a relief to get away from the historical text wherein farmers dressed up like redskins to protest a tax on their homemade whiskey. So what, he thought.

"Well, Queenie left for L.A. to nurse her friends leaving me high and dry with no money. I visit Dwight in the mornings and then I waitress."

"What do you want from me?"

"I don't know. I needed to talk to someone. Queenie's not answering my calls and you and I have a relationship of some sort."

"I suppose so." He wondered what it was though every time he thought of their woodpile coupling he was hopelessly stimulated.

"I thought I should tell you that the Chadron land sale went through. Actually it's a hundred and twenty acres north of Crawford, which is near Chadron and Fort Robinson where Dwight's hero Crazy Horse was murdered."

"How convenient."

"Fuck you."

After she hung up he walked down to the New York Deli and had a corned beef and sauerkraut sandwich on rye (with hot mustard), then stopped at Snowbound Books and bought a new text on the life of Crazy Horse by an Englishman and also, at the suggestion of the proprietor, a book of essays by the poet Gary Snyder called *The Practice of the Wild*. Poetry was very low on his list of interests but he liked the title and felt that he needed a break from history which after all tended to be a record of national bad habits.

On the walk home he was further irked by a thaw that
made the snow soft and slushy. He had felt the warmer air
from the south through the window in the middle of the
night and left for Big Bay well before dawn. He had hoped
to reach one of his brook trout spots back on the Yellow
Dog Plains but the melting snow clung to his snowshoes and
the going was hard. He returned to his vehicle and tried the
Bushwhacker skis but had forgotten to buy a pole to replace
the one that was missing. He got stuck in a melting drift and
fell over sideways yelling "Goddamnit" to the natural world.

His habitual postlunch nap failed due to a recurrent
problem with acid reflux and he didn't need to taste the
sandwich again. He had found some old vinyl records of
Diane's and thought that listening to Berlioz's *Requiem* might
elevate him but the old record player wasn't quite up to
speed and besides the music only elevated his melancholy
over Diane. He decided on a midafternoon jolt of whiskey
though he knew it was a mistake. He had seen the unpleasant
television ad warning seniors about overdrinking. In the ad
an old man had a beer while fishing in his rowboat but then
gradually moved up to a six-pack, not a threatening amount
to Sunderson. He lay down on the sofa with the obnoxious
afternoon sun pouring down on him through the living room
window, half dozing and praying to a god unknown for a
December blizzard. His thoughts were errant. To wit, if
there are ninety billion galaxies how many religions are in
the universe? Could he make a beef stew like Diane did without fresh sage? Soon after their divorce he had neglected the
heating element in her small greenhouse next to the garage
and the herbs had all frozen. Mona had retrieved a science

blog for him a few days earlier that claimed religion had a biological inception similar to our aesthetic perceptions. Even other mammals like cows and killer whales enjoyed Mozart. When they were in Florence and Diane had insisted on a three-hour walk through the Uffizi he had wondered about going that long without cigarettes but then had had goose bumps a half dozen times and had quite forgotten the existence of cigarettes. He came away convinced that art books were a hoax compared to the reverence of standing before the actual painting, a reverence ordinarily only elicited by the natural world. Was this religion? Probably.

Something like that since he had read the piece hastily. Unfortunately he slept for a few minutes and reclaimed the past by dreaming of Diane screaming close to his face, "I can't live any longer with a man who sees the world through shit-stained glasses." This happened the day before she left. She never swore so it truly got his attention, albeit tardily.

He was sweating and not from the sun through the window, which had disappeared. He pretended that the briefest of sobs was a hiccup and poured a very large whiskey, swallowing it in a couple of gulps. As an investigator he didn't generally believe in suppressed memory but had not previously admitted this scream to himself.

He threw on a jacket and bolted the house not wanting to make his way through the bottle of whiskey. He was wearing street shoes which were wet within a few blocks and he stumbled on a curb and nearly fell when the power of the big drink hit full force then he walked more slowly. He made it out to the city park, Presque Isle, for a gorgeous sunset which somewhat subdued his panic but not completely. He was brooding over a case that had preceded their separation and over which Diane had become very angry. In a small town far to the west three upstanding young men had seemingly kept a girl just over eighteen hostage in their deer cabin for three days. They had stowed her clothes outside and she was nude and hysterical when a visiting hunter came to the cabin. The perpetrators were out hunting and the girl had refused to run for it without her clothes. She was from a "trailer trash" family and when the local prosecutor talked to her father he said that she had always been "haywire." It was a dicey case indeed and when he had described it to Diane she demanded a prosecution full-speed ahead. Sunderson was less sure. When he talked to the perps who were all married with young children they were remorseful and used the excuse that they had all been drinking too much, an excuse all too often honored by some judges with a "boys will be boys" attitude. The prosecutor and Sunderson had agonized over the matter and decided against going on with the case, which would permanently injure the young men with felony convictions. The girl was trying to withdraw the charges under the pressure of her parents. They could have gone ahead anyway with the initial charges but the prosecutor felt too vulnerable in the community and chickened out. Diane was enraged when Sunderson had stupidly said, "She'll get over it," then went on to explain he couldn't continue without the prosecutor which was less than true. Oddly, in a follow-up inquiry the young woman seemed to be doing well having moved off to Duluth with a friend.

He was utterly fatigued and wobbly when he completed the nearly two-hour walk home, much longer than necessary because he had made a wrong turn and had walked toward a small rented bungalow they had lived in during their happier times early in their marriage. He could barely acknowledge his mistake but then blamed it on his age rather than on a questionable mood.

When he reached the house there was an unfamiliar car parked in front and the kitchen light was on in the late afternoon winter darkness. He walked across the yard then peeked around a maple tree and could see Diane and Mona chatting at the kitchen table. He stood there not wanting to go in his house and face the music but then realized there was no music to face. He slicked back his hair and entered through the porch door with a thoroughly fake smile. Get a grip on yourself, he thought.

"My goodness but you look good. Mona said you've become a fitness buff." Diane was grinning with no backspin.

"Retirement is more complicated than I thought it would be so I've been walking a few hours a day." He wished the open whiskey bottle wasn't on the table. To his surprise Diane poured herself a shot.

"I was wondering if you could drive Mona to Ann Arbor and then over to Kalamazoo to look into colleges? My husband is too ill for me to leave."

"Of course. I'd be glad to." This was a lie. He had a peculiar fear of heavy traffic.

They left to go out for dinner without inviting him. He wouldn't have gone but was still slightly miffed in the manner of a girl who didn't get invited to the prom. Before they left Diane said that she and her husband wanted he and Mona to come for Christmas. He accepted when he noted Mona's eagerness though in truth he'd rather stay home and suck a dozen raw eggs. He sighed wanting a whiskey but decided to delay it for after he had done a little reading and cooked supper. Diane, always prim and proper, looked ten years younger than her age of sixty-five. Marion had observed that in the past decade women were staying younger much better than men. He wanted to talk to Marion but he was off in Albuquerque, New Mexico, with his wife for a meeting on Indian affairs after which they were traveling to Guadalajara in Mexico for Christmas vacation. He opened D. H. Lawrence's *Studies in Classic American Literature* but something not clearly definable was nagging at him. He called Carla.

"What are you wearing?" he asked impulsively.

"A blue cotton skirt for work. White cotton short-sleeved blouse. It's warm here. Robin's egg blue bikini panties. You want to try some phone sex?"

"Yes and no but not really."

"I want your thick fat cock in my mouth," she laughed.

"Never mind, please. We've tried very hard and Mona's a computer whiz but we can find little information on King David's past except some French stuff, and almost nothing on his childhood."

"You're out of luck. I've known him the longest, three years to be exact, and he's said very little except he was brought up in a bunch of foster families in California. He went to college a couple of years somewhere in Oregon to study acting and anthropology. He knows a lot about Indians. That's about all I know. He's certainly unfaithful to his lovers but you get used to it. I worry that he's burning himself out with Viagra and Cialis. I know he has prostate problems. No wonder."

"Why does he go for the young stuff?"

"Are you taping this?"

"No. That would be illegal." He was amused by this.

"The young girl thing is theological. He sees himself as a god with a small *g*. It's important a girl's first sexual contact be with him if she is to live a powerful life. They are actually not of illegal age in most countries."

"I see," he said, but he didn't. He knew all of this in bits and pieces but it certainly didn't make a cogent whole.

"He thinks modern times suck and for health we must return to old-timey pagan life. We do a lot of drum dancing and free sex. He says that he is many persons."

"Do you believe this?" He was trying to ignore the mental image of Carla's butt glistening under the porch light near the woodpile.

"Some days I do and some days I don't. I'm mostly in love with him which is hard work."

When he hung up Sunderson was mostly amazed at his own sloppiness. In his long experience his habit was to locate the problem criminals, "the person of interest," as they are currently referred to, and then bear down hard. While unwrapping a piece of thawed venison and pouring a small drink it occurred to him that when he got interested in this case he was nearly retired and he likely subconsciously wanted to prolong it to give himself something intriguing to do. How could cult members willingly sacrifice their underage daughters? How could Abraham be willing to sacrifice his son Isaac? How did religion derange the human mind? Would the Shiites and Sunnis ever stop killing each other? Why did the Catholic Church want to ignore pederasty?

He fried some spuds and then his slab of venison me-
dium rare, still troubled that King David hadn't committed
a provable crime though he knew from cultural history that
some of the grandest crimes aren't technically against the
law. They were simply the way people in power behaved.

The venison and fried potatoes with an amber glass
of whiskey would have been even better if it weren't for
his errant thinking. The year before his computer crime
colleague had told him that there were four million child
porn sites. This was hard to believe but there was no reason
for the man to lie. About a week later as a favor to Marion
he had appeared at a middle school "career carnival" and
talked to an assembly about jobs in law enforcement. He
had been amazed at how widely varied the sixth, seventh,
and eighth graders were. Some looked like mature high
school students but many were just kids. In the question
and answer period a diminutive girl with thick glasses and
braces had squeaked, "I don't think you guys should shoot
people. It's not Christian."

"We don't unless they're trying to shoot us," he had
answered. "In forty years of law enforcement I've never shot
anyone." He did not mention a drunk man on his front porch
aiming a shotgun at him. He was betting that the shotgun
wasn't loaded when the man's very large wife jumped him
from behind crushing him to the porch floor. Afterward
Sunderson discovered the shotgun was loaded.

Now at the table forking in the last of the nearly bloody
venison he recalled talking to the little girl after the assembly
was over. She said she was twelve and read a lot of mysteries because she wanted to be a detective when she grew

up. The obvious point was that a girl that age was King David's favorite prey and an adult male who tampered with such a girl should be permanently imprisoned as hopeless scum. There was a fairly specific theory and practice of law enforcement that gave an appearance of sane equilibrium until you put a particular human face in place and then your stomach would begin churning.

He fell asleep a full two hours with his head on his arms on the table and then woke up and reheated some brackish coffee. He began reading D. H. Lawrence quoting Crèvecœur, "I must tell you that there is something in the proximity of the woods which is very singular." And then hunters, "The chase renders them ferocious, gloomy, and unsociable; a hunter wants no neighbors, he rather hates them, because he dreads the competition . . . Eating of wild meat, whatever you may think, tends to alter their tempers . . ."

With a bellyful of venison Sunderson was unsure of the complete truth of what he read though it was more true than not true. He went on to read about Fenimore Cooper and Lawrence's strange speculations on Native Americans which were totally unpleasant and nearly deranged. Not wanting to be kept awake by this lunatic Englishman he pushed the book aside and washed the dishes after which he turned on the television for the eleven o'clock news, pleased to see the forecast for a foot of fresh snow. When the news segued to Afghan car bombs he flipped through satellite channels until he arrived at *Co-ed Confidential*. The young ladies didn't look like coeds but certainly had nifty bodies. He was embarrassed when Mona walked in the unlocked front door and caught him at his movie. She looked distraught.

"So what's wrong?" he asked.

"I don't think Diane's going to want you back when her husband dies."

"It never occurred to me she would."

"She doesn't want to take care of another man. She wants to travel a lot."

"She always did. I was the slowpoke."

"It's just that I was hoping you two would get back together. With Mom being such a ditz you were nearly my real parents." Mona had tears in her eyes and slumped down on the sofa beside him suddenly grinning at the television. "Why watch these piggies when you can see me through the window?"

"No comment."

"We're in luck. I looked it up and they're playing *Faster, Pussycat! Kill! Kill!* in ten minutes!"

She was sitting too close to him on the sofa but he decided to ignore it. He had a couple of nightcaps but each time he sat back down she drew closer again. She boldly lit a joint and offered him a hit which he declined. He also ignored the illegality of the joint though he was slightly troubled when he glanced over and saw a condom in the purse from which she drew the joint. The movie *Faster, Pussycat! Kill! Kill!* was magnificently loathsome and trashy with three bathing-suit models punishing men for their lechery far out in the desert. They ran over men with cars or bashed them in the head with big rocks, an unpleasant reminder of his Arizona misadventure. Mona fooled with the clicker and on an adjoining channel was *The Diary of Anne Frank*. That's entertainment, he thought. He fell asleep and awoke at 4:00 a.m. covered with an afghan. Mona had kindly turned off the television. The star of the *Pussycat* movie had been an actress named Tura Satana, likely not her real name.

The morning's mail brought a postcard from Albuquerque and a letter from Roberta which he pushed aside with consternation. He could count on one hand the letters received from Roberta. One about ten years before had been so abrasive it took him days to recover, the key sentence being, "Bobby only found true happiness in his life when he discovered heroin." He had a bowl of nasty raisin bran to steady himself before opening the letter.

Dear Big Brother,

I must say that I thought you looked totally awful when we saw each other but Berenice said you were in much better shape than you had been the previous week before you went camping. The question is why an old man should unnecessarily put himself in harm's way and get himself nearly stoned to death? Who do you think you are? You should spend a lot of time pondering this question. You should spend all of your time fishing and camping, your childhood passions, when you're not reading. I remember a couple times when you took us camping a few miles south of town. Once you went off fishing and I stayed in the tent reading Nancy Drew. I think I was eight and you were fourteen. Meanwhile Bobby roasted a whole bag of marshmallows and puked and we had to drag him down to a creek and wash off the sticky marshmallow

stuff that was even in his hair. Bobby and me were
frightened that night when you crawled out of the tent
saying that you heard a bear trying to get our food.
You came back into the tent saying you had driven the
bear away with a burning torch. I had peeked out and
saw that it was a small raccoon but didn't say anything
because a bear made a better story. How I admired you
back then. You were such a kind brother to Bobby.

Now is a different matter. I have witnessed divorces in
long-term marriages and one of the partners always falls
in a hole like a well pit and it takes them about three years
to crawl out, if ever. Diane didn't make her profession
her whole life like you did. Your moderate alcoholism
makes you emotionally inelastic and you can't seem to
crawl out of the hole of your inevitable divorce. It makes
me mournful to think you should have been a history
teacher. You are a kind man not a tough guy. I would
like to retire early, come back, and take care of you but
I couldn't bear to live in the area of my childhood.

Love, Roberta

Of course the letter made him angry. He dressed
warmly in near tears and set off for a walk in the falling
snow and was gone for four hours. By the time he reached
Presque Isle in about forty-five minutes the anger had passed
because he was able to admit to himself that she was right
on every count. The idle idea of throwing himself off a cliff
into Lake Superior amused rather than alarmed him. He
had work to do.

Two days later they were off for Kalamazoo and Ann
Arbor. Diane and Mona had organized a precise itinerary
including hotels and appointments. Diane had irritated Sunderson by renting them a nice Hertz car for the trip feeling
that his twelve-year-old Blazer with a hundred and seventy
thousand miles on the odometer was vulnerable. She had
rented the car without telling him saying that it was a "treat."
As a civil servant from a relatively poor family he had chosen the path of ignoring their finances and when Diane had
tried to involve his interest in her inherited money he had
refused to cooperate. Any amount over a thousand dollars
set off a red light in his noggin and that was what the rental
car would cost for the four-day trip. Sunderson felt like one
of the limo drivers he used to talk to at the Detroit airport
early in his career when he was on surveillance for a mob hit
man supposedly coming in from New York City. The drivers were there waiting for "bigwigs," a name referring back
to the seventeenth and eighteenth centuries when a man's
importance could be determined by the amplitude of his wig.

They left an hour before dawn with Mona not excited
about colleges but about a computer discovery: to wit, she
had started over from ground zero in the investigative process. Instead of using the Peace Corps dead mother's name,
Atkins, she had tried the French father's name, Peyraud,
while surveying Carla's clue of Dwight attending an Oregon college twenty-five years before. Bingo. Dwight had
attended Reed College for two years in 1983 and 1984.
Mona then managed to communicate with a retired anthropology professor who recalled Dwight with amusement and
distaste. Dwight had been arrogant and overbearing though

a brilliant student. He had had a Mohawk haircut, a thin strip of hair down the center of his skull, wore martial arts clothing, and had a cadre of male and female students following him around. Mona's ingenuity depressed Sunderson. He and Roxie at the cop shop had clearly begun with the wrong name, the wrong presumptions. The sixteen-year-old neighbor girl was a better detective.

Mona typed on her laptop and listened to CDs of John Cage (which drove him batty), Pink Floyd, and Los Lobos, the latter with traces of rhythm that made him stupidly sentimental about his time on the border. His mistake in not searching Dwight's father's name kept reminding him of the term "unforced errors" in tennis. He had Mona reread the professor's e-mail pondering the last sentence about Dwight's disappearance during a summer visit to the Haida Indians on the Queen Charlotte Islands off British Columbia for a research paper. Sunderson recalled a few things about the Haida from talking to Marion. They believed that wolves and killer whales were the same creatures, taking up separate forms on land and water. Sunderson felt he should research native shape-changing since that seemed to be a continuing motif.

Five hours into the trip at a gas station near Cadillac he abruptly demanded that Mona change from her short skirt to slacks. An hour before she had curled up and dozed and he could see her blue undies and a bit of pubic furze and had come up on a semi too fast. What was this thing about blue panties? Diane had always worn white.

Mona returned from the service station laughing and waving the new *Rolling Stone* at him. She read a quote from the cover girl, an antic starlet named Megan Fox: "Men are scared of powerful, confident vaginas." What in God's name could this mean, Sunderson wondered. Had the starlet's parents read this and been embarrassed for their daughter? He was unsure of parental emotions but then here was Mona, nearly a stepdaughter, who of course was capable of saying something this preposterous.

"Imagine having a vagina as powerful as Arnold Schwarzenegger in his prime," Mona laughed. "You could chew up unsuspecting men."

The city of Kalamazoo, their first stop, didn't last long. He said the college looked *homely* but she said that he was looking at western Michigan. They drove to the top of a hill to Kalamazoo College but then Mona said, "Too small," and demanded that they proceed to Ann Arbor.

"But you have an appointment in the morning."

"I'll e-mail them." She suitably placed her laptop on her lap. "I won't be able to meet with you tomorrow because my father has died. How's that?"

"Wonderful dear."

They proceeded to Ann Arbor arriving in the confusing dark at the Campus Inn with Mona playing expert navigator with MapQuest on her computer screen. He was utterly fatigued from ten hours of driving so they had a dismal room-service dinner including a bottle of white wine in his quarters of their connecting rooms. He had a whiskey from the pint in his suitcase and glanced only once through the connecting door as she changed into jeans to take a walk. He felt a jolt in his nuts, then stared down at his half-eaten club sandwich. Will this pointless lust never end he thought?

Three hours later at midnight she still hadn't returned and he was near tears of frustration. She hadn't responded to his calls on her cell but then he discovered she had left it behind on the coffee table in her room. He must have paced a solid mile unaware that he was merely another father waiting up for a wayward daughter. His black mood had begun right after Mona left when Diane had called to say that his old friend Otto had died of a heart attack. He had difficulty accepting this as fact. He and Otto had fished for brook trout together a half dozen times a summer ever since they were ten years old in Munising. Otto owned a small construction company that specialized in building summer cabins for downstaters and the recent economic downturn had nearly bankrupted him. Otto could drink a case of beer in a long evening and was addicted to sausage in all its various forms. In a day of fishing he would eat a whole package of raw hot dogs. He would use a pound of ham in a sandwich and was locally famous for his expertise at roasting whole pigs and would devour the bronzed skin in portions of a square foot. Diane and her friends would euphemistically refer to Otto's problem as an "eating disorder."

The news of Otto had brought with it a momentary fear of death which Sunderson dismissed in favor of worrying about Mona wandering the nighttime streets of Ann Arbor. When she got home he intended on locking his side of the connecting doors to prevent the possibility of sexual mishap whether peeking or something more serious. When he was a senior in high school and full of confusion and near depression his dad had counseled him by saying, "You've got to boil down your life and figure out what you want."

Remembering this made him feel oddly hopeful and he took his notebook out of his briefcase.

1. On the map of Ann Arbor I note a park along the river where I can walk in the morning. Television weather says it will be unseasonably warm.

2. In e-mails with Carla, Mona has discovered that within Dwight's followers there are seventeen couples with daughters of eleven, twelve, or thirteen in age. Of course historically cults are often involved in illegal sexual license. This was possibly true in the Waco affair and the recent activity of the Mormon apostasy group on the Arizona-Utah border.

3. Boiling it down what truly angers me is Dwight using fake Indian material to fuck young girls. Given my knowledge of the suffering of American Indians for five hundred years this is doubly monstrous. It's been a decade since I could bear to read about this suffering which only talking to Marion puts into perspective.

4. Carla said that all the women in the cult dance naked around the bonfire while the men beat on drums after which Dwight selects one or two of the young ones for his "blessing." This happens every evening.

5. How could the parents allow this except through the delusion of religion? Carla said that in Arizona Dwight threatened one mother with his pet rattlesnake. She was trying to hide her daughter who had been made "uncomfortable" by Dwight's big dick.

6. This all sounds like a bad dream but it's reality. I have to put a stop to this. The irony is that I wouldn't

have all of this information without the criminal Carla-Mona connection and Carla's belief that I could get her sent to prison.

7. I just now leafed through Snyder's *The Practice of the Wild* and read, "Walking is the exact balance of spirit and humility." I am unsure of what he means except that in a walk of a couple of hours the first half hour is full of the usual mental junk but then you just zone out into the landscape and are simply a humanoid biped walking through the snowy hills and forests or along Lake Superior's frozen beaches. You don't bother trying to comprehend this immense body of water because you're not meant to.

8. Mona still not back and it's eleven. It helps to write it down. Why? It makes it concrete. D. H. Lawrence on the subject of Indians is very irritating but I have to remember that this stuff was published in 1923, nearly ninety years ago. He thought the demon in our continent was caused by the unappeased ghost of the "Red Indian," the inner malaise that brings us to madness. What am I to make of this?

9. I have to do a little reading to figure out again what Christianity is. It certainly cooperated in the destruction of approximately five hundred tribes.

10. Back to Dwight: he is using *Indianness* to enact his pathological sexual desires. This is unforgivable and deserves death, but his is unlikely.

He shuffled from the small desk to an easy chair where Mona woke him up at midnight. He had gotten pretty cranked up over Keith Olbermann but not enough to keep him awake. He had spilled his drink on his crotch which made it look like he pissed his pants. His Uncle Bertie, a commercial fisherman, used to say that any day you don't puke or shit your pants is a good day so Sunderson was ahead of the game.

"I was worried about you," he muttered.

"I just walked around town and had a couple glasses of wine with some students. I love it here."

Sunderson decided to let sleeping dogs lie rather than begin an interrogation. She was standing in front of him and his eyes focused on her visible, protuberant belly button between her sweater and jeans. There was an urge to lick this mystery. She pulled him out of the chair and led him to bed, helping him disrobe down to his boxer shorts.

"Get outta here," he said, following her to the door and locking it.

On the way home a day and half later he was happy because Mona was happy, perhaps the happiest he had ever seen her. For the seven-hour drive home he had packed a cooler with the three hundred bucks worth of stuff he had bought at Zingerman's Delicatessen, a place where Diane had gotten FedEx food for special occasions. A thaw had caused the spending binge. Fifty-five degrees in December! And after shopping he had ordered what was to be the best sandwich of his long life, a real pile of brisket on rye slathered with the hottest horseradish possible so that tears of pain and pleasure came freely. The moon was to be nearly full and when they reached Marquette he intended to take a couple-hour moonlit walk out to Presque Isle.

On the way home he described to Mona a freakishly

difficult case that he had finally solved the year before. In a
small school system in the eastern U.P. twelve thousand dollars had been embezzled. The only possible guilty parties had
been the school superintendent and his secretary, a minister's
wife in her midfifties, a graceful and intelligent woman, albeit
rather dumpy. After a number of questionings about computer and accounting accesses he determined both of them
to be clean. On what he decided was his final visit he talked
to the school janitor who seemed somewhat retarded and
had a speech impediment from a cleft palate. They smoked a
cigarette in the parking lot and chatted. No one notices janitors in their green suits. To Sunderson the janitor had tried to
present himself as stupider than he was and had let the word
"ubiquitous" slip through while talking about students and the
meth epidemic. It occurred to Sunderson that the janitor had
ready access to the office computer after everyone left for the
day. Back in the school he checked old yearbooks and noted
that the janitor and the school secretary, the minister's wife,
were classmates. He took a big chance and suddenly asked her
over coffee, "Why are you fucking Bob the janitor?" Bingo.
She fell apart, confessing that she and Bob were going to run
away with the money held in a bank account in the Soo. They
were headed to Milwaukee where Bob had a job lined up at
the famous Usinger's sausage factory. Why did every other
man in the U.P. seem to be named Bob?

Mona laughed hysterically. "The sweetest most religious girl in my class is a blow-job artist. She told me it was
like conducting an orchestra."

Sunderson was puzzled by this but let it pass. When
they reached Marquette Mona made them mortadella and

provolone sandwiches and then he headed out on his walk. The moonrise was stupendous forming a glissade of light on quiet Lake Superior and making the freshly fallen soft snow on the beach a nearly daytime white. He walked fast and raised a sweat, pausing only to talk to Professor Eathorne whom he had met in various taverns. Eathorne was throwing a ball for his yellow Lab who was able to find the ball hidden in the soft snow. Their language is in their nose, Sunderson thought. Where is mine? Maybe he should get a yellow Lab, he thought, to counter loneliness. Dogs need a lot of petting, which might have been a better way to conduct his marriage. Eathorne taught human geography, which among other things dealt with why people were where they were, a germane question in human history. Running into Eathorne gave Sunderson a dose of oxygen. There were all these areas of human inquiry that were intriguing. He thought he might begin auditing some courses at the university and stretch his mind beyond the confines of history.

Christmas dinner made him jealous of Diane's dying husband. How can you be jealous of a dying man? It takes work. They lived high on the edge of a steep slope that overlooked the harbor. He was a gentle and obviously melancholy soul and when he and Sunderson went into his den it took a while to permit their chat to go fluidly. His son had sadly enough dropped out of medical school to enter the movie business in L.A. while his daughter happily enough was a marine biologist at Scripps south of San Francisco. Neither had married so there were no grandchildren. Sunderson sipped rather than gulped his whiskey, always a temptation, and stared at a half dozen bird and animal prints that were splendid including a javelina.

The man said that they were first folio Audubons. Sunderson said he had seen a number of javelinas down on the border.

"Diane said that you were down their chasing an evil cult leader who preys on young girls," he said with a hard edge in his voice.

"I haven't been at it long, a couple of months, and I doubt I'll be successful. The problem is getting one of his followers, a parent, to testify against him."

"When my daughter was growing up a banker down the street had a discreet but unhealthy interest in her. I warned him and he broke into tears. He thought he was in love with a twelve-year-old. Then a friend of mine, an old classmate, who practiced in Omaha was caught and prosecuted for the same Lolita syndrome. It often comes from a man who lacked social contact with girls his own age between, say, age eleven and fourteen. The pathology is in the inability to control the urges."

"The problem is of course the permanent scar tissue left behind." Sunderson was unable to admit that he hadn't read *Lolita* though Marion had advised him to do so. He grew nervous watching Diane's husband wince a number of times.

At dinner Diane was perfect as usual. Sunderson over-ate, mystified by the deliciousness of the roast beef, which Diane had ordered from Chicago. The Burgundy wine was the best he had ever put in his mouth, and the good doctor asked Diane to open a second bottle for which Sunderson was grateful. He was also grateful for the way Mona amused and cheered the man. She was sitting on his right and had him laughing until quite suddenly during dessert he fell asleep. Diane's eyes flowed with tears.

PART V

Chapter 17

In January the cold winnowed him. It stayed near zero during the day and twenty below at night for a week. In order to walk he had to wear an irritating face mask and he went less far in the woods out of timidity. He carried a compass and wood matches in a small aluminum tube, also candles in his vehicle in case it broke down. It did on a country road south of Trenary with a metallic, hacking cough. Two candles plus the afternoon sun kept the interior well above freezing. He dozed, content that he would live through this and remembering his cell phone was on the coffee table in the living room. He had turned on the warning lights and overcame the irksome clicking sound by turning on the NPR station to a rather dreary Haydn piece and mulling recent developments in the case. Mona had shown him an e-mail from King David sent through Carla. "Carla tells me that you're extorting information from her. You better be careful,

kiddo. You're no longer a law officer." Sunderson replied,
"It is unwise to threaten someone from jail. I need only to
send your message to Maui officials to get your sentence
extended. However, I want you out of jail so I can get at
you." To Carla he said, "You should behave yourself. I need
only to call the prosecutor to begin extradition on you for
sexual abuse of a minor." He wanted Mona to add, "Mona
is now willing to testify," but she refused. She was stirring
a short-rib-and-lentil soup at his stove and said, "Carla got
me drunk and stoned and ate me out. I can't say that. I'm a
big girl not one of those kids King David is fucking with."

A logger towed Sunderson to a tavern in Trenary and
pointed out the hole in his engine drooling oil. "You've
thrown a rod," the logger said. "Your Blazer is shit-canned,
buddy."

He signed the title over to the logger who could use a
vehicle for spare parts for the price of a hamburger and a
beer. Marion picked him up in an hour. Sunderson got his
gear out of the woebegone junker.

"Aren't you going to say something sentimental?"

"Good-bye, darling," he said, patting the hood. The
hard part was when he found his dead dog's teddy bear
under the backseat.

When they got back to his house Mona was frying a
chicken and had also made succotash, one of his favorites.

"I'm being nice so you won't run away like my dad did."

He and Marion looked at each other feeling uncomfortable at her frankness. She was wearing a pair of turquoise
earrings Marion had bought her on a trip to Albuquerque.

"Carla e-mailed to say that Queenie's grandma died and

she's going to inherit a lot more money. The cult is definitely moving to Nebraska in April."

Sunderson exhaled over a whiskey thinking that he would have time to get all of his ducks in a row whatever that meant. He would walk, read, and intermittently hibernate for three months and then, by God, he would somehow close the case.

In the morning he bought a used, gray Subaru with only sixty thousand miles on it, then stopped at Snowbound Books for a copy of *Lolita*. He had a painful lunch with Diane which she had requested. She talked a lot about her husband's white corpuscle count and other medical details and barely touched her food which he, typically, finished. He was down fifteen pounds in the nearly three months since retirement, which made him ponder on the scales whether or not he had a fatal disease but then figured it must be the addictive walking. By the end of lunch she was in tears and he was near tears. Outside she hugged him good-bye and he shuddered at their first real physical contact in over three years. Life could be so merciless.

He fled out to the Skandia area for a hike. The temperature had risen to a balmy ten degrees above zero and he made a three-hour circle on a packed snowmobile track, which made walking without snowshoes easy. When the car came in sight after the lovely mindless exhaustion he wasn't ready to go home yet and stopped and built a small fire out of dead pine branches to keep himself company. He was thinking about back after 9/11 when he had attended two law enforcement conferences in Canada on the cooperative efforts to prevent terrorism. The problem seemed unlikely indeed in the Upper

Peninsula but the U.S. government was paying the tab and
the chief ordered him to go. The first was in Toronto and
the meetings were mostly pathetic nonsense but the city was
wonderful. He met a now retired Toronto detective named
Bob Kolb and they talked for hours in taverns and restaurants about trout fishing and grouse and woodcock hunting.
There was another meeting a few months later in Calgary
wherein much the same material was repeated so that one
day he and Kolb skipped a couple of sessions to see the zoo.
Strange to say Sunderson had never been to a zoo and the
event comprised the beginning of what passed for him as a
spiritual life. Soon after entering they saw a group of giraffes
and Sunderson stared long and hard at a very young giraffe, a
weanling, feeling goose bumps sweep up and down his body.
Simply enough, the animal seemed impossible. How could
it exist? Of course he had seen pictures but they had meant
nothing. How could this creature have been invented? He
had taken several college science courses and he was a devout
evolutionist but he suspected a *mind* had to be behind this
sublime creature, maybe what Indians called the Great Spirit.

There were repercussions that continued onward to
the present time. A trout wasn't just a trout any more than a
crow was simply a crow. This spirit of attention wasn't with
him often but often enough. Marion was better practiced in
this spirit of attention and when Sunderson visited Marion's
remote cabin he learned a great deal from him. Once they
had found a dead yellow-rumped warbler which Sunderson
had kept and put in a plastic bag in the freezer to remind
him of the ineffable. A creek or river would also change the
texture of his spirit so that staring into the moving water

would make his brain tingle as it had in his childhood when *wonder* is nothing special but an everyday event.

Stooping before the fire his back and butt were chilled with drying sweat. When his job confused him he often reread from a letter Kolb had sent years before now kept in a tiny plastic envelope in his wallet. Kolb was responding to Sunderson's note on how simple it must be to work in the U.P. compared to an immense city like Toronto. "No surprise but the TV networks, the news media, and I imagine most writers, have got it wrong. Crime is not interesting, it's pathetically predictable. Nothing has changed since Cain slew Abel. Greed, jealousy, mental instability, and economic deprivation remain the prime ingredients. Religion has a place as well. Today substance abuse and moral lassitude thicken the gravy. The interest is in the circumstances, not the act, and not necessarily the people directly involved. Witnesses seldom tell the same story. For any detective, geography notwithstanding, police investigation involves hours of grinding boredom interspersed with moments of shit-your-pants excitement. The latter keeps the adrenaline junkies in the game."

Sunderson watched the fire die. He shivered and anticipated the soup Mona said she would make out of venison shanks and neck plus barley and his favorite vegetable, rutabaga. Sunderson didn't realize that he had been a good detective because he was utterly ordinary like a root vegetable. He didn't separate himself from others like the Romantic hero, writers, painters, famed athletes. He made warm eye contact and spoke slowly in the grungy local accent. "Let's have a brewsky, hey?" People were disarmed and told him everything. His day job had been total consciousness.

Chapter 18

Winter passed quickly. He hit a long stretch of the best aspect of retirement which was freedom, the texture of which he had never totally experienced since before the age of twelve when he had begun working. He studied maps over breakfast and when he arrived at various destinations the only significant decision was whether to use cross-country skis, snowshoes, or whether there were solid enough snowmobile trails to go on foot. He had an upsetting pratfall with Roxie one evening when he couldn't get it up, rarely a problem. The throbbing, warm clothes dryer didn't work and she was chewing and snapping Dentyne the odor of which he never cared for. She wept and lapsed into bad grammar. "I don't turn you on no more."

And the novel *Lolita* was nearly unreadable what with the hero Humbert Humbert being a perverted nitwit bapping a thirteen-year-old girl and covering up his crime with

layers of intricate thought and language. Marion counseled
him on this problem.

"Fucking is fucking but what adds a good measure
is the aesthetic backdrop. There are a dozen reasons for
his criminal lust but they are inseparably intertwined. Remember what you said after talking to that drug cartel guy
in Nogales, about sex, religion, and money being knotted
together and impenetrable like the structure of a bowling
ball? Desire is like that and the cues are subtle and infinite."

Sunderson mentally backpedaled when he recalled
making love to a slumming sorority girl he had met in a
boring but required sociology class. He had bought sandwiches and a six-pack and they took a long car ride. It was
early June and they had made love in a foot-high wheat
field near a creek out near Fowlerville. It was her idea and
they had never made love again but this one occasion was
lunar. When they had finally risen it looked as if deer had
bedded in the wheat.

He had become obsessed with Deloria's *Playing Indian*
until he had to put it away for a while. And Mona required
time. Her mother had made a horrid three-day visit and her
father had the dealership deliver a compact Honda which
Mona had left in the drive until it was covered with four
feet of snow. She had also begun dating a freshman from
Northern Michigan University, a diminutive but bright
physics major from Newberry. Sunderson was embarrassed
over his vague jealousy when he detected they were sleeping together. During a brief thaw he had grilled steaks for
himself and Mona and described to her a peculiar case near
Detroit where a boy barely over eighteen had made love to

a girl barely under eighteen and had been prosecuted for statutory rape.

"Hey, fuck you fucking hypocrites. You'd love to lock up Romeo and Juliet," she exploded.

It took a full half hour to calm her down decisively. She ate with her hands and chewed at her rib steak angrily. He reflected how intolerant the young are of adult ironies and that a compendium of our sexual laws might exceed the size of the Chicago phone book. The effort to keep us from maiming each other often goes awry. The mating schedule of dogs and cattle seemed more reasonable and depended on a biological alarm that only rang once or twice a year. Humans were cursed with the sexual persistence of mice.

Chapter 19

Sunderson kept a terse journal of the season, a "winter count" in native terms, biding his time until he could drive to Arizona in April and track the departure of the cult from Tucson to Nebraska.

He had a close call near Grand Marais while heading the few miles down the beach to revisit the dunes and Au Sable Falls. He should have known better on the bright sunny afternoon that he might not beat the massive black front coming from the northwest toward town. He didn't and the fifty-knot winds and driving snow made him fearful. Luckily he could hear the harbor foghorn above the wind and there was a jumble of ice near the shore so when his way was blocked by ice piles he bore to the right. There were frozen tears of pleasure when he reached the township park and could see the lights of the tavern. Driving home was plainly impossible so he checked into a motel and headed to the bar questioning what he loved about his bedraggled landscape aside from its carpet of forest and clearings, the rivers, creeks, swamps, countless beaver ponds, and the terrain, occasionally rolling and hilly but mostly flattish in western terms. It had been entirely cut over by the timber barons except for a few minimal shreds of land, and after that pulped relentlessly of its second, third, and fourth growth for the paper mills, and mined to exhaustion of its iron and copper. Maybe it was the hundreds of miles of Lake Superior shoreline, much of it undisturbed, that saved the area, or even the Lake Michigan coast to the south, more pleasant, much less ominous than Superior so that even the people a hundred miles to the south were gentler and less cranky. He also thought his love for the area rose from the indefatigable creature life, his beloved trout and the thousands of bear, deer, otter, wolves, beaver, and other creatures, even loving the ugly and slow porcupine, the millions of birds and wildflowers. It was so good to live in a place largely ignored by the rest of the world.

Chapter 20

He rather liked the idea that he was leaving for Arizona on April Fool's Day, a Saturday. He had hoped to leave at dawn but Mona who had come over to make him a cheese omelet and fried spuds had become clingy, a homely little word but *au point*. She was in her robe, pj's, and bunny slippers at the stove sniffling a bit and he thought goddamn the lame parents who abandon their children. One generation teaches the next to behave poorly ad infinitum. It all made him recall Dickens's *Bleak House,* which he had read in college and which made him feel like he was trapped in a dentist office every time he picked it up. Given how Sunderson had grown up with empathy for the poor it was not a far reach. His mother was always making truly poor families mountainous casseroles and his dad would deliver a couple of cords of split hardwood to keep them warm.

While eating breakfast his emotions were in his throat
so he looked at topographical maps of the Chadron and
Crawford area in Nebraska that Mona had ordered for him
with the cult's one hundred sixty acres north of Crawford
highlighted in pink. Mona pretended to be reading a book
about the human genome but he had noted during the half-
hour breakfast that she hadn't turned a page. They had
embraced at the front door with his hands around her waist
through her open robe encircling her flannel pajamas. He
was startled when her body appeared to be humming.

"Come back to me. Don't die," was all that she said and
he was well west of town before the lump in his throat began
to disappear. Why wasn't she a sensible age like forty-five?
Time herself was askew on this spawned-out earth.

The little good-bye supper the evening before had been
confusing. Marion's wife Sonia had brought over the same
Mexican dish, *carne adovada*, that Melissa had made in Nogales
and Sunderson was goofy enough to wonder if this coincidence was a good or bad omen. Sonia was always pissed off
in her life's work of defending Indian interests but this evening she concentrated her angry energies on Dwight and the
cult. Marion had idly mentioned the Jim Jones massacre in
South America and Sonia tore off like an ICBM on the evils
of a religion that could con over nine hundred people into
cyanide suicide. Marion and Sunderson had tried to slow her
down by raising the point that Dwight aka King David hadn't
been very successful, never managing more than a hundred
followers. This didn't work but then Sunderson knew the
secret through Marion that Sonia had been misused as a girl
by an uncle. Sonia drank her wine in gulps and shrieked that

since Dwight would be arriving in Lakota country she hoped they would "scalp the motherfucker." Mona, meanwhile, had been unusually quiet struggling with the melancholy of Sunderson's leave-taking so that when they kissed good night she didn't try to put any hip into it but had looked at him so somberly that he had doubled up on his nightcap when she left. The extra whiskey had a negative effect when he reached bed as his mind kept bringing up the old photos of the bloated bodies of Jonestown with the deliquescent flesh bursting against the confinement of the clothing.

Given a number of snow squalls and a sleet storm that froze on the roads it was late the second afternoon before he reached the Chadron area, which he wanted to reconnoiter before heading to Tucson for the planned cult departure within a week. If there were a change of plans he didn't want to be caught waiting in the wrong place. He had descended from Murdo, South Dakota, to Valentine, Nebraska, then headed west to Chadron, mightily impressed by the oceanic sweep of the Sandhills, the slight greenish tinge of the first grass of spring, and, when he peed off a side road, the peerless call of the meadowlark in the air that he figured must have reached forty-five degrees, the low-range cutoff for comfortable brook trout fishing.

In the mental comfort of solitary driving he felt that he had attained equilibrium sufficient for the mission at hand. He was somehow going to get the nutcase fucker into prison where the authorities would hopefully throw away the key. Still there was a nagging lack of confidence that intermittently hit him over being in an unfamiliar territory, something that had led to a miserable failure in the Nogales area. On their

trip to Italy he had been jealous of Diane's competency. She
had refreshed her university Italian, studied maps and local
history, and was familiar with the contents of dozens of mu-
seums, and also restaurants which she researched through
friends, travel guides, and the Internet. Meanwhile, before
dawn and haunted by the usual jet lag, he sat in an eighteenth-
century Florentine café of surpassing beauty brooding over
a case that had arisen the day before they had departed on
vacation. Over west in the Sagola area a retired miner had
stomped his old wife into a condition near death. Normally the
local sheriff's department would have handled the case totally
but the stomping was so severe that it raised the possibility of
attempted murder. The point was the "no exit" aspect of his
job. How could he truly *be* in a Florentine café when he kept
seeing in his mind's eye the old woman's knee that looked
like a bright purple bowling ball? She had lisped through
swollen lips, "I don't want my Frank to get in no trouble
with the law." How many times had he heard of this defense
of the guilty? The population at large had no real idea of the
amount of domestic malice. The grand prize had been won
by a drunk who had screwed his two-year-old baby daughter.

He was anxious to survey the cult site north of Crawford, about fifteen miles from Chadron, but first checked
in to the pleasant lodgings Mona had arranged for him in
Chadron. There was also a fax from Mona that had likely
been read by the desk clerk but he didn't care. "Please keep
your cell phone on and charged. I need daily contact with
your lovely voice that sounds like a coal shovel grating on
cement. I lucked out and raised a chat room of an encounter
group of people recovering from being ripped off by cults in

America. One of them was a rich lady from Petoskey who
had temporarily joined up with Dwight. We exchanged
e-mails. She had dropped out because the longhouse accom-
modations near Ontonagon weren't up to snuff. She also
wanted something more 'Oriental' as her yardman was an
Indian and wasn't very spiritual. As an initiation fee Dwight
wanted 10 percent of her net worth which in her case was a
lot of money. She admitted that she had long been a 'spiritual
adventurer' with a lot of cult experience. She also enjoyed
the primitive sex. Anyway Dwight charges poorer members
a minimum of twenty grand. I wondered why Carla didn't
tell us any of this but Carla said that if any member breaks
secrecy Dwight insists that they'll be reincarnated as an
amoeba buried in a dog turd. Dwight received his dispensa-
tion from the gods while living with the Haida Indians on the
Queen Charlotte Islands off the coast of British Columbia.
I asked this lady why people would fork over that kind of
money and she said that Americans don't believe in the
value of anything unless it's expensive. Salvation and good
future lives don't come cheap. Dwight really wanted her
cash and declared that she was at the seventeenth stage out
of a hundred. Everyone had to have a spirit creature and
hers was the sandhill crane. Most poorer members are given
the porcupine with which to enact mimesis, or the beaver
so they'll work hard. Nifty isn't it? Love, Mona."

Driving toward Crawford Sunderson reflected on how
Mona liked to make him feel uncomfortable especially since
he no longer peeked at her. Of greater concern was the
idea that everything Dwight was offering was readily available for free to anyone who took the trouble to read a few

ethnographic texts, or better yet more accessible anthropo-
logical material, or visit modern tribes during powwows.
You didn't have to put in that much effort to get the gist but
then it took a lifetime effort to internalize the messages assuming you could manage the indeterminate quality of faith.

When he reached the small road that led north to the
area of the cult property his thinking rattled to a complete
stop when it occurred to him that he had the advantage of
growing up with the knowledge of Indians that was likely
exotic and alien to others. His dear friend George, an Anishinabe, whom he had hiked and fished so much with when
they were twelve, had a peculiar relationship with ravens.
They'd ride their bikes from Munising out to a creek near
Melstrand. A dozen or so ravens would follow them and
George said they were from south of town where he lived in
a trailer with his pulp-cutter dad and a crazy sister. George
was a great mimic and talked to the ravens and they talked
back with easy glibness. Late that summer when George got
hit by a car while riding his bike on Route 28 there were
ravens at the burial service led by a big bearded male George
could hand feed. At the moment Sunderson figured that one
reason he was so pissed about the cult is that Dwight was a
blasphemy against the spirit of his friend George.

Sunderson drove south a few miles but only until the
blacktop ended and the road became muddy and rutted. He
was met by an oncoming three-quarter-ton pickup covered
with mud and a man who waved him to turn around, yelling
through his open window, "You ain't going to make it." When
Sunderson turned around he saw in the distance two cowboys on horseback driving a herd of cattle toward the west,

the obvious answer though he had never been on a horse. Like it or not he'd have to masquerade as an old cowboy to conceal himself.

In a tavern in Crawford through the efforts of a friendly bartender he made a deal with a very tall mixed-blood Lakota to take him up to the cult property. The man's name was Adam and he was having a burger with his daughter who looked about eleven and was introduced as Morning Star, nicknamed Petunia. Adam was drinking coffee which was a good sign of reliability. When Sunderson told him the location of the property Adam said it had been bought by religious "kooks" partly as a camp for kids. Yes, indeed, Sunderson thought, kids are the thing. Staring at Adam he recognized the ex-alcoholic in him, possessing as he did many of Marion's hesitant mannerisms.

Sunderson had a fine, fatty rib steak in Chadron, slept well, and was back at the junction turnoff at first light. Adam was standing there rolling a cigarette with two mounted horses. Sunderson felt very awkward mounting and admitted this was his first time. Adam only said, "Don't fight it, sit easy." It turned out to be a thirty-mile cross-country roundtrip and that evening Sunderson thought of it as a day that would live in infamy as he applied ointment to his raw ass. He was rather proud that he had only fallen off once and that was when they were going down a steep embankment and he slid forward down the horse's neck into a small muddy creek. Adam had hoisted him back on the saddle as if he were a pillow. Sunderson was down from two hundred to one eighty but it was still no mean feat.

At the property, which wasn't much more than an abandoned farmhouse, a shed, a Quonset hut, and a ramshackle corral, Adam told him that a friend of his up in Pine Ridge had an order in for thirty-three high-end tipis. He had met the woman who bought the property and had been kind enough to give Morning Star a nice pair of earrings. He hoped to get on the crew that would set up the tipis and remodel the farmhouse. There was also talk about building a log lodge.

Adam unpacked some elk salami and fry bread from his saddle bag and they sat against the old house out of the gathering wind. Sunderson asked that his own visit be kept confidential explaining that he was a retired detective looking for a missing person. Adam said that he figured Sunderson to be a cop. Adam said he had quit his job butchering and skinning buffalo up in South Dakota because he wanted to get Morning Star out of the Rapid City area. He had quit boozing two years before but his wife couldn't so he packed up and brought his daughter down to Crawford near where his father had broke and wrangled horses on a big ranch. Sunderson said that he was headed for Tucson and would follow the cult up this way and hoped that Adam would rent him a horse so he could pass for a cowboy while looking for the missing person.

"You might need another lesson," Adam said, pointing to Sunderson's horse which had been improperly tied to the corral and gotten loose.

"I'm sorry," Sunderson said, feeling shamefaced.

"Sorry won't mean shit if you have to walk fifteen miles," Adam said, then walked over and opened the door of the Quonset hut, hooting into the darkness. Out of curiosity the horse walked over to see what the fuss was about and Adam grabbed its reins.

A couple hours later back at their vehicle in the

midafternoon Sunderson slipped getting off the saddle and hit the ground with his right foot still stuck up in the stirrup. Adam lifted him up and detached the foot, "You are not yet a cowboy," Adam said.

After a long restless night trying to find a comfortable position for his improbably sore ass Sunderson packed up before dawn feeling less than grand having taken six ibuprofen and drinking a half-pint of whiskey to fall asleep. His childhood prejudices against cowboys and horses had returned but then he thought that out this way horses were the only practical way to get around for centuries. He would have to go into a Goodwill store and buy some used cowboy duds. He knew that if he kept a safe distance neither Dwight, Queenie, nor Carla would recognize him.

After steak and eggs and hash browns he headed out of town feeling glum about the evident connection of religion and death. "Jesus died for our sins," the Lutheran minister used to say. Over nine hundred people at Jonestown committed suicide for whom in particular, an unknown God? Why were Sunnis and Shiites eager to blow themselves into hamburger? To Sunderson the purpose of life, simply enough, was life. He had never been willing like a sophomore atheist to deny anyone their hope of heaven. His mom, for instance, seemed perfectly confident that she would join her dead husband in heaven. Only the beauty of the Nebraskan landscape kept him from smothering in his mental detritus. He had noted many times how particular aesthetic aspects of the landscape could shut down the mind's dithering. During the last two months of the summer preceding the divorce when Diane had moved to a friend's cottage over in Au Train he had gone fishing every day after work not, certainly, in hopes of catching fish but to assuage his torments over her. A creek is more powerful than despair.

He pulled off on the road's shoulder and took out his topo map identifying Crow Butte, which the first rays of the sun were hitting with a transcendent glitter of light, the light moving almost imperceptibly downward as the sun rose. He thought that Diane had been right on the money when she said that he saw the world through shit-stained glasses but now the lenses seemed to be clearing.

Driving hard he made Tucson in late afternoon of the second day. He got his old room back at the Arizona Inn on the northwest corner of the hotel property and glassed Dwight's rental. There was a large, new, black Chevrolet Suburban parked in front, a car favored by drug tycoons, but no sign of activity. He craved doing some closer snooping but it was important not to be detected. He called Mona out of loneliness and she said that her obnoxious mother was there for a few days talking about selling the house no matter that the market was low. Out of anxiety she had called Diane who said she could live with her.

"I miss you," he said.

"Not as much as I miss you," she responded.

He drove over to the diner where he had met the stocky girl who had advised him to camp up in Aravaipa Canyon. She seemed delighted to see him but was very busy so he ate slowly until the supper crowd was sparse. She was a bit solid for his usual taste but then he was a man of the U.P. where the larger woman is favored likely due to the wickedly cold climate. She finally sat down with him and they talked about his fine camping week before he posed a question.

"Would you like to make some money?"

"You're too cute to pay for sex," she teased.

He made a lengthy explanation because the subject was too complicated for shorthand. He offered two hundred bucks and she agreed to knock on Dwight's door the next morning and join the cult. There was the problem of the demand for an initiation fee but then maybe it could be delayed. Charlene was her name and she came up with the idea of using a check from a defunct account of her ex-husband which he said was clearly illegal.

"From what you told me about him he's unlikely to go to the law."

Sunderson agreed and then suffered a poignant bout of desire for her. She sensed this and said she was already late in picking up her son from the babysitter. He'd be in day care in the morning and she'd stop at Sunderson's room after she visited King David, a name she was fond of. She gave him a brief hug out in the parking lot which made him hopeful but he was full of free-floating anxiety and drove over to Randolph Park where he walked an hour in the last fading light of the early April day. He was damp with sweat when he paused to watch dozens of duffers driving golf balls under the lights, doomed to go parless because hardly anyone was good at anything. The golfers reminded him of his own inept efforts to learn tennis twenty years before. It looked easy on television but wasn't. After three lessons he figured the sport was something you had to start young and gave his new racket to a kid down the street.

In his room he was restless and couldn't go further with Deloria's *Playing Indian* but then he had already been through the book twice and tonight the subject utterly enervated him. Mona had stuck a Donna Leon mystery in his briefcase and he drew it out. He had been absolutely averse to mysteries because of his profession but then, after all, he was retired now and Mona's recommendation had credibility. He was soon immersed in the mind of Commissario Guido Brunetti and an atmosphere he and Diane had loved during their three days in Venice. He was an hour into the book and having his nightcap deciding to turn out the lights early when an idea hit him with a jolt, not too strong a term. Why not go against all law enforcement ethics and have Mona construct some convincing prosecutor's office stationery saying to Carla that she will be prosecuted for her conduct with Mona unless she turns evidence against Dwight for sexual abuse of minors? He could show this letter to Nebraska cops and they would come down on Dwight. Why play fair with this scumbag? Of course there was an outside chance he could be caught for forgery but it would be unlikely if he mailed a copy of the letter from Chadron. The idea was amusing enough that he fell asleep thinking of Charlene's ample ass.

He was awakened at 6:00 a.m. by an uncomfortable dream about Jesus. It started in the Uffizi in Florence where he had been separated from Diane and couldn't find her and one of the countless *lachryma Christi* paintings started talking to him in a foreign language, maybe Aramaic, trying to give him directions to find Diane. Jesus alternately smiled and wept but he recognized this Jesus from Bess's, the old hotel in Grand Marais where the painting of Solomon's Jesus was covered with a curious glass shutter that allowed a smile or tears from different angles. While eating a double order of pork sausage accompanied by oatmeal as penance Sunderson figured that he was hardwired for Jesus from all the church and Sunday school in his childhood. He doubted that he could go into a church without a sense of irony but then he was a modern man at the crossroads trying to go in all four directions at once.

He drew a lawn chair from his patio up to the locked wrought-iron gate to the street from which he could glass Dwight's house. When a starched white employee came by he pretended to be bird-watching what with the area being saturated with twitchers. He was, in fact, looking at a tiny olive bird he knew to be a warbler when he segued back to Dwight's rental where he saw Charlene walking up the porch steps right on schedule at 9:00 a.m. She came out of the house at 9:30 and when she parked in front of the hotel he whistled and waved at the gate. She looked mildly pissed and concerned.

"He tried to get me to blow him."

"Did you?"

"Fuck you. No. I told him I had a tooth extracted yesterday, the best excuse. He called me a liar but took a rain check. Anyway I'm now a nine-thousand-dollar member. Everyone except two women named Carla and Queenie are camped out by Bonita. They leave at dawn in three days. Men are always saying that they're leaving at dawn but they rarely do."

"Where's Bonita?" It sounded familiar to Sunderson. He wondered how many times he had heard the tooth extraction trick.

"North of Willcox. There's nothing much there except a state prison. King David said he lived in Willcox a few months as a foster kid. You passed through Bonita on the way to Klondyke and Aravaipa where you camped."

They went into his room where she seemed quite

uncomfortable. This was a disappointment to his hopes for lovemaking. She took a photo out of her purse.

"I can't make love to you because you look like my Uncle Harvey in Missouri." She passed him the photo. There was a distinct resemblance over which he felt silly. He thought of saying "just keep your eyes closed" but he knew that pleading was a fatal tactic.

He checked out of the Arizona Inn mostly because Charlene said that Carla and Queenie told her they went there for lunch and the prospect of being seen was ghastly. He stopped at a camping store and bought a cooler and a coffeepot and a cheap summer sleeping bag and then went to an Italian deli called Roma that Charlene had told him about, buying bread, coffee, salami, mortadella, and provolone. The weather channel had said that it would remain warm with no rain in the immediate future.

As he drove east toward Willcox his thinking was disturbed by an item he had noted in hundreds of interrogations. To a lesser or greater degree people seemed to think that there was someone else besides their obvious selves within them. It was a "you don't know the half of it" attitude. Marion had said kids often give themselves an alternate name in childhood. He wondered if this was connected to the *otherness* sought in religion or simple boredom with the way things were? He remembered reading in college that Zen Buddhists attempted to find their *true character,* but wasn't everything you were your true character? Or do we have an essence that is a core of a private religion? This kind of thinking tightened his temples so that he was happy he was going camping in Aravaipa well up the road from the cult.

He chose a different camping spot from his previous one and a little more remote. He swore when he heard a big rock scrape the undersides of his car and got out squinting underneath to make sure his oil pan wasn't punctured. He gathered an enormous amount of firewood and figured he'd build his campfire against a canyon wall so it would reflect heat back on his sleeping bag. He was diverted by thinking about an article he had read by the terrorism expert Jonathan White. One of the many ideas White talked about is how cults with some exceptions internalize their violence while terrorist groups externalize it. If you boiled Dwight down you came up with a malevolent bully. How he became that way was beyond Sunderson's interests. His mission was to stop the damage.

He took a late afternoon stroll quite overcome by the arrival of spring, the multifoliate greening in the rock crevasse of the canyon walls, the mesquite and oak that somehow grew out of stone, the grasses and flowers along the purling creek the sound of which had soothed him beginning in his childhood. In the natural world he had always been able to take a break from the sense of his own failings and limitations. It was beside a creek that he prayed that his brother could grow another leg. It was beside a creek that he decided not to shoot the teacher who slapped him so hard his face ached for days. It was beside a creek that he buried his dog and figured out how to swipe a puppy from a litter across town where the owner wanted ten bucks that he didn't have. And far later in life it was on a bank beside the east branch of the Fox that he accepted fully the reasons why Diane was leaving him and came to the realization that she should have done so many years ago.

Early the next afternoon after a splendid morning hiking new country and a cold bath in the creek he was alarmed and a little angry to hear a vehicle chugging slowly up the two-track toward him. It was Charlene and her four-year-old son Teddy in her battered old Isuzu.

"I decided that you're a lonely man needing my company," she said, getting out of the car with a grin.

He got little Teddy started building a dam in the creek, always an engrossing project, then he and Charlene went up behind a thicket and boulder with Charlene peeking out to make sure that Teddy was staying in the creek. "I simply can't do it. You're too much the spitting image of Harvey."

"I give up," he said laughing.

"Thanks, Harvey. I always thought you were an old jerk but now you're nice."

Luckily she had brought along some cold fried chicken because he had had Italian sandwiches for dinner and breakfast. She said that she noticed the cult was starting to pack up and clean up their site for a morning departure rather than the day after. He said he would check it out but wasn't concerned. He needed to be in Dwight's area rather than just waiting in Nebraska. She said that she was one of the fifty thousand young people majoring in environmental studies but then she would settle for a job as a park ranger. They watched Teddy continue working on the dam while chewing a chicken leg. She pointed out that males like building dams, it was a control factor. As a trout fisherman he hated dams so he agreed with this feminist point. He was disappointed when she had to leave in order to get to work for dinner hour. He invited her and Teddy to visit in the Upper Peninsula in the coming summer and said he'd send tickets. She said that of course she would come and kissed him good-bye. Teddy screeched and wept when taken from his dam.

He dozed for an hour leaning against the canyon wall in the sunlight. He had an unfortunate dream of being trapped and suffocating in a sauna of his friend Pavo down in Eben Junction but when he broke down the door and filled his lungs with cold air he wasn't the man he saw standing in the snow wiping off sweat. How could this be? Awake, the sun was very warm on his face and he idly recalled Carla telling him that Dwight didn't like sweat lodges because he was claustrophobic and people were *smelly* adding that all female members were required to shower twice a day, which accounted for the elaborate bathhouse near the longhouse.

He stood and stretched his limbs and then was drawn back to his dream. He was clearly inside the man running out of the sauna but it wasn't him. It was distressing. Are we also someone else? Do we have dream doppelgangers? One reason people come to a religion is to reach *otherness*, or so he had read. Marion had talked about traditions but such things spooked Sunderson as if he were a boy walking past a cemetery at night. He struggled to get back to earth by thinking of the newspaper Marion subscribed to called *Indian Country Today* edited by a man named Giago who among the nuts and bolts of Indian problems was quick to point out silly white rip-offs of Indian customs. Sunderson suspected that behind much of the costumery and rigmarole, the attraction of the cult was the supposedly full expression of sexual freedom, especially for Dwight.

In the late afternoon he abruptly cleaned up his campsite,

made sure the embers of his fire were dead, and packed the
car. On a short walk up the narrow canyon he had seen with
curiosity on his first trip he poked his head into a small side
canyon, not much more than a crevasse, and had seen a tiny
Anasazi petroglyph not half a foot high of a goat that seemed
to be bucking or dancing. He was uncommonly disturbed at
the sight of the goat. He would never know what the Anasazi
meant by the goat, which was one of Diane's nicknames for
him. Long ago on a camping trip they had danced crazily
around a fire to the Grateful Dead on the car stereo. When
feeling especially good goats are known to dance.

He drove slowly toward the cult area to avoid raising a
lot of visible dust on the road, then parked his car behind a
mesquite thicket and walked up the hill with his old Bausch
& Lomb binoculars. It was nearing twilight but he had an
excellent view of the large campsite with all the black Sub-
urbans parked in a neat row. He put a hand behind his back
to swivel his ass for a better view and got yet another cholla
spine in his hand. You had to carry tweezers in this country.
He noted that the ocotillo flowers and his favorite, the prim-
roses, were closing up with the disappearing sun. Back at
the binoculars he saw he had missed the immediate arrival of
Dwight, Carla, and Queenie. He counted eighty-seven people
bowing with young girls in the front. Carla leaned over to get
something out of the backseat wearing shorts. What a great
ass, he thought. Dwight wandered over to the open-faced
cook tent and smelled the pots. Carla had said that unlike
most cults with all sorts of dietary rules Dwight was a real
meat and potatoes guy. Dwight patted the plump lady cook
on the head and she knelt, opened his robe a bit and planted

a kiss evidently on his pecker. Jesus Christ! This was the wackiest bullshit he had ever witnessed in a long life.

He was so enervated he drove all night, eleven hours in a row, finally collapsing at the rest stop on Interstate 40 between Santa Rosa and Tucumcari, New Mexico, sleeping deeply and drooling with the spring sun beating in the window. After washing up and getting a thermos of coffee at a gas station he called Mona. He had been brooding in the night about the ethics of sending the phony letter from the prosecutor to the Nebraska authorities. The odds of getting caught were so-so but he would also be making Mona culpable. When he had mentioned it on the phone the other day she was impulsively up for it but during the night he had developed doubts. The state police in Michigan had earned ubiquitous respect for being straight arrow, above reproach, and he had always played by the book. No matter how much he wanted to nail Dwight committing a felony to do so illegally would be a curse to carry the rest of his life since he was a memory junky and never forgave himself for anything.

"Hello darling."

"I've been thinking about the letter we were going to concoct from the prosecutor. Let's forget it."

"I could tell by your voice you didn't really want to. Hemingway said good is what you feel good after."

"I never liked Hemingway." He had a cigarette cough and gasped.

"Neither do I but what he said was true. The good thing in my life now is that I'm disowning my parents on the grounds of gross negligence and Diane's adopting me."

"You're kidding me?"

"No, we've talked about it for hours. She's got a lawyer working on it. It's late but I could use an actual mother. What do you think?"

"I think it's wonderful."

He was fueled by a giddy happiness for hours and then set about making a mental listing of a plan.

1. Buy old cowboy clothes in Chadron.
2. Move to Crawford to be closer to action.
3. Rent a horse from Adam.
4. Learn how to saddle it.
5. Stow car with Michigan plates. Rent old pickup.

He reached the cult site north of Crawford late the next afternoon pleased to see that Adam was part of a crew of fifteen men cleaning up the area and erecting the last half dozen big tipis, thirty of them in all on a flat out in front of the old house and corral. There were even a number of deep blue Porta-Potties and a water truck. He said hello to Adam's daughter, Morning Star, who was watching with some other kids and the wives of the workers in a near party atmosphere. There was a lot of comic banter about the coming cult. She said shyly that he could use her nickname, Petunia.

"Are these people crazy?" Petunia asked him with a smile. She was tall for her age, dark and handsome with a lilting voice.

"I'm afraid they are a little wacky."

"Dad said you might be an undercover cop."

"I don't think so," he said.

Adam came over with a broad grin saying that the cult front man was keeping him on for top-dollar wages for at least another week. He pointed at a man in a gray suit in the distance looking at the ramshackle house with a foreman. This made Sunderson nervous so he asked Adam if he and Petunia could meet him for dinner in Chadron.

Back in the car he felt he had to be careful because the man in the suit might be one of Queenie's Detroit lawyers who would wonder about a car with Michigan plates. He found a combination junk and old clothing and pawn shop in Chadron and outfitted himself for twenty bucks, not a bad amount to become another person. The used cowboy hat was sweat-stained and shapeless, a little large but it looked bona fide in the car mirror. He checked back in to his local Chadron motel in a state of delirious fatigue. He'd find a Crawford lodging in the morning.

When he walked into the restaurant in his new costume he could see Adam and Petunia in a far corner but neither recognized him until he was nearly to the table. They both laughed.

"Another piece of shit old cowpoke," Adam said.

They all had big rib steaks and Sunderson was surprised when Petunia bore down and finished hers first.

"She's growing like a weed," Adam said.

"Like a flower," Petunia corrected. She went off across the room to visit school friends.

"She's trying to fit into a mostly white world. She's the star of the seventh-grade basketball team," Adam said.

"Any chance I can rent that horse I rode last time and maybe you could help me find an old pickup to cover my tracks?"

"I got both at home. That motel outside of Crawford has fenced pasture for travelers pulling horses. I figured you're really not looking for a missing person."

"No, I'm tracking a bad guy. He's the cult leader with many names. If Petunia is out there, keep an eye on her. He's got freak hots for young girls. I got proof of this."

"I'd gut him like the buffalo I used to butcher," Adam said, his face tightened and clouded.

"I wouldn't blame you."

Sunderson reached Adam's at 6:00 a.m. with the first light just squinting low in the east but catching the top of Crow Butte with a glow of sunlight. He thought this whole Sandhills area was as lovely as any country in America, albeit subtly. It had been a haunted night with only a single nightcap to help him into sleep. He had long known that you had to pull back from booze when the pressure became acute despite the daily craving to dull the senses a bit, or quite a bit. When he had wakened at 3:00 a.m. he began brooding about the conclusions of Deloria's *Playing Indian* but then it was a scholarly book and scarcely the place for a white-hot rant. It was as if those playing Indian were saying, "Look at us. We're human and we can be like you, too. We know we took the land of over five hundred tribes and butchered a few thousand and ten million inadvertently died from our diseases and hunger in a two-hundred-year holocaust. But we're like you dressing up in your garb and dancing."

Only we weren't Sunderson thought in his middle of the night rambles through the mental swamp of our history. Sunderson recalled Disraeli saying as a Jew something to the effect of, "When your people were cavorting in animal skins mine were walking to the temple singing." We were Attila and the Huns without a singular Hun, only Andrew Jackson, the many General Crooks and Custers. With our jelly-like

good intentions in the manner of a PTA potluck with unrest
barely beneath the skin we were always sure we were doing
the right thing and it was unbearable as in Vietnam when we
realized we weren't doing the right thing any more than we
had done in the massacres at Sand Creek and Wounded Knee.
Our attitude had consistently been, "Have gun, will travel."

Adam had an old Chevy pickup from the sixties parked
by the house trailer, their home, up and running and attached a battered one-horse trailer, loading the saddled
horse he called Brother-in-Law.

"Take off the saddle when you put him down for the
night. There's two bales of hay in the trailer."

Petunia, though Sunderson preferred Morning Star,
called them for a breakfast of buffalo sausage and fried potatoes. He was surprised how pleasant this girl had fixed up
the interior of the trailer. There were wreaths of sweetgrass
and also dried wild turnips Adam's mother had picked out
in the country near Pine Ridge. Adam said that they were
reconstituted with dried corn in venison stew.

Sunderson packed his gear in the old Chevy pickup
and parked his own car behind Adam's trailer. Adam followed Sunderson to the motel to make sure he made it,
then dropped Morning Star off at school, then came back
to unload the horse. Adam had said, "This horse don't load
well," which meant that unloading Brother-in-Law could
also be a semiviolent mud bath.

"Good luck," Adam said waving good-bye and looking
at Sunderson as if he had doubts.

Sunderson was quite suddenly afflicted with the Great
Doubt himself and told Adam he had decided to wait a day

and make sure his plan was in order. Adam merely nodded though Sunderson felt that Adam suspected his plan wasn't all that firm.

Driving back to his Crawford room he had the intuition that after months of things going slow the pace had abruptly quickened. He called the Sioux County sheriff and was immediately patched through when he said he was a Michigan state police detective neglecting to mention "retired." They talked in generalities about the cult and Sunderson described himself as on vacation looking for a friend's daughter who was a member of the cult, mentioning that he knew the Great Leader had a taste for adolescent girls. The sheriff said that they were aware of certain rumors but hadn't received any complaints. They would move quickly if Sunderson noted any hard evidence. This call was an ordinary courtesy among law enforcement professionals but Sunderson was thinking he might need backup. He wasn't up to getting stoned again. It wasn't just the pain it was the prolonged recovery.

Sunderson decided to walk up Crow Butte and camp for the night in hopes of achieving clarity of intention. He packed his camping gear and light sleeping bag trusting in a warm night. He left behind his whiskey bottle with regret. Luckily the horse unloaded easily into the fenced area and he tossed out a half bale of hay. He stopped at a grocery store and bought a small steak, a block of cheese, and some crackers.

He drove as close as he could to the foot of the butte passing one NO TRESPASSING sign on a two-track figuring he could flip his expired badge. A good idea for keeping out of harm's way was to turn in the badge when he got home to Marquette.

He was two hours into a strenuously steep uphill walk when while taking a rest it occurred to him he had forgotten salt for the steak and, more important, a canteen full of water. He would have to live without both, unable to be angry because of the sublimity of the landscape and a comic memory of a dinner date with a bright schoolteacher two years before. They had gone to a nice little log cabin restaurant in Au Train but being in her company reminded him of trying to eat fried fish or corn on the cob without salt. You only had to remind yourself flippantly of the thousands of men who had died for salt on the ancient trade routes. Human history was so basically berserk that he easily imagined one man strangling another for a one-pound sack of salt at an oasis in the Gobi. Once a doctor had told him to knock off all salt for a week to improve his high blood pressure and it had been a disgusting experience, plainly time to find another doctor. Toward the end of the salt-free week he had sucked the tits of a hefty barmaid over in Newbury at the end of her shift on a hot summer day and reached bliss with the salt on her skin.

It took him nearly six hours to reach the top because of frequent pauses to still his fluttery heart. Also the climb was much more difficult than it looked from a distance where the crags, culverts, and gullies were somewhat concealed. His mouth became quite dry but his struggle excluded worrying about a water-starved body. As a flatlander from the densely forested north he was totally without experience in climbing and though he could walk for hours the angle of nearly straight up exhausted him. During one short rest period he reflected that descending the next morning would be even more difficult because of the gravity of his body. It occurred to him that he would have made this climb as a boy or young man but lost the impulse for forty years, and now it returned as a nearly old man when certain aspects of the mind become captious and boyish again. He suddenly remembered he and Roberta pulling Bobby up a steep wooded hill in his red wagon soon after he came home from the hospital. In their churning climb they disturbed a yellow-jacket nest and each was painfully stung a couple of times. Bobby bawled like a baby and Roberta screamed "Goddamn God" which frightened all of them. In another hour towing the wagon they were out on the end of the timber boat dock where the men had just unloaded the logs and this big Swede who was the captain and a friend of their father's invited them along to Grand Island to pick up another load. Grand Island was only a few hundred yards away but the three treated the ride as if it were an ocean adventure. When they got home for supper Bobby yelled at the table that it had been the best day of his life despite the yellow jackets.

Sunderson found himself weeping as he climbed and asked his long dead brother, "What's going on out there if anything?" He was fairly confident that he was losing his mind but then it was a mind well lost. Men did a lot of silent weeping but rarely out loud. He paused to try to think of another but saw one coming and backed away. Before it starts you think you're going to burst and then you begin weeping like you did out in the woods the day that Dad died.

Time was misarranged, a quirky idea but unavoidable. If the timing had been right Diane would likely have been able to save Bobby in his heroin narcosis but toward his last years he wouldn't come home or see anyone except Roberta.

Sunderson had driven himself into a depression investigating heroin, even snorted a dose, but only came up with the
idea that the drug worked for those who want to feel nothing. A blank page. Zero. The emotions were all cessations of
emotion. Life became white on white paper. There was an
intriguing notion that life became photographs and for once
all horrors were at safe removal, totally immovable and at
rest. But then parts of the photograph began to move and you
needed more of the drug and finally you wiped reality clean.

At the very top there was a mound with a flat space
where he collapsed and slept for an hour waking sore but
refreshed with the unnerving perception that he could see
nothing but sky. This was an odd experience as waking always
offered peripheral objects such as a pillow's edge, a night
table, a door, a wall. He wasn't dead because the clouds were
moving and there was a huge front far to the south moving
from southwest to northwest that he hoped wouldn't push
his way. He had no idea what time it was because he had left
his cell phone with its clock back in the room with the pint of
whiskey. He smiled at the idea that what he was doing was
a vague parody of what Marion described as an Anishinabe
or Chippewa power vision where you spent three days and
nights on a hill without food, water, or shelter waiting for vision. The possible grandeur of such an experience was alien
to him. He had always refused the sophomoric notion that
life was a process of settling for less in favor of the idea that
sometimes life was good, sometimes bad. He mildly teared
thinking how much Diane would have liked it up here.

He had to sit down because his legs trembled with exhaustion so that even seated they jerked and flopped. "How could

she have saved Bobby when she couldn't save me" was the
question that gagged his mind. Halfway through the marriage
Diane had tried to convince him to quit and get a graduate
degree in history. Her best friend at the time was the wife of
the superintendent of schools so it wouldn't be hard to get him
a high school teaching job. The trouble with this idea, and it
was hard to admit it to himself, was that in twenty years of cop
work he had become a bit of an adrenaline junkie. A classroom
smelling of chalk dust and the Spanish rice wafting up from
the lunchroom and possibly the ozone odor of sloth emerging
from the skulls of students was a poor substitute for playing
Lone Ranger in a souped-up Crown Victoria chasing a perp
on a log trail through the woods throwing out a rooster tail of
mud, or taking a photo of the son of an obnoxious politician
making a cocaine buy outside a bar. This wasn't the kind of
thing you could explain to Diane simply because she was a
hundred percent grown up. Her ducks were in a row, as they
say, and she was a genuine public servant.

Turning this way and that he had a clear view of the
four directions: east toward Chadron and far away home,
far south toward the ominous roiling storm, west toward
Fort Robinson and the murder of Crazy Horse, and north
where the Lakota had been driven and resettled for the third
time in a short period simply because we wanted the land.
He made out the speck of Adam's trailer in the distance
and was a little consoled that you couldn't kill a people *unless you killed all of them*. The exception of reading Deloria's
Playing Indian was tolerable because it was a clinical study
of the absurd ways we tried to adopt customs of the people
we had attempted and failed to turn into permanent ghosts.

He had read the histories of the main Indian tribes
before he took a course in Greek myth and history so that
he tended toward the error of seeing the Greeks in American Indian terms. No groups could be less similar than the
Greeks and the Hopis and a twenty-year-old student brain
became goofy trying to force them to cohere. His favorite
professor had advised him to back away and gave him a
monograph with limited conclusions on how one year the
United States government failed to give the Lakota their
food allotment. Some ate their horses and survived but others refused and starved. The professor's point is that you
can't draw large conclusions unless you can draw small,
accurate conclusions. Sunderson was unsure as he had
noted that academics were forever carping about large-
scale brilliant writers like Bernard De Voto in favor of their
own minimal conclusions about the Westward Movement.

He was pleased when his legs stopped trembling, which
put him in mind of all of the variations of his own hubris. His
daffy Uncle Albert, his dad's oldest brother, made it through
World War II poorly, losing a dozen friends at Normandy and
was over the hill far enough that he survived on half-disability.
He was married for years to an Ojibway woman way up in
Mooseknee on Hudson's Bay but she drowned while fishing
and Albert moved back close to home over north of Shingleton and east of Munising. Albert was plainly odd, walking in
the woods and chanting nonsense and fishing. It was he who
got Sunderson started on his lifelong brook trout obsession,
a beautiful fish indeed and also delicious. Sunderson and his
father would take a casserole to Albert on Sunday or Albert
would drive his old Model A crusted with swallow shit from

sitting in a barn near Trenary for twenty years. Albert would
pick Sunderson up at dawn and they would be off for the day
exploring creeks with a bag of sandwiches. The damage was
done by a ditty Albert sang incessantly in mocking tones,
"Just make the world a better place." The trouble was that
at age seven Sunderson took these words seriously from his
insane hero and never questioned his abilities. Of course he
could climb Crow Butte at age sixty-five. Of course he would
make the world a better place. Of course he had to destroy the
Great Leader to save the innocent, both children and adults.
The worst criminals were those who took advantage of weak-
ness through greed, lust, and religion. The fact that many of
the cult members were college graduates stymied him. The
fact that someone could get an *A* in biology at University of
Michigan and not understand their own biology left him quite
muddy. Dwight was beating the child because it was a child.

But how about retirement? How about letting the mind
rest? How about moving over toward L'Anse or Iron Mountain and escaping the scenes of crimes, his own and others.
At least Mona was becoming part of his own extended family and disappearing as a sexual being. She was the only
example he could think of that showed self-control. You
could think it through all you want and you're still going to
get a hard-on over the wrong person and human peace is
blown away. At least a tinge of incest made it taboo. Quitting drinking was out of the question. His cop mind needed
a constant supply of adrenaline.

Just before dark he cooked his steak over a small fire
of pine, never done in his homeland because the meat would
taste like pine resin. His dad used to say, "A Saltine is a feast
to a starving man," but the crackers and cheese were nearly

impossible because his mouth couldn't raise enough spittle to effectively chew them. He coughed over and over and a small group of crows that had been hanging around since his arrival scolded him. The tough steak was better because it had some juice and despite the fact that the pine flavor and lack of salt would normally make it intolerable. After this supper and one of the best cigarettes of his life he took his leftovers thirty yards down the slope, returned to his perch, then watched the crows haggle over the food. They were survivors.

Curiously, rather than thinking through the case of the Great Leader, he could think of nothing, not even Diane or his long life. His mind was full of only the grandeur of where he was as if he was trout fishing in the sky. His muddled brain couldn't begin to compete with the rising three-quarter moon and the immense thunderstorm far to the south.

He tried to fall asleep too early without success and felt he'd pay a thousand bucks for a few aspirin. He got up and walked in circles and tried to stretch out his lumpy muscles. He kept being revisited by the image of time going out the door but never back in. Where did this come from, this huge wooden door? The image arrived because it was true. It wasn't an abstraction. The neurons made a painting of his anguish. It was the nursery rhyme where all of the king's horses and all of the king's men couldn't put their marriage back together again. Diane's face was a dozen miles south near the actual storm and the upcoming storm of her new husband's death. Twenty years before they were visiting her parents near Ludington and went for dinner and dancing at a restaurant on the shores of Lake Michigan. They danced at least an hour to a rather schmaltzy Glenn Miller orchestra but loved it. Diane wouldn't make love in her parents' home so they stopped at a motel when they left the restaurant. It was a sublime night and the memory of it made him think his head would burst with tears. It was he who caused their marriage to stop dancing. Now his only fallback position with Diane and Mona was to become a perfect gentleman. After a single beer crazy Uncle Albert would walk in tight circles moaning and after a bender had to be confined in the VA for the last three years of his moaning life. When he was growing up everyone local remarked on Sunderson's father's good manners, now called for in his son's life.

He struggled to drag his mind away from critical issues by pondering an article Mona had faxed him about these large moths that migrate by the millions from Nebraska to Wyoming and Montana and alight at an altitude of eight thousand feet on scree. Dozens of grizzly bears appear and eat up to ninety pounds of protein-rich moths apiece in a day. Staring at the immense thunderstorm moving from the east to the southwest he wondered how this could be? It was certainly a mystery that more deserved to be solved than the inscrutability of wife beating.

Now he saw Mona convoluted in the storm and recalled that the first time he saw her nude on the bed the lust was like a stomach cramp. What in God's name did such lust mean? He was happy when there was a grand lightning stroke and the image of Mona was gone, clearly an experience that belonged to demonology as if the most haunted house of all were biology.

At dawn he felt creaky but had never slept so well in his life. He made a slow, perilous descent from the top of Crow Butte.

Chapter 21

Sunderson thought afterward that they were by far the longest three days of his life. Without the suppressed violence of the present they reminded him of the nasty heartache of homesickness in late spring at college turning in papers and taking exams before he could make the long drive north toward home. It was a lump in the throat time.

The first day the whole idea of using a horse as camouflage for his pretense was most unfortunate. Nearly two hours into his ride while skirting a mudhole the horse became slightly mired and frantically bucked Sunderson off. He watched despondently as the horse ran off in the direction they had come and then he walked toward the cult site perhaps three miles away. It was raining, which at least washed off the mud stuck to his clothes. As he neared the site he was pleased to see a big bonfire behind the house. The workers were burning trash and all the members kept to their distant tipis in the rain. He dried off before the hot fire.

Adam wasn't disturbed about the horse saying that it knew the direct way home better than any human. Most fortunate for Sunderson was that Queenie and Carla had flown off that morning with the guy in the suit on the charter for Denver with a big list of supplies to buy for the new location. Sunderson was put to work by the foreman for ten bucks an hour chipping dried mud off the half dozen new all-terrain vehicles, the noisy four-wheelers that haunt mere walkers in the wild with their insufferable racket. He kept an eye on Dwight's distant tipi thinking that Dwight was the only one with an off chance of recognizing him, remote because of the costume and the idea of being out of context. His outfit made him as invisible as a man in a green janitor suit in urban areas. No one notices janitors. It was, however, comical to Sunderson that he was cleaning up the machine he hated most other than snowmobiles. That night he was totally the exhausted geezer, ate a burger at the bar, and slept twelve hours.

The next morning, Saturday, life warmed up in every way. It was bright, clear, and sunny and by ten warm enough to be without a coat. Sunderson was put to work with a hammer, nails, and a crow bar repairing the collapsed portion of the corral. Dwight had decided that in harmony with the countryside the cult should have horses and commissioned Adam to secure a dozen rideable quarter horses and give lessons to those without experience. From the corral he watched Adam and Petunia perhaps a hundred yards away, teaching most of the young people horsemanship. He noted the great majority of girls over boys and wondered how this was organized. Dwight was an onlooker in a mauve robe and Sunderson noticed that he was standing fairly close to Morning Star.

At noon there was a picnic to which the workers were invited but Sunderson hung back at the corral and Adam brought him a sandwich.

"He seems like a pretty nice guy," Adam said.

"I was a state police detective for nearly forty years. You'll have to trust me."

"True. I've been suckered by a lot of white folks."

Sunderson sat in the pickup eating the sandwich and glassing the scene. When Adam was off leading a horse and rider at a brisk walk he saw Dwight hold Morning Star's hand and his blood pressure rose precipitously, but then she got in a car with a friend and they were driven off to a Girl Scout meeting.

He had dinner with Adam and Morning Star in the trailer. She was enthusiastic because the cult was hiring her at good wages to teach riding with her father on weekends. Dwight had told her that his nickname was King David which she thought was funny.

"He's such a wonderful man," she said.

Sunday was bright and sunny but with a brisk wind from the south. The workers had taken the day off and Sunderson ensconced himself near a window upstairs in the old house having packed two wretched bologna sandwiches and a thermos of coffee. Petunia was teaching three girls about twelve how to saddle a horse and he was amazed at the ease at which she pitched the saddle onto the horse. She was a

strong girl indeed. He was relieved for her that King David
hadn't made a move but also pissed off that it hadn't come to
a head like he knew it would.

It was nearly noon when Queenie and Carla drove
in with a Suburban jam-packed with supplies from the
plane. Only one male member volunteered so Adam was
made busy unpacking the supplies and carrying them to
the cook tent and various tipis. Sunderson's heart jumped
when he saw King David lead Morning Star into his tipi
while Adam was coming out of the most distant tipi. Within
a few minutes he heard a scream and Morning Star ran
out of the tipi in her panties with Dwight stopping at the
open tent flap. He looked dazed until he saw Adam running toward him with a drawn knife. Dwight jumped on
an ATV and sped off at top speed. Adam swiftly mounted
his horse and gave chase but fell behind because the ATV
could do fifty on the road but then Dwight made a fatal
mistake and turned off the road heading cross-country
toward Crow Butte.

"Jesus Christ," Sunderson yelled, moving to a back
window watching the figures become distant. He ran downstairs and luckily one of the ATVs he had cleaned was still
parked near the corral. He took a few frantic minutes to
figure out how to operate the machine but then he was off
and moving. He could see that Dwight was still well ahead
but Adam was gaining, while he was a full mile behind. The
only reason that he didn't want Adam to cut Dwight's throat
is he'd go to prison and leave Morning Star fatherless.

Now Dwight slowed moving up the initial slope of
Crow Butte, slowing even more as the slope grew steeper.

Sunderson could see him look back at the quickly gaining
Adam then gun the powerful ATV, shooting up the steep
slope until it became almost vertical whereupon the machine flipped backward in a big arc with Dwight clutching
the handlebars until it hit earth landing on Dwight and
both man and machine rolled down the hill so that Adam
had to dodge on his horse. Adam dismounted taking out
his knife.

Sunderson was yelling "no" over the roar of his machine as he came up the beginning of the hill. He feared
flipping and jumped off still yelling "no." Adam turned to
him as he crawled and scrambled up the slope to Dwight's
side. Dwight was on his back with the left side of his chest
clearly stoven in and a leg twisted under him. His head was
also cocked at an impossible angle and was the only thing
about him that moved. He yawped a primitive sound like a
heron then gurgled up puke and blood.

Sunderson and Adam only looked at each other shaking
their heads then turned away from the now bleating body.

Epilogue

Sunderson had only taken a few careful steps down the steep hill when he heard a howl that froze his soul. He turned in panic and saw that Adam had lifted Dwight high with his big rough hands around his neck and was shaking him like a terrier does a rat, not a fond memory for Sunderson, or Dwight for that matter.

Of course King David lived. No one has ever been able to kill the Devil. He is everywhere with us. The State of Nebraska and Sioux County were puzzled about a possible prosecution for attempted sodomy and rape. Should millions of dollars be spent incarcerating an acute quadriplegic with no operable parts except a head that talked in a language no one could understand? Morning Star had given frank testimony. Indian girls are generally tough what with living in two worlds. Sunderson skillfully minimized his own part in nailing Dwight. He presented himself as merely a retired

Michigan state police detective looking for a missing person. He certainly didn't mention the rag doll shaking incident. It wasn't that the crime was swept under the rug, only that law enforcement and justice are as messy as life herself and why spend millions trying to punish an eggplant?

The Devil was medevaced to the big regional hospital in Rapid City where his condition was stabilized, the lowest common denominator, for a month or so whereupon he was flown to Santa Monica, California, where Queenie and Carla decided to live. Dwight was kept in a small guesthouse that was converted into a colorful hospital room. Young women can't be expected to spend their lives on dead meat so there were around-the-clock attendants, three of them in eight-hour shifts, who played alternatively the kind of music Dwight loathed, heavy metal, rap, and country.

Sunderson drove home to Michigan by a circuitous route at a leisurely pace attempting to allow himself to decompress. He tried to avoid thinking about the big issues like love, death, freedom, or religion, much less money. He drove north to experience the emptiness of North Dakota knowing that an underpopulated landscape can draw off the poison. In a good if eccentric restaurant in Fargo he ate a big plate of barbecued beef ribs betting in his mind that the cult would dissolve as they usually do with the loss of the charismatic leader who could put a number on a member's state of development. Some cult leaders have predicted Armageddon and are at a loss when the world fails to end and just keeps plugging along through the indifferent cosmos. There had always been a trace of a dog barking in Dwight's voice and now he would bark no more.

He reached home in time for the opening of trout season on April 23, but it was largely a joke because half a foot of fresh snow fell. He fished anyway at a beaver pond near Marion's cabin sensing the weight of the snow gathering on his hat. He caught two modest brook trout and fried them with bacon fat for lunch with bread and salt. He spent most of May at Marion's cabin not quite ready for a steady diet of people.

By June and the beginning of the obnoxious bug season that would last at least a month he was back in his home study. There was simply no dealing with the mosquitoes, blackflies, and deerflies unless it was very windy at which point he would launch himself back into the woods.

He had dinner with Diane and Mona once a week after taking Diane's declining husband for a ride out in the summery landscape. Mona had moved in with Diane and now acted a bit more girlish rather than prematurely womanly. Her ditzy mother hadn't protested the change in her daughter's parentage and had immediately sold the house to a young academic couple with a little money on the side. Sunderson couldn't help but pull out the Slotkin book for a little peek at the attractive wife. One stellar morning he had caught her doing yoga in a skimpy leotard and his blood pressure ascended. What was this yoga thing? Wasn't it also a religion? He had been pleased on Memorial Day when it was an untypically hot day and Mona had bathed nude in a spring hole in the creek that he hadn't watched but fled back into the woods. A girl needed a father figure not a lecher. He bet that Adam would keep a close eye on Morning Star.

Soon after he had returned home he had bought a pedometer and now on an unpleasantly warm Labor Day weekend he checked his mileage, startled that he had walked seven hundred miles in four months, an average of five miles a day. This was neither here nor there except to remember that such diverse figures as Thoreau, Kierke- gaard, and George Bernard Shaw had said that you could walk yourself into serenity. He doubted that but walking and fishing filled his life in a way that his work had long ceased to. He knew he wouldn't become as well mannered as his father but kept a fairly tight lid on his irascibility. He was charged with assaulting two college students but the charges were dismissed when it was determined they were setting off cherry bombs near Sunderson's garage. That made the *Marquette Mining Journal* with "Retired Detective Subdues Athletes with Clothesline Rope."

He didn't drink less on purpose he just drank less by switching to wine, the quantity of which could be more easily controlled. With the help of a surveyor he blocked out an even square mile of state land near Marion's cabin having decided to do a flora and fauna identification and species count. His stack of nature guidebooks was becoming well thumbed and he liked the idea of investigating the nature of nature excluding the human species and its charnel-house history. Enough is enough.

On a Sunday morning before Labor Day he stopped by Diane's house to check out dinner plans just as a hospice worker and an RN arrived. Diane was making arrange- ments for a full day off and Sunderson and Mona took a short walk down to the beach near the Coast Guard station.

Mona waded in and said it was the warmest she had ever felt
Lake Superior. She was distracted with butterflies because
she was leaving for Ann Arbor and the university midweek.
When they got back to Diane's house a pile of camping gear
was stacked on the porch and the temperature was already
in the eighties. Diane's face was tight and distraught. She
told them her husband had suggested an overnight camping
trip while he came as close to euthanizing himself as possible
without the final step.

They drove east to Munising and then northeast to
the shore road, taking a dip at Twelvemile Beach which
was nearly empty, the often tempestuous water sullen and
placid. A dozen miles to the south beyond Kingston Lake
Sunderson found the two-track with difficulty. He was full
of anxiety that the pond he and Diane had loved and so
often camped at over twenty years before had somehow
been ruined. Not in the least. The two-track was nearly
impenetrably overgrown and Sunderson managed to knock
loose one of the sideview mirrors on Diane's newish station wagon, which she ignored. When they arrived at the
clearing, about seventy yards by seventy, two coyote pups
scooted off and entered a burrow up a hillside. Sunderson
grabbed a flashlight, walked up, knelt, and shined the light
in the tunnel. The male pup growled as if to protect his sister. The women took the flashlight and knelt down wagging
their butts in the air. They were both wearing clingy gray
cotton gym shorts. At the first stroke of desire Sunderson
looked up at the heavens but failed to feel heavenly. He
quickly set up his small tent facing east so he could catch
the first of dawn's light while the girls chose the far side so

that they could sleep in. He was told to turn around while they put on their bathing suits but he was already headed west for a walk despite the heat following a tiny creek that provided the pond's outlet. He looked down at the spring fumaroles burbling upward and the shadows of a small patch of lily pads with yellow knob flowers. Everywhere on the water's bottom where it was shallow enough there were the footprints of heron and sandhill cranes. At the far end the girls were screeching at the coldness of the water but finally submerged to their necks. He was looking forward to the roast chicken, potato salad, and wine Diane had brought but he first needed a two-hour sweaty walk and a swim. They would never be the kind of family that would live under one roof but they would be close.